BOOKS BY PAUL BISHOP

Hot Pursuit

Deep Water

A Bucketful of Bullets

Running Wylde

Nothing But The Truth (Almost)

Suspicious Minds

Lie Catchers

FEY CROAKER SERIES

Croaker: Kill Me Again

Croaker: Grave Sins

Croaker: Tequila Mockingbird

Croaker: Chalk Whispers

CROAKER: KILL ME AGAIN

FEY CROAKER
BOOK 1

PAUL BISHOP

**ROUGH
EDGES
PRESS**

Kill Me Again
Paperback Edition
Copyright © 2025 (As Revised) Paul Bishop

Rough Edges Press
An Imprint of Wolfpack Publishing
1707 E. Diana Street
Tampa, FL 33610

roughedgespress.com

Paperback ISBN 978-1-68549-679-1
eBook ISBN 978-1-68549-678-4

AUTHOR'S NOTE

Kill Me Again and the other original Fey Croaker novels are set in the late '90s. As such, the storylines represent the attitudes and technology relevant to the time period...

CROAKER: KILL ME AGAIN

CHAPTER ONE

LOS ANGELES, 1995

Fey Croaker looked up from the arrest report occupying her attention and saw Lieutenant Michael Cahill crossing the squad room toward her. As she watched his approach, she felt a familiar chill of anticipation wash over her. Goose bumps thrilled up her neck. Her Irish mother always told her the feeling came from someone walking over your grave. If it was true, Fey hoped they were walking softly.

"The first stiff of the new year?" she asked when Cahill was close enough.

The detective lieutenant shook his head in genuine amazement. "How do you always know when I'm coming to tell you we've got a cold one? It's spooky, Fey."

"It's instinct."

"I don't care if it's ESP. It's still spooky."

Fey took off her reading glasses and set them on her desk. "Where's the body?"

"Two-zero-zero-eight Mirrorwood." Cahill held out a pink phone memo with the scribbled information.

Fey took the note, glancing at it. Without her glasses on, she had to hold it at arm's length. "The new town-home complex above San Vincente and Barrington? What's it called? Oak Vista Estates? The one only dope dealers and Ferrari salesmen can afford."

"Yeah. It's a sure bet the homeowners' association isn't going to be real pleased about the situation. The people who live in the complex are paying through the nose for private security and all the other amenities."

Fey looked at Cahill. "Come off it, Mike. Those people put more money up their nose in a day than they pay in homeowners' fees. It's pin money to them."

"Anyone ever tell you you're a cynic?"

"Yeah. It's why I'm good at my job." Fey stood up and checked her watch. Eight-thirty. A hell of a way to start a day. "Who found the body?" she asked.

"The maid. She thinks it's the owner..." Cahill grappled with his memory and then pointed to the memo he'd given Fey. "I wrote the name down."

Fey gave the pink slip of paper another long-distance glance. "Miranda Goodwinter?" she read with a question in her voice.

"Sounds right," Cahill said. "Anyway, the body is female, white, fortysomething. Naked. The maid didn't take too close a look. Too much blood."

"So, no positive ID?"

"Nothing beyond the maid's guess, which is probably going to turn out to be good."

"I don't recognize the possible victim's name. Any political or big-time money overtones yet?"

Cahill snorted. "This is West L.A. Unless the stiff is homeless, there's always political or big-time money overtones. Do you think the Oak Vista Estates homeowners' board are going to stand by quietly while we go about our business? They're going to be screaming bloody murder to both the chief's and the mayor's office. If we don't solve this one in a hurry, our butts are going to be in the middle of the skillet."

The West Los Angeles Division was the jewel in the crown of the Los Angeles Police Department, the gem of all twenty-one geographic divisions. Many of L.A.'s richest areas, including Brentwood, Bel-Air, Cheviot Hills, and Pacific Palisades, fell within its jurisdiction.

Beverly Hills had their own technology worshiping police department bordering the West L.A. Division to the east. The city of Santa Monica had a similar setup on the division's west side, although they favored a more liberal mode. And the northern border along Mulholland Drive possessed some of the most expensive and isolated estates in the city, if not the world.

West L.A. was the rich filling in a money sandwich.

When Fey had first promoted into West L.A. as a Detective II with sixteen years on the job, Mike Cahill had taken her aside to explain the divisional facts of life. Things were handled differently in West L.A., Cahill told her, because the rich never went up the chain of command. Instead, they started at the top and let the crap roll downhill. The rich were different and expected to be treated differently.

This different treatment didn't mean the rich never went to jail. But it did mean officers better be sure of what they had before slapping the cuffs on some movie star's brat. It also made things very tough for an officer who stopped someone for drunk driving only to find out the lawbreaker was on his way home from a thousand-dollar-a-plate fund-raiser for the mayor.

Neither did the difference mean the rich automatically had all their crimes solved or all their property recovered. But it did mean a detective better be prepared to jump a little higher when a councilman's wife said there was a trespasser on her grounds while her husband was out of town on a junket. This was true even if there was no trespasser, and the only reason the wife had called was because she was lonely and horny and wanted some attention from the stud of a uniformed officer who she knew would respond to her 911 call.

Fey played the game with the rich very well. She was known for her *bedside manner* and for her ability to soothe even the most ruffled of feathers. She was also known to solve a lot of crimes and put a lot of suspects behind bars. In an enclosed world where reputation counts for almost everything, Fey was a rising star. The respect, however, was still grudging because she was still undeniably a woman in a man's world. A bitch in the locker room. Different generation, but the same prejudice.

After four years in West L.A., her abilities led to her promotion to Detective III. Two years later, she was given the homicide unit to supervise. It was the top detective spot in the division, and Fey was the first woman to ever head the unit. She was pleased at first to have overcome the barrier. Then she found out orders had come down from on high to put a woman in the spot, not because a woman, or specifically Fey, deserved the spot, but because a token had to be presented for public relations purposes.

Fey's initial reaction to this news had been anger. She almost stalked into Cahill's office to throw her badge and gun on the desk and resign, like in the movies. Cooler thoughts prevailed, though, and on reflection she decided it didn't matter what the motivation was for placing her in the position. She – Fey Croaker – was still in the position, and it was up to her to prove she could do the job, not because she was a woman, but because she was a hell of a good detective.

Fey had worked homicide earlier in her career as a

Detective I, and later as a Detective II. She had quickly learned the supposed differences between the rich and poor were only superficial. When you worked homicide, dead was dead. Murder had no respect for wealth.

Fey sighed and massaged the bridge of her nose with the thumb and index finger of her left hand. Her nails were long, but the blood-red polish on them was chipped.

She felt a deep sigh dissipate in her chest. You always wanted the first body in January to be easy, a self-solver. It set the tone for the rest of the year. This one felt rough.

She shoved together the paperwork she had been shuffling and stood up. "Have the coroner and the SID lab boys been notified?"

Cahill nodded his head. "The uniforms radioed for them as soon as they saw the stiff."

"How about an ambulance crew?"

"On the scene now."

"Good. Okay. Who are the blue-suiters on the scene?"

"Eight-A-Sixty-Four. Reeves and Watts."

Fey cringed. "Reeves? He wouldn't know a suspect if one came up and jumped in the backseat of his police car. He probably hasn't gotten any further in the investigation than trying to put the make on the maid. Watts is okay, but still very wet behind the ears."

Cahill gave a weary smile. "If working homicide was easy, we'd let someone from the mayor's staff investigate."

"Heaven forbid," Fey said, rolling her eyes before becoming serious again. "Do me a favor?" she requested. "Send the uniforms a message over the MDT to make sure they have the crime scene taped off and are staying outside the residence. The last thing we need is the crime scene contaminated by Reeves doing his kleptomaniac act or Watts flicking cigarette ash over all the evidence."

"Anything else?"

Fey took a breath before continuing. "Make sure they've got an incident log started and they're keeping the maid isolated from other witnesses."

"Will do," said Cahill.

"Oh, make sure they keep the ambulance crew there until we arrive. I'm going to want to interview them and find out what they touched or moved."

Cahill said, "Check." He had a lot of faith in Fey. She was very methodical in her investigations and didn't miss a trick.

Fey picked up the unit's sign-in sheet and stared at it. "I'll take Hatcher with me," she said, making a notation on the sheet.

"Why don't you take Colby?"

Fey gave Cahill a sharp look. It was very unlike the lieutenant to question who she assigned to a case.

Cahill caught Fey's glance and held up a hand in mock defense before she could retort verbally. "Colby asked specifically to be assigned to this one," he said in a conciliatory tone. "He knows the lay of the land up there."

"What does that mean?" She didn't like Colby. Supervising him was bad enough, but she loathed the thought of actually partnering him on a case.

"Because he dresses like a wannabe movie star with the taste of a two-dollar whore doesn't mean he knows the rich any better than the rest of us."

"Come on, Fey," Cahill said. "Give the guy a break. He's a good detective. He needs a little experience."

"Not to hear him tell it," she said.

As if on cue, Alan Colby came up the back stairs and cut a swath across the squad room. Tall and athletic, he walked past the random clumps of desks scattered around the room, and flashed a grin at Cahill and Fey.

"Was somebody talking about me?" he asked, picking up leftover vibrations of conversation. "My ears are burning."

"Grab your stuff," Fey told him as she reached down to take a shoulder-holstered Smith & Wesson .38 out of her desk drawer. "We've got a stiff waiting for us up in Brentwood."

"Hotdog!" Colby said.

"I'm glad you find death something to be happy about."

"Chill out, Frog Lady. I'm turned on by a challenge."

Fey halted in the process of slipping on her shoulder rig. "I won't tell you again, Colby. Don't call me Frog Lady."

"You've got to love her pose, don't you, Lieutenant?" Colby said, referring to the fact Fey's position, half in and half out of the shoulder rig, pushed her arms back and thrust her bosom forward as if it were an item offered for display.

"It's impressive," Cahill said.

Fey shook her head and shrugged the shoulder holster the rest of the way into place. "Why is it men never grow out of adolescence? If women were fixated on nothing but various parts of the male anatomy, then both sexes would be useless."

The lieutenant's secretary giggled when she overheard the comeback. Fey grinned at her. "It's like trying to keep a room full of five-year-olds busy," she said. The secretary laughed again.

"Come on, Colby," Fey told him. "You're slowing me down."

CHAPTER TWO

Despite Fey's disparaging words, Alan Colby would have looked good on the big screen. He had high cheekbones, full lips, and a shaggy mane of crow-black hair he was constantly being told to cut. His eyes were clear with an unusual bright green tint to the irises and a slight Oriental cast to the lids.

His lean build testified to long hours of workouts. He was ranked as one of the top thirty triathletes in the state. On two occasions, he had won gold medals in the Police Games, and on another, he had placed fourth in the Ironman competition in Hawaii. Working out was something of an obsession with him.

His clothes were straight from the pages of GQ— Italian suits and shoes, Oriental silk ties, and French cuffed shirts with expensive cuff links. He wore them all well on his tall whipcord body. He could easily have made a living as a male model. Fey had more than her share of battles with weight, and Colby's flaunting of his slimness only added to her dislike of the man.

Colby's smile was right off the silver screen as well. He could melt them in the aisles when he let loose with his trademark grin. Right now he was flashing his ivories at the maid who had discovered the body. It was making the interview difficult and driving Fey mad.

"Knock it off, Colby," Fey told him quietly. "Her bank balance isn't big enough to interest you."

"Meow," said Colby. He turned his grin in Fey's direction. "I love it when you show your jealous side."

"Why don't you go play in traffic?"

In all her years on the job, Fey had seen a lot of detectives come and go. Colby might be the current flavor of the month, but Fey kept telling herself he, too, would pass. He'd recently been assigned to homicide as a reward for breaking a huge car theft ring while assigned to the divisional Auto Theft Unit. Apparently, he was still riding high on the notoriety.

As the homicide supervisor, Fey had objected to being forced to take on a detective she wasn't comfortable around. In her mind, Colby's flashy clothes, flashy jewelry, flashy car, and flashy style smacked of corruption. She couldn't prove it, but her instincts were rarely wrong.

There had been a problem, however. The homicide unit was on a cold streak. They were suffering from four *unsolveds* in a row, and Cahill had insisted on an injection of new blood. As a result, Colby had simply flashed his Cheshire Cat grin and picked canary feathers out from between his teeth.

Nobody came out and said the cold streak happened because a woman was in charge of the unit, but the sentiment was clearly apparent. Fey was convinced, however, Colby had something on someone. She didn't want to admit to her own working-class snobbery by putting Colby's success down to talent and hard work.

There was another thing Fey didn't want to admit to herself. Down where her primal sexual instincts lived,

Colby's good looks tripped her switches. She disliked him, but physically he turned her on. She couldn't help her response, and it pissed her off to no end.

For his part, Colby did things specifically to irritate Fey. He hadn't been interested in the maid, but he knew it would upset Fey if it appeared as if he were. There was something about Fey that brought out the worst in him. If he looked at it objectively, she was a good detective, but he didn't think she deserved to be running the Homicide Unit.

The reasoning behind his feelings was something he didn't want to examine too closely. As in other unresolved relationships in his past, analysis might reveal personal faults to which he didn't want to admit. In the short run it was easier to accept the feelings and leave the reasoning locked up in a mental closet somewhere. You never showed any weaknesses, never gave anyone the edge.

When Fey and Colby had arrived at the security gates of the Oak Vista Estates, they found themselves doing battle with an overeager security guard worried the events of the evening would put his job in jeopardy. He insisted on checking their ID, and then radioed to another security guard, who was inside the complex with Reeves and Watts, to make sure Fey and Colby were authorized.

By the time the security gates were swung open to allow the detectives' beat-up sedan to pass through, Fey was fuming. "Wuss butt," she said, referring to the security guard. "He'll let the press straight in as long as they promise to take his picture."

On the other side of the vehicle, Colby was strangely quiet during this tirade. Fey looked over to see him staring out the passenger window at the opulence of the surrounding community.

"There's no way, Colby," she said.

Colby brought his attention around to her. "I don't follow you."

"There's no way you'll ever be able to afford one of these units on a cop's salary."

Colby shrugged. "Why not? You live in a house on a couple of acres somewhere to accommodate your horses and all the flies they attract. Bet it cost you a bundle in the California real estate market."

"I was lucky," Fey said. "I bought the property before the real estate boom." She felt angry because Colby had immediately put her back on the defensive.

"So, maybe I'll follow your example. I'll get married and divorced several times, take all my exes to the cleaners, and then I'll be able to move right in here. They'll be glad to have me. Having a real cop on the grounds would give the homeowners a sense of security. Plus, I don't need room for animals, and I don't gather flies."

Fey bit back. "Don't flatter yourself. You're no real cop."

The complex the two detectives were driving through looked like something out of *Architectural and Landscaping Monthly.* The exteriors of the two and three-story town homes were done in mock Tudor style and built over matching two-car garages. White stucco was crisscrossed with black oak beaming and highlighted with old-fashioned red brick or silver-gray quarry stones. There were perhaps 150 units, each attached to another unit by one common wall. Not one of them cost under $850,000.

The grounds surrounding the units were green and rambling with babbling brooks, low split-oak fencing, and other lush, expensive to maintain, features. An army of grounds keepers were kept busy tending the roses, trimming the mature oak trees, mowing the extensive greenbelts, and tending the private nine-hole golf course running across the back length of the complex.

Fey saw an ambulance and the black-and-white police unit parked in front of 2008 Mirrorwood. Reeves was standing beside the vehicle, the driver's door open. Next to him was one of the complex's uniformed security guards.

Through the squad car's rear window Fey could see Rusty Watts sitting on the passenger side talking to a woman in the vehicle's backseat. Fey assumed it was the maid.

On the townhome's front lawn, three men and two women all dressed in casual clothes or sweat suits stood in a group. Any of their outfits would have cost Fey two weeks' salary. One of the women walked up to the open door of the townhome, grabbed hold of the doorframe, and leaned in to peek inside.

There wasn't a glint of yellow crime scene tape to be seen anywhere. Fey could feel herself beginning to steam. Not the best frame of mind to start an investigation in which the first six hours were the most critical. She parked behind the ambulance. Both she and Colby climbed out.

"Get those people off the lawn, and get that woman away from the door," Fey told Colby. Turning on her heel, she started walking toward the squad car without looking back to see if Colby was following her directions.

Reeves straightened up and smiled when he saw Fey approaching. Each arm of his blue uniform shirt sported a pair of chevrons identifying him as a training officer. "Howdy," he said, in a put-on cowboy accent.

"What are you doing letting those people walk all over the crime scene?" Fey demanded, opening up with both barrels.

Reeves's smile turned to a look of confusion. He swiveled his eyes toward where Colby was herding the citizens off the lawn like a collie with too many sheep to tend. "There's nobody in the crime scene. It's upstairs in the bedroom."

"How long have you been on this job, Reeves?" Fey didn't wait for an answer, plowing straight on. "Didn't Cahill send you a message to tape off the scene?"

"It wasn't needed. We closed the door to the bedroom. It was enough to keep everybody out."

"How did you ever become a training officer?" Fey did not have much tolerance for incompetence. "This whole complex is a crime scene. Now, get off your dead ass, dig some crime scene tape out of your trunk, and get this area protected. And if I find you've smudged any prints by closing the door to the bedroom, I'm going to initiate a personnel complaint so fast, you'll be doing freeway therapy before the ink is dry on the paperwork."

Freeway therapy was the term for the *unofficial* department discipline of transferring an offending officer to the farthest division from his home. Reeves looked aggrieved and pained, as if he were a child being disciplined by an overbearing parent for no reason. He turned to slowly do Fey's bidding.

Fey knew Reeves would now start spreading the word about what a bitch she was, but it didn't bother her. She'd lived with it all her career.

If a male detective had chewed Reeves out, Reeves would have been seen to be at fault. The male detective would have been admired as a kick-ass, no-nonsense copper doing his job.

However, because she was a woman, other male officers would rally to Reeves's defense. Fey's outburst would be put down to PMS or some equally moronic placebo. It wouldn't matter if Fey was right, or Reeves was nothing more than a lazy drone who never did more than he had to in order to get by. Only gender stereotypes would matter—Reeves was a macho, fun-loving guy. Fey was a frigid bitch who complained about every little thing.

Fey leaned into the interior of the police car. She smiled at the woman who was smoking in the backseat, then looked at Watts. He was also smoking a Marlboro cigarette.

"Do you have a crime scene log started?" she asked Watts.

"You bet." Watts held up a sheet of paper attached to a clipboard. In a neat, precise hand, he had notated all incidents since he and his partner had discovered the body. Each entry bore a time notation.

Fey looked at the list and handed it back. "Good," she said. "I can even read the thing." She smiled. "Log in the arrival of my partner and I, and keep the list going until I tell you differently."

"Okay," Watts said. He was still a rookie and eager to both please and learn. Fey had seen him around the station and felt he had potential. Reaching over, Fey took the cigarette out from between Watts' fingers and took a long drag. "Filthy habit," she said.

"I know."

She took another hit and handed the cigarette back. "Did you light one of these up in the residence?"

Watts shook his head. "Who do you think I am? Reeves?"

Fey laughed for the first time since Cahill had handed her the squeal. She felt some of the tension flow out of her.

"No," she said. "I wouldn't insult you."

Colby materialized behind Fey's shoulder and started flashing his ivories at the maid in the backseat of the police car. She was a young and slender Latina with curly black hair and a scared look in her eyes.

"Did you get the names of the looky-loos?" Fey asked Colby when she became aware of his presence.

Colby displayed a handful of field interview cards. "They didn't take kindly to being questioned, but I charmed them all."

Fey rolled her eyes. "How about the ambulance crew?"

"It's Kyle Digby's crew."

"Great. Digby knows what he's doing."

"Digby said he walked a straight line to the body to check for vitals. Said it was a foregone conclusion. Victim's carotid was severed. Blood had spurted everywhere. Digby declared the victim dead on the F-six-sixty form."

"Okay, keep it to attach to the death report. Any of the other crew go inside?"

"Digby said only him. He knows how you like to keep the scene as virgin as possible. Kind of like your reputation."

Fey didn't rise to the bait.

Turning back to Watts, she said, "Get on the radio and whistle up another patrol unit to help secure the location. I want to go inside and have a look before the coroner and SID show up." She nodded toward the woman in the backseat. "The maid?"

Watts nodded as he picked up the radio mike. "Yeah. Lucia Cortez." He handed Fey an FI card with the woman's basic information filled out neatly in the assigned boxes.

Fey pulled back from the front seat of the police car and opened the rear door and slid in next to the maid. Colby took Fey's place on the front seat.

"Hello, Lucia. I'm Detective Croaker. This is my partner, Detective Colby. Do you speak English?"

"Yes." The maid bit the word off as if she were scared to let further sounds burst from her mouth.

Fey could tell the woman was extremely nervous. Her eyes kept bouncing around the interior of the squad car, making her seem like a frightened animal looking for an escape route.

Fey noticed Colby turn up the intensity of his smile when he noticed how lush the maid's body appeared to be under her tight black-and-white uniform.

"Knock it off, Colby."

"Yes, ma'am," he replied, turning up the wattage another notch.

Fey ignored him and returned her attention to the maid. "Lucia, I'm sure this was a terrible shock, but I need to ask you a few questions, okay?"

"Okay," the maid said, cutting off the word again with a firm clamping of her mouth. She'd finished the cigarette she'd been smoking and seemed at a loss of how to dispose of the butt. Fey took it from her and handed it to Colby, who put it in the gutter.

"How long have you been in this country, Lucia?" Fey asked. The immediate fear in the woman's eyes confirmed Fey's instincts. "It's okay," she told the woman, placing a reassuring hand on the maid's arm. "We don't care if you are here legally or not. You aren't in any trouble, and we aren't interested in deporting you."

"You no send me back?"

"No," Fey said. "When we are done here, I'll have somebody drive you to wherever you're living."

"But I have other houses to clean today. I get fired if I don't turn up."

"It's okay," Fey said. "Tell me who you are working for and I'll have somebody talk to them and make sure they understand. All right?"

The woman nodded. "Okay."

"Now," Fey said, "what time did you get here today?"

"Eight o'clock. My boyfriend drop me off outside." With the mention of a boyfriend, her eyes flicked again to make contact with Colby's.

"How did you get into the house?"

"I have a key. I let myself in by the front door. I called out to Mrs. Goodwinter, but she no answer."

"Mrs. Goodwinter? She's the woman you work for, the woman who lives here?"

"Yes."

"Is there a Mr. Goodwinter?"

"I not know. Mrs. Goodwinter, she live alone."

"How long have you worked for Mrs. Goodwinter?"

"This is only second week. She only move in. I come on Tuesday and Thursday for four hours, and then I go and clean for Mr. and Mrs. Barstow down the street."

"How did Mrs. Goodwinter come to hire you?"

The maid shrugged. "I see her moving in two weeks ago. I come over and ask her if she need anybody to do her cleaning. She tell me to start the next Tuesday." She looked at Colby again and self-consciously ran a hand through her hair. She re-crossed her legs, and there was a whisper of black nylon.

Fey glared at Colby. She returned to questioning Lucia. "What did you do after you entered the residence?"

"I thought Mrs. Goodwinter might still be asleep, so I went upstairs to check."

"You didn't start cleaning?"

"No. I didn't want to make no noise and wake up Mrs. Goodwinter and get her mad at me."

"Okay. You went upstairs to the bedroom. Then what happened?"

Lucia began to cry. "The door. It was a little open. I opened it the rest of the way and then I saw her on the bed." The maid put her hands up to her face and began to cry harder.

Fey put her arm around the woman. "It's all right," she said.

When Lucia calmed down a little, Fey asked her, "Did you go any further into the room?"

"No. I was too scared. I run down the stairs and outside."

"You didn't call the police?"

"No."

Fey looked over at Watts.

"The radio call came out as an *unknown trouble, woman screaming*. There was no PR or call-back number," Watts explained.

Fey spoke to Colby. "Use the mobile phone and call communications right away. I want the nine-one-one tape with the call on it and the printout with the address of the original call."

Colby grunted and slid out of the car.

"Are you sure the person you saw on the bed was Mrs. Goodwinter?"

"Yes.. No...I think so."

Fey patted the woman's arm again. "Thanks, Lucia. I'm going to want to talk to you again later, okay?"

"*Si*...Yes. Okay."

Fey climbed out of the backseat and walked around the car to the passenger side. She signaled to Watts, who climbed out to talk to her.

"Take care of her," Fey said. "I don't want anyone else talking to her. I don't want her to leave the scene. She might split on us and we'll never find her again. Don't let her out of your sight."

Watts looked confused. "You think maybe she did it?"

"No, I don't," Fey said. "But I'm not going to take a chance on being wrong."

CHAPTER THREE

Fey stood on the threshold of the victim's residence. Colby stood behind her, slipping plastic bootees over his Italian loafers. Carefully, Fey took a pair of latex gloves out of her pocket and pulled them on as if she were a surgeon preparing for an operation. A small satchel was slung over her right shoulder.

Taking a deep breath, she cleared her mind of all exterior input. This was the moment of an investigation in which Fey felt almost down to the core of her being. The split-second high before plunging into the deep end of a dank and seemingly bottomless pool.

Time was ticking.

It took six hours from the time a detective first received a murder call-out until the best chance of solving the case disappeared in a heartbeat. Twenty-four hours later the case began to slow down. After forty-eight hours the main leads were cleared off the desk and you began to start looking for anything you might have missed. At seventy-two hours the bell rang and the time on all your options ran out.

Beyond seventy-two hours, solving the case became a

long shot. A crapshoot. A needle-in-the-haystack proposition.

Seventy-two hours and time was ticking.

Fey checked her watch and made a mental note of the time. Colby would be following along behind her, making a hard copy of the same thing on his clipboard. He would already have notes of the time they had received the original call, how the call had been made, and who had made it. As they continued, he would be noting down the outside and inside temperatures and the weather conditions. All of these things could turn out to be no help at all, or they could turn out to be crucial at a trial held months or years later. Notes were far better in court than blurred memories, or memories influenced by every crime scene a detective had ever worked.

Fey stepped under the crime scene tape. Reeves had gone out of his way to string it everywhere like a dog marking his territory.

It was time to go to work.

The inside of the town house was opulent and beautiful. It was as if pages of an interior decorating magazine had been clipped out and given life. Large burnished squares of Italian tile with rough gray grout slid underfoot, leading the way into the spacious open floor plan currently in vogue.

Exposed beams crossed the high ceilings to tie in with the Tudor exterior. Across the back of the house, large windows and French doors spilled light through gauzy eggshell draperies. The tiled floor was decorated with expensive throw rugs ranging in styles from Aubusson to Oriental to Persian. Couches and chairs with lots of cushions were seemingly scattered at random but were actually placed at aesthetically strategic spots. The beige textured walls sported rounded corners as if the house were designed to be lived in by someone who had to be kept away from sharp edges.

Fey memorized it all with a glance before walking in a careful line directly from the front door to the curved stairway. With her hands down by her side, she walked slowly, looking ahead to where her next foot would fall, making sure no piece of vital evidence would be disturbed by her passage.

Behind her, she could feel Colby correctly dogging her footsteps like a child following his father through the snow.

At the top of the stairs, Fey stopped again to take in the surroundings. She was conscious of the weight of the gun hanging snugly in its holster under her arm. She tested the air as if she were an animal sensing for danger. There was almost no *probability* the suspect was still on the scene, but it was always a *possibility*.

When Fey had first been assigned as a detective trainee years earlier, she had come across a murder suspect hiding on the shelf of a walk-in closet twelve hours after he'd done the dirty deed. The incident had been like lightning striking, a once-in-a-career instance, but the chance still had to be considered.

The magazine-perfect decorating theme was continued on the townhome's upper level. Fey thought it was beautiful, expensive, and charming, but impersonal. There seemed to be no mark anywhere of the owner's individual personality other than to say she didn't have one. The fact there was no pattern was a pattern in itself.

All the doors to the rooms leading off the landing were open except for one. Fey realized the closed door, having been shut by Reeves, hid the crime scene. She walked to the door and looked at the door handle. Any chance of prints on the doorknob had probably been screwed up by Reeves, but she didn't want to compound the error. Taking a Swiss army knife from the satchel, she selected the longest blade and shimmed the door with all the adroitness of a professional burglar.

The door swung open and Fey felt the electric charge of anticipation, fear, and discovery zip through her. The room was picture perfect—a murder captured on canvas by an old master—another leaf from the decorator's handbook. This time it was an illustration of the use of white. Every shade from stark to eggshell to lace was represented by either the carpet, the chairs, the bed, the lampshades, the comforter, the walls, or the ornate plastered mantel across the white fireplace bricks.

Sunlight streamed through a large open window, highlighting the pale white body of the victim as it angled across the four-poster bed. The head and right arm were off the mattress, pointing toward the floor. The acute angle of the head exposed the ragged wound across the side of the neck. The hand at the end of the long, graceful right arm touched the floor in a pool of congealing blood.

The impact of the white-on-white-on-white was heightened by the dramatic slash of dark red, which arched like an angry brushstroke from one side of the bed, across the white wall and the off-white window sheers, to speckle out across the flat white ceiling.

A trail left behind by the soul as it fled the body.

Fey felt Colby behind her, not touching her, but still pushing her to enter the room.

"What's the matter?" he asked, when she still didn't move. "Not scared of dead bodies, are you?"

"I've seen more naked dead ones than you've seen naked live ones."

"You picking out your lovers from the morgue again?"

Fey grunted, but still did not budge. "Hold your water and try to learn something."

"What's to learn?"

"There is something alive in this room, and it isn't the body on the bed."

Colby stiffened. "A suspect?" His voice was disbelieving.

Fey shook her head. "No. I don't think it's human."

"What are you talking about? Ghosts or something?" The tone in Colby's voice had turned from disbelief to ridicule.

"Give me the clipboard."

Colby handed the board over Fey's shoulder. She took it from him without taking her eyes off the scene in front of her. Using the pencil attached to the board by a length of twine, she began to sketch the crime scene on a clean sheet of paper. She worked fast with sure strokes, creating almost a piece of art—a still life of death—as opposed to the more typical drafting floor plan, which she would leave to Colby. When she was done, she handed the board back to her partner.

"Well," he said.

"Well, what?"

"What about this nonhuman presence?"

"It's not ready to come out yet." Fey smiled to herself. She knew she was getting to Colby.

"You're weird," Colby said, forcibly pushing his way into the room. "Are you some kind of witch or something?"

"Thanks for using a *W* instead of a *B*."

"Not much difference," Colby said.

"Follow me and take your notes." Fey started to move toward the body. Her eyes scanned the floor and she was careful to touch nothing. When she reached the body, she began talking softly and slowly, giving time for Colby to write it all down.

"Victim is female, white, red hair. Approximately five feet four inches, one hundred twenty pounds. No obvious scars or tattoos visible. Lots of freckles. Emerald green fingernail and matching toenail polish. The body is naked and there are no obvious signs of bruising or other contusions or abrasions. There are no apparent foreign objects protruding from the body. The mouth is open slightly and is smeared with red lipstick. The smear appears to have occurred before death, possibly through a kissing motion, as opposed to a smear consciously applied by the suspect."

Fey moved around the bed to get another view. She noted a pale green nightgown on the floor and pointed it out to Colby. He flipped the pages on the clipboard and made a note of the position on his crime scene drawing.

Fey continued her dialogue. "The victim's legs are slightly spread open and there appears to be a white discharge seeping out of the vaginal area. There are no apparent foreign objects, and there are no visible signs of a struggle."

Returning to the side of the bed where she'd started her examination, Fey crouched down and examined what she could see of the body's sides.

"Postmortem lividity appears normal for the position of the body," she said, knowing lividity was the bruising occurring in a dead body when the blood settles. She knew if a body had been moved, the lividity would not be consistent with the body's new position. She reached out and touched a pale white arm. "Rigor is present."

Next, she turned her attention to the wound. "The victim has an approximately two-inch gash on the right side of her neck appearing to have severed the carotid artery." The autopsy would come later and give the official cause of death, but Fey's observations would start the ball rolling. "The wound appears to have been made by a sharp object other than a knife because of the tearing of the skin. Possibly an icepick-type weapon." Fey looked up at Colby. "You getting all this?"

"I'm a happy little stenographer. Want me to sit on your lap?"

"Shuuuush..." Fey held up a hand.

"What?"

"Shut up." Fey's voice was quiet, but insistent.

Silence.

Colby shuffled his feet. Fey shot him a dirty look.

A cry sounded faintly, like a baby with a pillow over its face.

"What the hell..." Colby said.

The noise sounded again.

"Where is it coming from?"

Fey slowly crouched beside the bed. The dust ruffle at her feet moved slightly.

"I think we've found ourselves a witness," she said as a sleek white cat suddenly jumped into her lap.

Colby shook his head in disgust. "You and your inhuman presence. How did you know about the cat?"

"Experience."

"My ass."

"If you say so."

"Come on."

"I used my eyes, Colby." She was pleased she'd got his goat. "I saw the cat hairs on the tiled floor downstairs. They were the only things not left behind by the decorator in this entire place."

"But how did you know the cat was in the room?"

"Because I know cats."

The animal was really yowling now, as if it were trying to tell Fey everything it had seen. Fey wrapped her arms around it and stood up. She thrust the bundle of fur at Colby. "Take him down to the car and secure him."

Colby fumbled with his clipboard as the cat squirmed around. He'd been so shocked when Fey handed the cat to him, he'd accepted it automatically.

"Leave a window slightly cracked so he can get air, but don't leave it down enough so he can get out. Then see if the photographer has arrived and send him up."

"I'm not an errand boy, Frog Lady." Colby was indignant. Pressing the squirming cat and clipboard to him with one hand, he tried in vain to brush cat hair off his suit jacket with the other. Frustrated, he raised his voice. "I ain't no freaking cat-sitter."

Fey turned slowly to look at him. "Consider yourself lucky." She smiled evilly. "This is probably the closest you're going to get to a pussy until this investigation is over."

CHAPTER FOUR

"Who shoved a burr under your partner's saddle?" Eddie Mack asked as he came in through the bedroom door. Camera gear sprouted from his body like fruit on a tree. "He looked like he wanted to strangle the cat."

Fey laughed. "Adversity is good for him. It helps build character." She turned from her study of the body to greet the new arrival. "How are you, Eddie? Busy shift?"

"I'm okay, but busier than a set of jumper cables at a Mexican wedding. I had a triple over in Newton. Before there, I handled a drive-by in Seventy-Seventh."

"Welcome to Los Angeles where we treat you like a *King*," Fey said, cynically referencing the Rodney King incident. The sentiment had become a catchphrase for the continuing explosion of violence in the city.

Eddie swiveled the strobe on one of the cameras slung around his neck. He was a short man made ugly by thick black hairs blossoming from his nostrils, and a tennis-ball-sized lump on his neck. He was stuffed into a mish-mash of clothing even a thrift store would reject, but his equipment was state-of-the-art and in pristine condition.

He'd bought all the equipment himself, knowing the city would never pay for it. "You want the usual shots with an extra set?" He'd worked with Fey before and knew what she expected.

"Yes," Fey said. "Make 'em sharp, Eddie. I want to crack this one fast."

"When have I ever given you anything but my best work?" Eddie sounded wounded.

"Never, Eddie."

"Exactly."

"How about sticking around and shooting anything the print people come across?" Fey asked. Taking photos of prints before they were lifted made sure you still had a usable piece of evidence if the print disintegrated during the lifting process.

"No problem." Eddie looked up from fiddling with his equipment. "Oh, I get it," he said, realizing why Fey was being so careful. "This is your first stiff of the new year."

"It won't be the last."

Eddie guffawed then glued his eyes to a viewfinder. Without waiting any longer, he started triggering film. "Nice set of gazzongas for an old broad," he commented, viewing the body from behind the defense of his lens.

In the bursts from the strobe, Fey looked at the dead woman with the big gazzongas. It made her sad. Even in death, the woman was not safe from the vicious bite of sexual innuendo.

Who were you? Fey silently asked the body. *Who were you?*

Backing away to the door, deep in thought, she almost collided with the coroner, Harry Carter.

"Sorry," she said, stepping aside.

"Getting a little too wrapped up in your work as usual," Carter said.

Fey smiled. "Trying to solve this one without any clues. Cart-before-the-horse time."

"Coming up with answers before you know what the questions are? If anybody can do it, you will." Carter was an older man and enjoyed the role of father figure. He also liked Fey and was one of her big supporters.

"What's the head coroner doing here anyway?" Fey asked him. "I thought you'd become too much of a big shot to come out in the field anymore. I expected Simms or Wiley."

"Simms is out with the flu, and Wiley got himself caught stealing gold fillings. Big investigation going on."

"Really?" Fey said, slightly shocked.

Carter rolled his eyes. "Down at the coroner's office we're no different than police officers. We're our own worst enemies. The political-damage-control types have been trying to keep it out of the papers, but the story is going to leak eventually."

"Good grief. So, as a result you get to come out and play with the common folk."

"It makes a nice change. Beats the pressures of doing celebrity autopsies."

"You won't get a book out of this one," she said.

Carter had made a big splash with a nonfiction book recounting the stories behind the deaths of numerous celebrities on whom he'd conducted autopsies.

Carter shrugged. "Who needs to write another book? The publishers have got some hack to grind out a new series of mysteries featuring a coroner as the main character, some kind of high-priced *Quincy*. They're going to publish them under my name. I talk to the hack a couple of times on the phone and then sit back and rake in the hefty advances and royalties. When the books come out, I make the book-signing rounds as if I wrote every word, assure everyone the next installment is well under way, and then leave the public and the talk-show hosts thinking I'm some kind of Renaissance man. I don't even have to read the things."

"Sounds sweet."

Carter shrugged expressively. A smile split through his beard. "It's a living." He hefted his black bag. "Better get to work."

Fey smiled back and let him slip by into the crime scene. Two men from SID, the department's Scientific Investigation Division, followed through behind him. One would be a latent-print expert, the other would be a specialist in biological stains. Fey didn't recognize the stain specialist, who was lugging around a huge Woods lamp, but she did know the print man. He nodded a greeting.

"How are you, Steve?" Fey asked.

"Can't complain. Nobody would listen anyway even if I did."

"Let Eddie Mack follow you around and pop a few flashes before you lift anything."

"You want anything else special?"

Fey smiled engagingly. "I know it's a big place, but can you give me a top-to-bottom?"

"You got it."

Fey smiled again, said, "Thanks," and left them to it.

Before she retraced her steps to the front door, she made a quick search until she located a covered cat litter box in the small downstairs bathroom. Fortunately, it had been recently emptied. She lifted the covered litter box by the plastic handle on the top and carried it with her.

As she passed by the living room, she heard Colby call out to her.

"Look what I found." He held up a woman's handbag.

Fey shook her head. She shouldn't have let Colby off

the leash. He was like a two-year-old who keeps getting into the kitchen cupboards. There was a lot more they should have done before starting to root through hand-bags and wallets.

She kept her temper in check. The damage was done. Getting pissed would only make things worse.

She walked over to stand next to the formal dining table, where Colby was laying out his finds. She set down the litter box.

Colby handed her a California driver's license.

"Miranda Goodwinter. Like the maid said," he told her.

Fey took the small card and looked at the flash-flat-tened picture. There was no doubt it was the woman upstairs on the bed. The harsh photo had brought out all of the age lines relaxed by the death repose.

"Did you find an address book?" she asked, flipping the license back onto the table.

Colby riffled through the pile of items from the handbag – wallet, makeup, short-handled brush, hair clip, assorted papers, matches, cigarettes, checkbook, keys.

"No address book, but there's some other ID in the same name," he said. He handed Fey a stack of plastic and cardboard rectangles taken from the wallet.

"Any photos of friends, relatives, ugly babies?" Fey asked as she shuffled through the stack.

"Not in the purse. And I didn't see any on the walls or furniture. It's something I always check for."

Fey raised her eyebrows.

Colby cut loose his maddening grin. "Ease up, Frog Lady," he said. "You might not like me, but it doesn't mean I'm a bad detective. If you'd loosen up a bit, you might find I'm not too bad at other things either." His implication was clear, his grin turning into a leer.

"Come back and see me when you reach puberty, Colby," Fey told him.

Colby laughed, unoffended. "Everyone tells me you're a tight-ass."

"I'm as watertight as a duck's ass, Colby. Don't forget it."

"Yes, ma'am."

Fey shook her head at Colby's sarcastic tone. It was another one of the many irritating things about him. One second, he could display the professional sense all top detectives develop, and the next moment, he acted as if he'd never outgrown the phase of male development where sex was a dirty joke and women were something to snigger about while smoking cigarettes behind the school gym.

The combination of traits did not sit well with Fey. She liked people to either be one way or the other. It made them easier to deal with. With someone like Colby, she didn't know which way to jump. She could rely on him in some areas but had to keep her defenses up in others. It was a stress inducing situation. So, rather than attempt to walk a tightrope between the characteristics, Fey simply distrusted Colby in all areas, making it very hard for her to be objective about him.

Fey looked down at the cards in her hand again, shuffling through them for a second time. "Did you notice anything strange about this ID?" she asked.

"It's all current issue," Colby replied, back in professional mode. "The driver's license, the credit cards, the Auto Club card – all of it is fresh."

"Good answer," Fey said. "You get to move on to the bonus round."

"It's as if this babe was brand-new," Colby continued. "If it weren't for her stretch marks and wrinkles, she could have just popped out of the womb."

"Interesting analogy, but not far off," Fey agreed. "New condo. New ID." She surveyed the room. "All the furniture looks new."

Colby agreed. "Even the television has a protective covering on the screen."

Fey walked over to the coat closet and pulled it open. Inside the closet, several expensive coats hung on the rack. Fey checked the sleeves. Two had the manufacturer's tags attached. "Fresh from the boutique," she said.

Picking up a checkbook from the pile on the table, Colby looked at the balance. "She opened this account with ten thousand dollars." He looked further. "Two checks are gone. They're the ones you have to fill in the name and address part until the printed ones arrive."

"Does she have a car?"

"The uniforms ran a DMV on the new Beemer in the driveway. It's registered in the name of our victim. If it is her name. I'd say she was running from something, but she didn't run far or fast enough."

Fey's silent words echoed in her head again. *Who were you?*

"She's run before," she said. "The ID and the rest of this setup is too sophisticated for a first-timer. Go upstairs and tell Carter to get a second set of prints off the corpse and run them through FIN." The Fingerprint Identification Network would kick out a match if the victim had been printed anywhere for any reason such as military, criminal, professional licensing, and so forth. "Also tell him we need a dental chart. Maybe we'll get a line on her from her teeth."

"You suck eggs this way, Grandma," Colby said. His grin was as vibrant as ever. He moved without hurrying toward the stairs.

One day, pal, Fey thought, *your dentist is going to be handling you as a trauma case.*

CHAPTER FIVE

After setting the litter box on the back seat of the detective sedan, Fey waited outside until Colby and Harry Carter finally came down from upstairs. Reeves had at least done the job of stringing the crime scene tape properly the second time around. After he'd roped off as much of the house and grounds as he could, he had set up a second buffer of tape a little farther out. The public and the press would be kept behind the second buffer, but other police officers and brass could enter the VIP area. It was a technique to keep the crime scene protected while ensuring other officers on the scene didn't have to mix with the general public. It also provided an area for the police brass to preen themselves and to be seen importantly doing nothing.

Fey had checked in with Mike Cahill, who was standing in the VIP area along with the two other detectives assigned to Fey's homicide unit—Vance Hatcher and Monk Lawson.

Hatcher was tall and blond with a potbelly stolen from a stove. He favored old-fashioned polyester leisure suits, loud ties, and penny loafers. One of his shoes had a tarnished penny stuck in the slot. The other didn't. Despite appearances, he had the highest clearance rate on the team.

Standing next to Hatcher, Monk Lawson looked as if he came from another planet. Shiny black skin, muscles still compact from his days as a top collegiate sprinter, hair sheared close to his skull with a stylish razor slash running through it. He wore a purple shirt with a peach tie under a lavender suit. For some reason, he and Hatcher got along well.

"How did the Schaffer case go?" Fey asked him as she stepped into the VIP area. She could see a lot of the neighborhood residents gathered behind the second buffer of tape. Among them she also recognized the faces of several reporters from the local television stations. Bad news didn't travel anywhere near as fast as sensational-ized news.

Lawson shrugged. "Pretty much a piece of cake. Our witnesses were nailing him all the way down the line. His lawyer called a time-out, took his client aside, and came to us on bended knee for a deal."

The homicide unit was also responsible for investi-gating ADW cases, *assault with a deadly weapon*. Reginald Schaffer had taken a baseball bat to his neighbor's head when the neighbor let her poodle crap on his perfectly manicured lawn. Almost killed the woman. Did kill the dog.

"We cut the deal?"

Lawson smirked. "We figured, why should we? Juries don't like people who are cruel to animals. If he'd have hit the broad, he might have had a better chance. But when Schaffer smacked the dog out of the ballpark, he signed his fate. We turned down the deal, and Schaffer copped out anyway."

"Sounds like he didn't have much of a choice."

"Rock and a hard place."

"Good job," Fey told him. Lawson simply nodded.

Fey turned to Hatcher. "How about you?"

"I got the Taylor spousal abuse filed, but the district attorney referred it over to the city attorney's office. We only got a misdemeanor count filed."

"What! His wife took twelve stitches under her eye from where he punched her."

Hatcher held up his hands placatingly. "What can I say? The DA felt it was provoked."

Fey shook her head in disgust. "She tries to stop her husband from spending the rent money on booze, and it justifies him popping her one? She should have known better than to provoke him. She should have at least waited until he came home drunk before making him punch her out."

"Come on, I didn't reject the filing," Hatcher said, still on the defensive. "I argued the case, but you know the DA's mentality in these situations."

"I know it, all right," Fey said. "It's the same mentality as believing every woman who wears a short dress is asking to be raped."

"How come you never wear short dresses?" Colby asked as he walked up with the coroner on his tail.

"I don't want to distract you from what little work you do," Fey retorted quickly. Monk Lawson laughed. Like Fey, he didn't care for Colby. Monk's mother and four older sisters had raised him to respect women. Colby's sharp tongue might score a lot of points with some of the other guys, but Lawson looked on him with disdain.

Lawson liked Fey. He found her to be a fair and sympathetic supervisor. She could be tough when she had to be, but she didn't throw her weight around needlessly. Lawson also respected her because she didn't seem to notice he was black. As long as he did his job properly, she didn't send any extra flack his way.

Colby, on the other hand, had a chip on his shoulder the size of a redwood. Lawson knew it pissed Colby off to work for a woman. Somehow, Colby had it in his head the situation belittled him. Colby had never been directly disrespectful toward Lawson over the issue of race, but Lawson believed sexism and racism had much in common. If Colby was overtly sexist, he was most likely racist as well, only he hid it better.

"What have you got for me, Harry?" Fey asked the dapper coroner, who was now standing next to Colby.

"I'll have more later, naturally, but right now I can say your stiff has been dead for about eight to ten hours.

From the type of wound, you're looking for a weapon with a sharp point, but not a knife."

"Ice pick?" Fey asked.

Harry shook his head. "More like a screwdriver. Flathead, not Phillips."

"What else?"

The coroner shrugged and consulted a small notebook. "The weapon was used in a slashing motion. Right to left, making your suspect most likely right-handed. Carotid artery was flayed open. Victim bled to death in about ten seconds. The suspect probably caught some blood splatter. The victim shows evidence of recent sexual activity. I may be able to tell you later how recent, and if it was forced. Otherwise, the big news is she definitely dead." He looked at his watch. "Time for me to go to lunch. I have a date."

"Thanks, Harry," Fey told the coroner. "Will you be handling the autopsy?"

Harry checked another page in his notebook. "I've got two others lined up for this afternoon." He thought for a moment, looked at his watch again. "If you want to be there, how about tomorrow morning around ten? If not, I'll have the results typed up for you and sent over by late tomorrow afternoon."

"I'll be there," Fey said.

Harry bobbed his head in acknowledgment.

Two coroner's assistants brought the body out of the town home's front door, wrapped in a black body bag. Press cameras began to whir, and the gathering of citizens behind the second barrier began to surge forward imperceptibly. Everyone wanted to see something even when there was nothing to see. It was the same phenomenon as mile-long traffic jams for fender benders already off to the side of the road.

"What's your next step?" Cahill asked Fey.

She thought about it for a moment or two. "If you want to give the press a statement, Colby and I will go back inside and do the crime scene search."

"What about the maid?"

Fey nodded toward Lawson. "Do you have time to take a formal statement for us?"

"No problem," he replied. "I've got a couple of lukewarm leads on the Bradshaw caper to run down, but those can wait until this afternoon."

"Great. When you're done with the maid, you can send her home, but make sure we have some way of contacting her again."

Lawson turned on his heels with military precision and moved off in the direction of Reeves and Watts' squad car.

"Do you want me to help with the search?" Hatcher inquired.

"I think we can handle it," Fey told him. "I don't want too many cooks. Can you head back to the station and get today's paperwork handled? Make sure we don't have any surprise bodies in custody." Hatcher was a *detective two* and therefore the unit's second-in-command. He was in charge when Fey took a day off or was on vacation.

"Do you want me to split the new cases between Monk and myself?"

Aside from murders, suicides, other suspicious deaths, and ADWs, the homicide unit also investigated spousal batteries where someone was in custody, kidnappings, and various other felonies.

"Yeah. Leave Colby and me clear to work this for a while. When we get done here, we'll all gather back at the station for a powwow." Fey looked at her watch. "Say, three o'clock?"

"Sounds fair. I'll tell Monk."

Because all of the unit's detectives were tied up investigating a fresh murder didn't mean the rest of the unit's workload screeched to a halt. There were still citizens who didn't care how busy the detectives were, continuing to keep hitting each other with blunt instruments, shooting at each other, chasing each other around with knives, kidnapping each other, and basically raising hell in general. Murder took precedence, but life and crime rolled on.

Back inside the town home, Fey and Colby prepared for a major systematic search of the premises. They split up the rooms on the second floor, with Fey taking the crime scene bedroom, the master bathroom, and one of the spare bedrooms. Colby took the two other bedrooms and the guest bathroom. When they were done, they would switch rooms and check each other's work.

Fey felt like a voyeur as she pawed through the dead woman's bedroom drawers. Searches were the worst kind of privacy invasion, looking for dirty little secrets in the nooks and crannies of another person's life. Fey always felt there was something perverse about the process, as if she were a sneak thief rummaging around for a pair of dirty panties with which to abscond.

She also had a bad feeling about the whole case in general. It was too antiseptic. Almost staged. A place for everything, and everything in its place. Either the victim was incredibly anal-retentive, or she'd had the money to go out and order everything brand-new to fill up the drawers and cupboards. A life assembled by the numbers – *I'll take four of those, two of those, and three of the others. Oh, and give me a couple of those red ones over there.*

The dresses in the closet were a uniform size eight, with shoes to match each outfit. None of the shoes showed any signs of wear. The clothing was expensive, mainly in blacks, reds, and maroons. There was a half dozen white blouses, a dozen pairs of slacks, a couple of casual summer dresses, three business suits, and two formal gowns. The clothing was top quality, even down to the two sets of designer sweats.

In another drawer there was enough lingerie to stock a small Victoria's Secret. It ran the gamut from skin-flick kinky to modest weekday-labeled panties. It boasted of an active sex life, but like the clothing in the closet, the lingerie appeared brand-new.

The only thing in the bedroom with any apparent history was the jewelry in a large fabric-covered chest. There were a couple of unique pieces Fey thought might be traceable if they had trouble getting a line on the victim.

Again, there were no address books or Christmas card lists. No compilation of tax returns or monthly bills, not even a payment book for the new BMW. Fey had a feeling the car had been bought for cash. There were no photo albums, no memento knickknacks, no used ticket stubs, no cherished stuffed animals. No detritus of a life lived.

From all appearances, Miranda Goodwinter's life was

as limited as a blow-up doll sitting on the shelf of an adult bookstore. Somebody used her as a depository for sexual lust then deflated her and cast her aside. There didn't seem to be anything else. She'd been alive, and now she was dead.

And dead was nothing more than dead.

Who were you? Fey asked silently again, looking at the rumpled sheets where the body recently reposed.

She stripped the sheets from the bed, turned the mattress over, checked under the bed and in the night-stand. No clues, and no murder weapon.

In the master bathroom she found fresh, name-brand makeup, an unopened box of sanitary napkins, tooth-paste, a single toothbrush, various hairbrushes, and assorted other products. There were no prescription drugs, no illegal drugs, and still no clues.

"Anything?" Colby asked, sticking his head in the door.

"No," Fey replied. "How about you?"

"Sterile, baby, sterile. This place has been picked wholesale out of a catalog. The victim, whoever she was, didn't bring anything with her from any sort of past life. It's like she didn't exist before she moved in here."

"Let's do the downstairs."

Splitting up the rooms again, Colby drew the living room, the den, and the attached garage. Fey took the family room, the kitchen, and the laundry room.

In the kitchen there were three glasses in the sink and a bowl of chips and dip on the counter. The dip was rapidly souring. Fingerprint powder had been splashed over everything in sight.

The refrigerator yielded milk, a couple of grapefruits, three bottles of good champagne, and a half dozen cartons of yogurt in various flavors. Not exactly the cook-at-home type, Fey thought.

The cupboards were mostly empty except for a brand-new set of pots and pans. There was a new set of glasses and an everyday set of china and silverware.

Under the sink was a trash basket. Fey spilled it out on the floor. The only thing of interest was two empty champagne bottles of the same brand as in the refrigerator.

A little bit of luck popped up out of a kitchen drawer filled with the receipts for all the furniture and decorating. Fey set those aside with the empty champagne bottles to deal with later. They might be all they had to work from in trying to reconstruct the victim's background.

There was nothing on the notepad beside the phone. Fey ran the lead of a pencil sideways over the top sheet, but there was no residue from anything previously written on the page above.

With a deep sigh, she turned her attention to the laundry room. There was a new washer and dryer in matching pastel colors. Next to them on the floor was the first sign of normal life Fey had encountered, a large plastic basket with dirty laundry plopped into it.

Fey opened the front-loading door of the dryer. A big fluffy white towel spilled out. Fey pushed it back in and shut the door again. She checked the washing machine tub. Empty. Methodically, she checked the contents of the washing powders and soaps on the shelf above the appliances. Nothing.

Looking at the laundry basket, Fey bent down and picked through the soiled underwear and towels.

Almost automatically, she again noted the underwear was expensive. It should have been hand-washed, not dropped in with the towels to be run through the normal cycle. Maybe the victim was planning on separating the items later.

Fey looked at the towels again. She took off a latex glove and felt them with her bare hand. She brought a bundle of the towels up to her nose and inhaled. The commercial term *springtime fresh* ran through her mind. The towels were clean.

Feeling her pulse increase, she turned back to the dryer and opened the door again. The white towel spilled forward. Fey grabbed it and pulled it clear.

She crouched down to look into the drum. "Crap," she said under her breath.

CHAPTER SIX

"What do you have there?" Colby asked loudly. Fey's concentration had been so centered she hadn't heard him approach.

"For hell's sake, Colby!" His voice had startled her. "Are you trying to give me a heart attack?"

Colby grinned. "Keeping you on your toes."

"You're getting awfully close to stepping on them. When you do, I'm going to cut you off at the knees."

"I love it when you talk dirty," Colby said in a high voice.

Fey ignored him, turning back to the dryer. Colby bent down to look in as well.

"*Oh, crap* is right," he said. With the latex gloves still on his hands, he reached into the drum and began to pull out banded stacks of fifty and hundred-dollar bills. There seemed to be a never-ending supply.

As the stacks grew in front of the dryer, Colby turned to Fey. "What do you say, Frog Lady?" he asked. "Fifty-fifty?"

Fey couldn't quite believe he was serious. She'd felt

the young, flashy detective was bent, but this was a bit too obvious.

Colby suddenly upped his offer. "Okay, you're the boss. How about sixty-forty?"

When he still didn't get any response from Fey, Colby reached back into the dryer and pulled out another handful of banded bills. "There's still a lot of money in here. How about I promise to keep my mouth shut for a seventy-thirty split? Can't be fairer. I've got bills to pay and an image to keep up." He reached back into the dryer again and pulled out two non-monetary banded bundles.

Fey's face had turned seriously red during Colby's monologue. When he turned to face her with the two new bundles in his hands, she was about to boil over.

He grinned. "A joke, Frog Lady," he said. "Believe it or not, I've got more money than I'll ever need."

"Stop calling me Frog Lady. You're beginning to seriously piss me off. Maybe you do have more money than you need, but I doubt you have more than you want."

It was Colby's turn for a reddish flush. "You may think you're a hell of a detective, Frog Lady," Colby emphasized the derogatory nickname, knowing there was nothing Fey could do as long as he didn't use it in public, "but you know nothing about me. One of these days, you'll climb down off your high horse long enough to see things as they really are."

"What are you talking about?"

"You've got it made. Because you're female, you get to live in a coddled little world on this job. Nobody wants to upset you in case you beef them or pull a Franchon Blake and sue the city because you got passed over for a promotion. You flash your legs or your tits, and up the promotion ladder you go."

Fey laughed. She couldn't help herself as the guffaws and giggles flooded out of her. The absurdity of Colby's thought process almost doubled her over with hilarity.

She leaned back against the washing machine, wiping away a tear of amusement. "You ought to be onstage at the Comedy Club. You crack me up."

Colby stood silent, a grim look on his face.

"You are a jealous and confused little boy." Fey actually reached out and put a hand on Colby's shoulder. "I'm sure the two women lieutenants who were on my detective oral board were real impressed when I flashed my tits at them." Fey erupted into another fit of laughter.

"You can't deny the only reason you got the *detective three* spot in this homicide unit is because you're a woman. Everybody knows pressure came down from the chief's office to give the spot to a female."

"May be true, maybe not," Fey said, finally calming down enough to catch her breath. "But it's no different than any of the other favoritism-type promotions in this or any other department. There are guys who get promoted because they go to the same church as someone else. There are people who get promoted because they've got themselves a rabbi who has been molding them in their own image for years. Others promote because somebody somewhere says we have to have a certain number of blacks, Hispanics, or Asians at certain levels. And every once in a while, someone will get promoted because they deserve the promotion in the first place.

"The real world is not a redneck, lily white, male-bonding, white-hoods-and-keep-the-blacks-and-women-in-their-place world anymore. I'm sure you think it's a shame, but it's time to grow up. You pulled a lot of your own strings to get assigned to this unit and this case. All your sour grapes and crying-in-your-beer stuff is nothing more than the pot calling the kettle black. As far as you're concerned, it's only favoritism when somebody other than you gets the spot."

"That's not what I mean."

"Really? Because it sounds like what you mean."

"But…"

Fey dropped her hand from Colby's arm. "I don't have time for any more buts today, partner. Let's get on with what we're doing. Time's ticking."

Colby didn't quite know how to respond.

Fey shook her head, a wry smile racing across her mouth. "Let's call a truce, okay?" She pointed at the last bundles Colby had pulled out of the dryer. "What are you trying to strangle in your poor reverse-discriminated white hands?"

"Some truce," Colby said, staring down at his hands as if he'd forgotten they were attached to his arms.

After a second, he turned and dropped the bundles on top of the washing machine. He popped the rubber band on the larger bundle and sorted through its contents. "Interesting," he said, trying to get past his emotional outburst.

Fey picked up the other bundle and unwound the rubber band around it. She flipped through the contents. "Another complete set of ID in the name of May Wellington. Victim's photo on the driver's license."

"Same here," Colby said, shuffling through the other bundle. "Only the name on this set is Madeline Fletcher." He looked up at Fey. "What kind of scam was this woman running?"

Fey flashed back again to her silently repeated question. This time, she voiced it aloud. "I wonder who she really was."

Colby waggled his eyebrows. "I guess we're going to have to make like detectives and find out."

Fey waggled her own eyebrows, as if the two of them were engaged in a Groucho Marx impersonation contest. "Let's hope when we confirm her true identity, we'll also find who killed her."

"You must be dreaming, Frog Lady. Life is never simple."

CHAPTER SEVEN

The cat yowled incessantly all the way back to the police station.

"We should stick the damn thing on the roof and use it for a siren," Colby complained, holding his hands to his ears.

"The animal is upset," Fey said. "How would you feel if you saw someone murdered right in front of your eyes?"

"You can't compare how an animal feels to how a human feels," Colby grumbled. "Cats don't care about anybody. The stupid animal is only upset because it lost its meal ticket."

"You really are Mr. Sensitive. I bet you volunteer to work off-duty security jobs protecting animal research labs."

"Screw you."

"Snappy comeback."

The cat turned up the noise a notch. Colby twisted around and flailed his left arm at the animal, who was crouched on the backseat of the vehicle. The cat lashed out and clawed Colby's hand deep enough to draw blood.

Colby screeched. He stuck his lacerated hand in his mouth and, in a lightning motion, whipped his 9-mm Beretta out of its hip holster.

The cat was faster than Colby, sensing what was coming and diving for cover under the front seat.

Fey was faster than both. As Colby turned back to the front of the car, planning to stick his gun under the seat and blast the cat to hell, his nose collided with the barrel of Fey's wheel gun.

"Whoa!"

Colby reached out to knock the gun away, but Fey shoved it forward against his forehead. He froze.

Fey was still driving with her left hand, switching her gaze between Colby and the road. "If you hurt the cat, I'll plaster your brains across the landscape. If you don't think I'm serious, please test me."

The cat had gone silent.

"No problem," Colby said, finally. His face had blanched, his eyes wide and shocked.

"Put your gun away," Fey said.

Moving slowly, Colby slid the 9-mm into its holster. He snapped the safety strap across the top.

Fey lowered her revolver then reached across her chest to shove it into its shoulder rig. She put both hands back on the wheel before stopping for the traffic light at Santa Monica Boulevard and Butler. When traffic cleared, she turned right on Butler to cover the last five hundred yards to the police station.

Pulling into the small police only parking lot, she found a slot and braked to a halt.

Colby was sitting straight ahead, staring out the windshield.

"You're a madwoman," he said, without looking at

Fey. His voice and tone were matter-of-fact almost as if he were in shock.

Killing the ignition, Fey leaned her head back against the headrest. She sighed deeply. "Colby, I don't know if you are a good cop or a bad cop. I've got a feeling you could be a hell of a detective, but it's going to take a major attitude adjustment."

She expected some kind of response, but Colby kept his mouth shut.

"Ever since you were assigned to this unit, you've had a King Kong-sized chip on your shoulder," Fey said, her voice low. "I don't know what you have against women – maybe your mother took you off the tit too soon – but if you don't stop busting my chops, you're going to find out I play hardball with the best of them."

Still no response from Colby. He was a sullen child enduring a lecture – the less response, the sooner the ordeal would be over.

Fey took a deep breath and let it out. "If you don't like working for a woman, Get Cahill to sign a transfer. But understand, you're going to go before I do. You may be a hotshot, but I've earned my stripes, whether you think so or not. I'm entitled to the respect you would show a man in my position."

Colby still didn't look at her. "Are you through?" he asked.

Fey sighed again. "I'm through."

Without saying anything more, Colby got out of the car. He slammed the door and walked away.

"I tried," Fey said aloud to herself. She reached over to get her purse from the backseat. As she did so, the white cat emerged from hiding and hopped up next to the purse.

He let out a pathetic yowl.

Fey petted him. "I'm sorry, boy," she said. "Are you hungry?"

The cat yowled.

Fey knew it was silly to think the cat was answering her, but she couldn't shake the feeling the cat was trying to communicate in its own fashion. Her fingers scratched the top of the cat's head, receiving a purring noise in response.

"I'll have to figure out what to do with you later," she told the animal. "Right now, I've got to go play detective."

The day had turned cool and overcast. Fey didn't feel bad about leaving the cat in the car, but she did take the time to fetch water using an old, inverted hubcap as a bowl. She put the water on the passenger-side floor-boards and left the animal to its own devices.

Inside the station, she headed for the upstairs squad room. On the way she nodded to a few of the uniforms with whom she was friendly. She checked the homicide unit's box in records for new crime reports. It was empty.

Taking up almost the entire second floor, the squad bay was a beehive of late afternoon activity. Fey had used the back stairwell leading directly into the work area.

There was a front stairwell for citizens, which ended in a small lobby area. It was decorated with silk trees and a large, framed flag from the 1984 Olympics. There was also a bulletin board with pertinent information for citizens – including an 800 number for complaints if someone didn't get exactly what he or she wanted.

When Fey first saw the 800 number posted, she'd realized police work was changing. Too much had happened in reaction to the Rodney King arrest to let the department be the world leader in policing it had once been. Fey loved the job, but like many of her contemporaries, she was now looking forward to her retirement, when she could get out of the city and never look back. She'd be glad to leave it to the politicians, liberals, and hidden-agenda loudmouths to fight over, hyenas stealing from a lion's kill.

The incident involving Rodney King – a black man whose violent arrest had been captured by an amateur cameraman on videotape – had shocked the world. The video had been shown on television over and over, ad infinitum, until there didn't seem to be a single place in the world where it wasn't a source of dinner conversation.

All L.A. cops, good or bad, found themselves trying to explain to aggressively inquisitive friends and relatives an incident no *straight* could understand.

Cops understood it, though. They might have been appalled and sickened, but they understood it. While the politicians and police brass fought one another for scraps, the working cops held their heads up and did their job. Rodney King or no Rodney King, there were crimes to solve, people to protect, and criminals to put in jail. Life and crime went on, and there wasn't anyone else willing to jump in and do the job....

Be a cop? Are you crazy? Those suckers get shot at. Not me, man.

The unprecedented media coverage of the trial of the officers who'd arrested King, the politically motivated destruction of L.A.'s police chief, and the findings of the Christopher Commission assigned to investigate the LAPD in the wake of the King incident resulted in hundreds of knee-jerk measures – like the 800 number hot line for complaints against the police.

Fey had read the Christopher Commission report cover to cover. In her mind it made the Warren Commission report on the John Kennedy assassination look like gospel.

Behind the detectives' lobby there was a long hallway hiding several interrogation rooms, a cot room, a small cubbyhole for the division's computer nerds, and a softly decorated, nonthreatening room for interviewing rape or child abuse victims.

The other side of the lobby led into the squad bay. One end of the bay was walled off to form a good-sized room for the fraud and forgery investigators. There was another small office, with windows looking out into the bay, for the detective lieutenant in charge of the squad, Mike Cahill. The rest of the room was taken up with clusters of desks assigned to different divisional investigative units; juvenile, Sex Crimes, Robbery, Burglary, Auto Theft, and Homicide.

Phones rang, files were filed, cases were assigned and investigated, suspects and victims were interviewed, jokes were told, coffee was poured, administrative details were handled, audits were audited, photo lineups were composed, and once in a while a crime was solved, if you were lucky. Cops didn't need to worry about job security.

At the homicide unit's desks, Vance Hatcher had his feet up talking on the telephone. Monk Lawson was talking to two patrol officers. Monk raised a hand in greeting when he saw Fey.

Dumping her purse beside her desk, she slipped out of her shoulder rig and slid it into a side drawer.

Hatcher hung up the phone. "You look fried," he said to Fey.

She dry-washed her face with one hand. "I'm okay."

"Where's Colby?"

"Off somewhere sulking," Fey said. "Actually, I hope he's gone to see if he can rush the FIN run on the victim's prints."

"We'll be lucky to see it before the end of the week."

"Colby claims he's got a contact at the FIN unit who can expedite things."

"Probably some little groupie who can't wait for him to get into her pants."

"Probably," Fey said. "Though I have no idea why."

Hatch laughed. "He might not be your cup of tea, but I've seen him pull a few rabbits out of his hat. If he says he has a contact, it's probably true."

"If you say so."

"How's the new case?"

"It's going to be a rough year," she told him. "It always is when the first murder is this complicated."

"We might get a break," Hatch said.

"Unlikely. This one is right out of the *Twilight Zone*." Fey plopped into her chair. She picked up a file from her inbox and checked it. "The sixty-day follow-up on the John Doe transient is due," she said to Hatch. "Did you or Monk come up with anything further?"

Hatch grunted. "It's a loser. You know what this division is like. We've got the very rich and the very poor, and never the twain shall meet. Both groups ignore each other. Both are closed communities to working coppers." He shrugged. "The victim was murdered in a drainage ditch probably fighting with another wino over a short dog. The suspect who did it has probably frozen to death by now while sleeping rough in the sheriff's area. We'd never hear about it. Even if we did, there'd be no way to put it together."

"Write it up as best you can," Fey said. "Let's keep the paperwork on schedule." She pulled out another file. "What about the Bradshaw caper?"

"Monk's baby," Hatcher said.

Hearing his name, Monk Lawson finished his conversation with the two police officers and came over to join the confab.

"I think we've got enough on Bradshaw's brother-in-law, Lance White, to go to the DA," he said.

Fey could tell Monk was holding something back. Hopefully something good. The unit needed a break. "Not what you said when we last talked about the case," she said. "What's happened since?"

"Lance hasn't surfaced since the killing. The victim's wife, Shirleen, finally broke down and admitted she'd told good old Lance all about the times Bradshaw beat her. Lance threatened to do something if it happened again."

"Did it happen again?"

Monk's even white teeth appeared between his lips.

"Don't keep me in suspense," she said, waiting for the black detective to be more forthcoming.

"On the night of the murder," Monk said, "Bradshaw split Shirleen's lip for supposedly making a pass at a guy in a bar. Shirleen says she and Bradshaw were both drunk when it happened, but she got pissed because blood from her lip dropped on her new blouse. She took off with a full mad-on and went to cry on Lance's shoulder."

"Which got Lance worked up," Fey said.

Monk nodded agreement. "He grabbed a genuine Louisville Slugger and headed out of the house. Shirleen says she thought he was going to go over and scare the hell out of Bradshaw, but Lance came back forty-five minutes later looking like the devil was after him. He wouldn't tell her what happened but threw a bunch of clothes in a suitcase and took off. It's the last time anyone saw him."

"Do you believe her?"

"It took me long enough to get the story out of her. Yeah, I believe her."

"I don't mean about what happened. I'm talking about whether anyone has seen or heard from Lance."

"Monk looked thoughtful. "You light have a point. Give me a little time. If I can get her to tell me where he's hiding, we'll set up a surveillance – let her lead us to him."

"You've got motive and opportunity," Fey said, "but I don't see enough for the DA."

"I saved the best for last. I found the murder weapon," Monk said, a twinkle in his eye.

Fey raised her eyebrows.

Hatch took his feet off the desk, leaning leaned forward. "You didn't tell me," he said to his partner.

Monk enjoyed being the center of attention. "I have to keep one or two surprises."

"I give up," Fey said. "Where did you find it?"

"The murder happened on a Wednesday night, but the body wasn't called in until late Thursday afternoon."

"So what?" Hatch said.

"I was looking at the crime scene photos, saw there were several empty trash cans curbside. I checked the trash pickup schedule and found the refuse trucks go through about ten a.m. on Thursdays."

Hatch caught on immediately. "Between the time of the murder and the time it was called in."

Monk was almost dancing with the excitement of his discovery. "It gets even better," he said. "I contacted the refuse company and talked to the guys who pick up on Bradshaw's route. Turns out the driver has a ten-year-old kid who's really into playing baseball. When he saw a perfectly good bat sticking out of Bradshaw's trash can, he pulled it out and kept it. He was saving it to wrap up for his kid's birthday next week."

"I don't believe it," Fey said, although it was obvious she did. "Great detective work."

"The trash truck driver was real upset having to give up the bat. He's got a whole brood of little trash pickers, money is tight. The bat was probably going to be the only gift the ten-year-old got for his birthday. I was so happy to find the murder weapon, I went out and bought a bat, a glove, and a ball. The guy cried when I gave them to him."

"Really?" Hatch asked.

"It was amazing. Big old muscular guy. Big fat tears running down his cheek. The man loves his kids."

"Nice thing to do," Hatch said.

"Trying to do what was right."

"Enough male bonding," Fey interrupted. "You and your partner can go out and hug trees and beat war drums on your own time. Tell me about the bat."

Monk picked up an SID report from his desk. "I took the bat to the lab. They complained about how busy they were, but finally came across. Even though the trash driver had cleaned it up, they were still able to find traces of blood in the wood. It's a match for the victim."

"How do we tie the bat to the suspect?"

"Shirleen's statement. She saw Lance take it when he left to have a chat with Bradshaw."

Fey's face took on a wary expression. "It might fly," she said, eventually. "Maybe enough to get the case filed. When are you going to present it to the DA?"

"Tomorrow."

"Keep me posted. Don't let the DA continue the case for further investigation. We want a filing or an outright reject. We need the crime clearance."

"You got it," Monk said.

"You done good, son," Hatch told Monk.

"Absolutely," Fey agreed quickly. She wished she'd been the first to offer the compliment, but she found giving praise hard. She had trouble feeling if she praised someone, it gave license to take advantage of her in the future. There were a lot of mixed signals for women who supervised men. If you tried to be one of the boys, you were considered easy. If you took a more reserved roll, you were an ice queen. Finding a middle ground was something Fey was still striving toward.

"What about this new caper?" Hatch asked.

Fey put the files she'd been checking back into her inbox. "It's going to be a problem. What do you make of these?"

Fey pulled the three sets of ID from her purse and handed them to Hatch.

The money from the dryer was in the trunk of the police car. They would count it later and book it into evidence, but Fey didn't want to do it in a squad room full of well-intentioned, but nosy detectives not involved in the case.

Working his way through the cards and papers, Hatch passed each piece to Monk as he finished with it. The faces of the two men creased with concentration. Fey marveled, as always, at how good detectives managed to compartmentalize their thought processes.

All thoughts of the Bradshaw case, or the John Doe transient, or the day's earlier court appearances and other activities, had been swept away in favor of total attention to the issue at hand. It was very existential, each case existing strictly within its own absurd universe, unaffected and unrecognizing of anything outside its own universe, total attention to the here and now.

The ability to compartmentalize, to not be overwhelmed by the demand for attention on too many fronts, was essential to the emotional makeup of a good detective. However, the trait was hell on interpersonal relationships. Spouses and offspring often felt closed out, unable to break into the other universes a cop kept to himself, and therefore felt ignored or unimportant. This often led to divorce or alienation. Perhaps, Fey thought, they could now lodge their complaints with the 800 number instead.

"Unreal," Monk said, setting aside another piece of the victim's identity collection. "Miranda Goodwinter; May Wellington; Madeline Fletcher. Who the hell was this woman?"

"My question exactly," Fey said.

Hatch walked over to the small office the detectives used as a coffee room. He came back carrying a small tray with three personalized mugs filled with steamy black liquid.

Fey gratefully took her mug. "You heard about the citizen who runs into the police station and tells the desk officer there's a dead cop lying naked in an alley across the street. The desk officer asks how he knows it's a cop if the body is naked."

"Because he's got an erection and coffee pouring out his ears," Hatch said, stealing the punchline.

"Wise guy," Fey said. She knew it was an old joke because there were now too many women on the force to make the punchline valid.

Fey became serious again, fingering the IDs now on the desk. "This is a problem."

Hatch took a sip of his scalding brew. "Monk and I will keep up with the old stuff, and catch anything new, so you and Colby can stay on it."

"Thanks," Fey said. "If we don't break this one fast, the lieutenant will have our heads served up on a platter with apples stuffed in our mouths."

"Won't he be happy with the Bradshaw result?" Monk asked.

"He'll be happy, but it will only keep him off our backs for a while. We had eight unsolveds out of twenty-two dead bodies in the division last year. Not a great batting average. Up until this break with Bradshaw, we've been riding a four-body losing streak. The brass are getting antsy. I know my butt is on the line."

"The unsolveds aren't your fault, boss," Hatch said, concerned. "The last four have all been nowhere cases. We've worked them to death, and with the exception of Bradshaw, the clues closet is bare. Nobody could have done more."

"Not an answer I can take to the next supervisors' meeting They'll chew over Bradshaw and then ask why we haven't worked the same kind of magic on the other cases. They won't care if baseball bats in trash cans only come along every millennium."

Hatch shrugged, turning his attention back to the identification on the desk. He was surprised he'd been promoted as high as D-2. He knew he was a good detective, but he'd never been good at playing the promotional politics game. He also knew he wouldn't want the added responsibilities Fey carried as a D-3.

He didn't have ambitions beyond the pride he took in doing his job. He had no desire to promote, or do anything else, until he retired in another couple of years. Then he and Lorraine were going to grab his pension and take off for their retirement cabin outside of Seattle. Nothing but fishing and sipping. No dirtbags, no politicians, no *stinkers*, *floaters*, or babies with their heads bashed in. After a while, maybe his nightmares would go away.

"This ID is really good," Hatch said as he worked his way back through the papers. "Driver's licenses, Social Security cards, credit cards, even library cards."

"You get tired of one life and step into another like a snake shedding its skin," said Monk. "The ultimate goal of conspicuous consumption."

"Then there's these," Fey said. Dipping back into her purse, she brought out the other documents from the dryer drum. "Birth certificates, school transcripts, passports." She spread the papers across her desk. "Plus, down in the car, we have a nice round million in cash."

Fey wasn't sure what tipped her off to take a second look in the dryer. Maybe instinct, or perhaps experience. After twenty-two years on the job, there wasn't much difference.

Hatch whistled when Fey mentioned the money.

"A million in cash?" Monk asked in disbelief.

"Yeah."

"I haven't seen so much cash since I worked dope," Hatch said.

"I've never seen so much cash," Monk said. "Can I go down and get it? I want to run my fingers through it. Smell it. Take it home and stuff it in my pillow to dream on."

"Down, boy," said Fey. "You'd never be able to get it out of the car. I've got an attack cat watching it."

Hatch laughed. "I heard about the cat. Colby was pissed."

"What else is new?"

"What are you going to do with the vicious beast?"

Fey shrugged. "If we can't find a relative, which doesn't appear likely, it's off to the animal shelter."

"I know better," said Hatch. "You come across as a hard-ass, but you won't let the cat be put down."

Fey smiled. "You're probably right. Constable and Thieftaker won't mind a cat around the stable."

"Not unless they're friends with the mice," said Hatch.

Monk was frowning. "Who are Constable and Thieftaker?"

"My horses," Fey said, and pointed to a photograph under her desk blotter of two well-groomed quarter horses.

Hatch picked up one of the passports from Fey's desk. He flipped through the pages before setting it down again and picking up another. "Maybe we should send this stuff over to Questioned Documents. See if they can tell us what is forged and what isn't."

"You have something in mind to do with the results?" Monk asked. Like Colby, he was a D-1. Unlike Colby, he was always ready to learn something new.

Fey answered for Hatch. "Forgers are like painters. They all have a distinctive style. Unique flairs or special touches. Sometimes it's an ego thing, sometimes it's subconscious, but you can always spot the technique."

Hatch opened one of the passports. He showed Monk a page full of visa stamps. "A few years back there was a guy named Justin Otekan. An Englishman, he was reputed to be so good, museums hired him to paint replicas of priceless paintings from their collections. If they took the original down for security purposes, or restoration, they would hang Otekan's copy in its place. Nobody ever caught on."

"Your point?" asked Monk.

"Otekan was also known to produce perfect American passport forgeries. The only problem with the things was all of them had the same three visa stamps – Great Britain, France, Switzerland. If a passport had those three visas, chances were, it was an Otekan forgery."

"You're saying if we find out which of these IDs are forged, we might get to a forger who might be able to give us a clue to the victim's true identity."

"No flies on you," Hatch said.

There was a commotion on the back stairs. The three detectives turned as Colby swaggered into the squad bay. He looked smug and pleased with himself.

Mike Cahill also saw Colby enter. Sensing something

was up, he appeared as if by magic in the midst of the homicide unit personnel.

"I've got good news and bad news," Colby said, shaking a fistful of fax paper. "The good news is there was a successful hit from FIN."

He pulled out a specific fax sheet and scrutinized it.

"Ditch the drama," Fey said.

Colby was purposely drawing out the suspense. It was as if nothing she'd said in the parking lot registered. "Eleven years ago, our victim was printed after a shoplifting arrest in San Francisco. Her name then was Miriam Cordell."

"What's the bad news?" Fey asked, hoping Colby would get to the point if she played straight man.

Colby's grin widened. They were hanging on his every word. "The bad news is, ten years ago good old Miriam got herself murdered."

CHAPTER EIGHT

"How could she have been murdered ten years ago in San Francisco and end up freshly dead again this morning?" Fey kept her voice calm. The last thing she needed was Colby trying to make a farce out of this case. "Either the FIN people made a mistake, or we've got the first recorded case of two different people with the same set of fingerprints."

"The FIN people didn't make any mistakes," Colby said. His voice held a tinge of anger. "I called them direct after finding out about the situation. Instead of running the prints through the computer a second time, they hand-searched the records and pulled the hard copy of Miriam Cordell's prints from the shoplifting arrest. Then they used the hard copy to do a comparison with the prints we faxed them from our stiff. No question, they belong to the same person."

"No way."

"Don't climb all over me, Frog Lady. I'm only the messenger. You're the big-deal detective."

"Cool it, Colby," Mike Cahill said. He could see the confrontation coming and wanted to defuse it.

"What about the fax we sent?" Monk asked. "Maybe it wasn't clear enough. Maybe the prints are close, but not exact, and comparing off a bad fax copy makes them look alike."

Colby shook his head. "They said the first fax copy of the prints was clear, but I sent another anyway. Same result. Miriam Cordell and Miranda Goodwinter are the same person."

"The first name, Miriam, is consistent," Hatch put in. "Miriam; Miranda; May; Madeline. The M can't be a coincidence."

Fey shrugged, reluctantly. "I'll buy the prints," she told Colby. "But how did you come up with the stuff on the murder? I know it didn't come from FIN."

"I called SFPD direct after FIN told me the Miriam Cordell prints came from a shoplifting arrest in the Bay area. I wanted to see if they had anything else."

"And?"

"Their records unit ran the name every which way and came up with the One-eighty-seven report listing her as a homicide victim."

"What were the circumstances?"

"I don't know. The records unit could only tell me what was on the computer. The suspect on the murder report was listed as Isaac Cordell. Their computer showed two other connected reports – an arrest, and an arson report."

"Smart work," Cahill said.

"Thanks, Lieutenant."

"None of this explains how our victim managed to pull a resurrection act and then get herself murdered again ten years later," Fey said.

Colby turned to her. "I'm working on it. The detective who investigated the original case retired a couple of years ago. SFPD will contact him and have him call us."

"What about the original reports?"

"They're on microfiche in the bowels of San Francisco PD's Records and Identification Division. The supervisor said he'd overnight them to us."

"You touched all the bases," Fey said, grudgingly. "There isn't much we can do until the reports get here or we hear from the detective who handled the case."

"What do you want us to do while we wait?" Monk asked.

"Are you and Hatch clear?"

Monk looked over at Hatch.

Hatch nodded and said, "The new reports were light today. There's nothing can't sit on the back burner for a while."

"Then go back to the scene and canvas the neighborhood. Door-knock every unit until you find a witness. Keep a list of units where there's no answer. We'll pick those up later. Colby and I will meet you after we book our evidence into property."

"Who's going to start the murder book?" Hatch asked.

"I'll run it," Colby said. The murder book held all the case reports and memos for later reference.

"I'll do it," Fey said. "I want you to crank out the crime report and chase SID to give us anything they have from the scene."

Colby looked as if he was going to protest. Then he seemed to think better of it and shut his mouth.

Monk saw the action and smiled to himself. In Monk's estimation, Fey had her work cut out trying to supervise Colby. He also knew she was equal to the job. The fact Fey was a woman never bothered Monk, like the fact he was black never bothered her. He figured there were things in life put there to challenge you. Things you couldn't change. It didn't make sense worrying about them.

Even if he had the choice, he wouldn't change being black. After watching Fey do her job, he doubted she would give up being a woman. Being good at your job was Monk's bottom line. He'd worked for Fey long enough to see she was good at doing hers.

Monk and Hatch grabbed their jackets and headed for the door.

"Can I leave you kiddies alone?" Mike Cahill asked, once Monk and Hatcher had gone.

"Why would you even ask, boss?" Colby said quickly, before Fey could get in a reply. "We have no problems. Do we?" He threw a vicious smile at Fey, which Cahill couldn't see.

Internally, Fey felt her emotions flip-flopping. She didn't understand what was behind her ambivalence toward Colby. Sometimes, she could keep herself in check and treat him with nonchalance and superiority. Other times, when her guard was down, his inherent sexiness touched something inside her. Still other times, she felt violent and aggressive toward him.

This time her emotions settled into the latter area.

"We both have big problems," Fey told him. A cold fury at his goading escalated inside her. "My problem is trying to figure out who slashed Ms. Risen Again's throat. Yours is finding a psychiatrist you won't scare off after one session."

CHAPTER NINE

By the time Fey arrived home, it was midnight and she was almost dead on her feet. There was a note under her front mat from her neighbor, who took care of her horses when she couldn't be there. Thieftaker had a loose shoe, and Constable appeared to be off his feed. Fey groaned and took the note inside. She dumped it on the living room table along with the day's mail. She shucked her purse and jacket and returned to her car to get the white cat.

Fey expected the cat to be skittish after a day filled with extraordinary circumstances. However, after she had transferred the cat from the plain detective sedan to her own car, the animal had simply curled up on the passenger seat and gone to sleep.

Once on the floor in Fey's house, the cat began to whine and wrap itself around Fey's legs.

She set down the litter box she had also brought in from her car. "I know what you want," she said to the animal, bending down to scratch its head. "You must be starved."

The cat followed her into the kitchen and kept up a

constant racket of excited, if unintelligible, conversation as Fey opened a can of tuna.

All the way home, Fey had tried to decide what to call the cat. There had been no collar and tag with the animal's name on it, nor had there been anything in the victim's house to indicate the cat's moniker. Hell, there hadn't been anything in the house to indicate the victim's true moniker. It was the weirdest case of identity Fey had ever come across.

After much deliberation, Fey had decided on Brent-wood, after the area where the victim had lived. It had the equal amounts of class and irony of the best cat names. She tried it out now as she flaked the tuna onto a saucer.

"Here you go, Brentwood," she said as she set the food on the kitchen floor. "Good Brentwood." She stroked the cat's long back as it dived nose-first into the tuna.

The cat was totally oblivious to his new name. Fey realized she could have called him Attila the Hun as long as she fed him.

Watching Brentwood eat, she pulled open a kitchen drawer and took out a sealed packet of cigarettes. Fumbling with the packet in indecision, she eventually put it back and closed the drawer. She had quit the habit two years earlier, but the urge was still strong – never more so than when under the stress of a fresh homicide.

The rest of the day at work had been rough. The mountains of paperwork had been waded through, the press had been handled, and a large amount of shoe leather had been wasted canvassing the town home complex for witnesses without success. There remained a short list of units where nobody was home. Two of those units were close enough to the victim's residence to perhaps be of use, but Fey didn't hold out hope.

The facts surrounding the victim's multiple identities and the money found in the dryer had been kept back from the press. The last thing any detective needed on a case was a media circus. When the situation was under better control, she would tip a reporter who might get half the information right in print.

She put a bowl of water down next to the saucer of tuna. She moved the litter box to a corner of the kitchen, then left Brentwood to his own devices. Kicking off her shoes, Fey picked them up and carried them into the bedroom. She picked up her jacket along the way to hang in the closet.

The house was a long, low ranch-style design. It was set back against the foothills of the San Fernando Valley. There was an attached three-car garage and a half-circle drive. The exterior was a pleasing blend of red-tiled roof, adobe-colored plastering, and bleached split-rail fencing. The front yard consisted of low-maintenance cacti and yucca trees. A long strip of Kentucky bluegrass was kept in shape by a local kid for spending change.

Fey had bought the property after her first divorce. She had married young and wrong. She'd been looking for a way out of one abusive situation, found herself in another.

Her first husband had inherited a successful contracting business. After two years of putting up with his fists, Fey never felt guilty about taking him to the cleaners, as Colby had called it.

Once, when feeling extremely cynical, she told a therapist she had earned the money the old-fashioned way, with her body. The male therapist didn't understand the joke. She never went back to him again. The cost of earning money with bruises and broken bones was far too high for her to waste time with someone who had no concept of the price.

The house had been built after marriage number two. Fey had been on the job for two years when she found herself swept off her feet by Johnny Killerman. He was a dashing motor cop as macho and sensitive as his name implied. There was something about the black boots, the Harley, the macho mustache, and the last-of-the-cowboys image which still sent a tingle up her spine.

There had been no physical abuse this time, but Johnny was interested in only three things – motorcycles, guns, and sex. Romance, travel, education, reading, or any kind of police work not on two wheels was a waste of time as far as Johnny was concerned. He couldn't understand why anyone would be interested in anything else.

Johnny also had trouble with the concept of keeping his dick in his pants. Fey got tired of hearing other women talk about how good Johnny was in the sack. She also wondered how low some of these women's standards were. From her own experience, she knew Johnny was all acrobatics and no passion. After five years of playing mother to a man who refused to grow up, Fey packed her bags and walked.

She let Johnny buy her out of the house they bought together. She then used the money to start construction on her current residence. Bit by bit, she scrimped and saved to complete the structure. It took five years to complete, but she was happy and secure in the end result.

During those five years, Fey battled her own emotional demons. She drifted into casual affairs. She drank hard, she played hard, and she kicked butt on the street. She thought she was one of *the guys* until she realized *the guys* had a double standard. What was good for the gander was not good for the goose. A guy's reputation was enhanced by drinking and whoring, but a gal's reputation was ruined by the same behavior.

Marriage number three also came and went. Yank Conners was a hard-living hockey goalie with the Los Angeles Blades, a feeder team for the Los Angeles Kings.

For all his fierceness on the ice, Yank was a sensitive person in relationships. He sent flowers, wrote bad poetry, made love gently, and could listen with as much intensity as he could talk.

Life looked good, but then fate intervened. The Chicago Blackhawks bought up Yank's contract, offering him a starting position. Yank wanted Fey to come to Chicago where fame and fortune awaited. Fey wanted Yank to stay in Los Angeles where she had her own career.

She still remembered the night when they held each other and cried into the small hours of the morning. Marriage or career? Which was more important? Neither could determine if they had made the right decision.

Yank went to Chicago. The marriage lasted long distance for another year, dying with a whimper instead of a bang. Yank appeared before packed arenas for every game. Fey moved into her dream house to lick her wounds. Yank had shown her she was capable of a good relationship. Love, however, demanded a high price in compromise.

Yank's playing career was cut short by injury, but he found a spot for himself on the Blackhawks' coaching staff. He'd remarried and had three little prospective goalies.

He and Fey stayed in touch, even saw each other when the Blackhawks came to town. Their relationship was one of love's strange tangents, incomprehensible to anybody but those involved. They figured their ongoing relationship was their business, not his wife's or Fey's current lover.

The house was Fey's castle. She decorated the interior in country fashion –

straw dolls, gingham curtains, wood and fabric couches, and horse-related gewgaws.

The house put her close to her horses and was a place where she could be totally independent. She thought of it as the *Land of Fey*, an extension of her inner self. Lock the doors, run up the flag, and defend the walls against all intruders.

Her bedroom was neat and tidy. There were two phones with attached answering machines in the room. The answering machine on her dresser showed two messages. The machine on the nightstand held another.

Fey checked her watch. Eleven-thirty. She still had time. She ignored the machine on the dresser, pressing the message button on the nightstand machine.

"You have one message," advised the electronic voice. *Beep*.

"Hi, honey. I heard you hooked a real whodunit." Fey smiled, instantly recognizing the voice of Jake Travers. "I know you'll be out late but call me anyway."

Travers was an experienced deputy district attorney. He and Fey had become close friends over the course of winning several big cases together. After losing a big one, they had also become lovers.

"If you don't get back in time," the message continued, "I'll touch base with you in the morning. The Hansen case is coming up for trial next week, and we need to make sure all the wits are ready. Talk to you soon. Love you."

The machine voice took over again. "No more messages."

Love, Fey thought, reflecting on the message. Did she love Jake? Probably. But she loved her freedom more. Twice he'd asked her to marry him, but she had demurred. She was intimate with those pitfalls. She was too set in her ways, too comfortable with her lifestyle. She could be a friend or a lover, but not a spouse. She loved Jake, but he would never be hanging his suits in her closet.

She knew it was still before midnight, but she had things to do. Rather than calling Jake back, she slipped out of her work clothes and pulled on a pair of jeans, an old sweatshirt, and a pair of beat-up Jodhpur boots. Back in the kitchen, she poured a glass of red wine. She finished it quickly and then opened the sliding glass door to the back of the property, turned on the exterior lights, and went to see to her horses.

The rear yard ran back for a full acre before sloping sharply upward to meet the scrub marking the beginning of the foothills. There was a large, partially covered patio attached to the house extended out to surround a hot tub. Behind the tub was a five-foot brick wall with a wooden gate at one end.

Fey let herself through the gate and into the dirt corral area. The corral was surrounded by an iron-railed fence. It contained a wooden stable structure at one end. Her two horses nickered as they became aware of her presence. Trotting over to the iron-railed fence, they stuck their necks over for their noses to be nuzzled. Fey talked softly to both animals as she slid between the rails and entered the corral. Patting Thieftaker, a dark bay gelding, she checked the loose shoe on his left hind hoof. She swore softly. The farrier would have to come before the horse could be ridden again.

Constable was a black gelding with a gleaming coat and regal bearing. He stood two full hands higher than Thieftaker and was a recent addition to the family. Fey patted him and checked him over to see if there was any noticeable reason for him being off his feed. His right front leg felt slightly warm. If it was still warm in the morning, Fey knew she would also need the vet. With the cost of caring for two horses, Fey was glad she didn't have kids to raise.

Kids, however, were one thing she didn't have to worry about. Her father had taken care of the problem.

After checking the feed and water bins in the horse boxes, Fey left the horses and returned to the house. She checked her watch again. Eleven forty-five. She knew she'd better hurry.

Throwing off her clothes, she turned on the radio in her bathroom to catch the sports scores. From the shower she could hear the announcer rambling on about basketball scores and college sports. Finally, he got around to reporting the Kings lost their hockey game to the Chicago Blackhawks by a score of five to two.

Fey smiled as she dried herself, put on perfume, and slid into a soft nightgown. She would call Jake in the morning. A five-to-two win meant Yank would be in a very good mood when he arrived.

Life for the victim was over, but Fey learned long ago life went on for the living.

CHAPTER TEN

The following morning, Fey allowed herself an extra fifteen minutes sleep. Making love with Yank always left her feeling stress-free, relaxed, and deliciously naughty. The infrequency and the secretive nature of their liaisons added spice to the encounters. They were both friends and lovers, and their relationship had survived the long term because it did not suffer from the demands and everyday stresses normal romantic, dating, or spousal ties engendered.

Fey stretched her legs across the bed and felt an unfamiliar lump down by her feet. She opened one eye to peer down at Brentwood. The cat was perched at the bottom of the bed with his feet tucked in underneath him. His eyes were wide open watching Fey, seeming to will her awake.

"Good morning, Brentwood," she said.

The cat yowled back.

There was a dent in the pillow next to Fey's where Yank had slept. He'd told her the night before he would have to leave early since the team was catching a morning flight to Vancouver for another road game, this time against the Canucks.

She vaguely remembered his weight shifting off the bed while it was still dark outside. A little later, she had felt the brush of his lips against her cheek. With her eyes closed she had whispered an endearment and drifted deeply back to sleep.

Once out of bed, she wrapped herself in a white terrycloth robe and struck out for the kitchen. She put a pot of coffee on and put a saucer of milk down for Brentwood, who was more interested in attacking her fuzzy bunny slippers. She wrote a sticky-note reminder to pick up cat food and stuck it to her purse.

When she had a cup of coffee inside her, she put on ranch clothes and spent an hour mucking out the stable. Constable's leg was cool, and he happily munched into his morning feed. Thieftaker, however, had not fixed his own shoe. Fey left a note for her neighbor, Peter Dent, to call the farrier to take care of the problem.

Peter was a magazine writer with three horses of his own. Like Fey, he lived alone. Fortunately, he was also more than willing to take care of Fey's animals if she was gone or working overtime. It was a good arrangement. Fey likened it to a single parent's problems with childcare. Domestic horses, like children, did not take care of themselves.

After showering and washing her black shoulder-length hair, Fey dried off and stopped to examine her body critically in the mirror. At five-foot-nine, she was a big woman with a big bone structure. Hours of horseback riding kept everything firm and toned, but there was no denying she was ten pounds above her best weight.

Looking in the mirror, she realized her legs were still good, and the sharp bone structure of her face was wearing well. Her complexion was smooth, and her hair held a gleaming shine.

Her hands, however, gave away her age. She used lotion and kept her nails short but working with horses and spending hours in the sun took a toll.

Finally, she shrugged at herself in the mirror. She felt strong and healthy, which some days was good enough. She might envy the energy of the female rookies, but she knew the heartbreaks ahead of them. No way would she trade places.

Back in her bedroom she continued to ignore the flashing notification light of the dresser answering machine. While she dressed, she picked up the portable phone from the nightstand and called Jake. He came on the line after the first ring.

"Hello."

"Hi, kiddo," Fey said. Thoughts of making love to Yank zipped briefly through her mind, trying to push every guilt button they could find, but she shoved them aside.

"Hey! How are you?" Jake was always upbeat in the morning. "What's this about bodies coming back from the dead to be murdered again? Don't you have enough work?"

"Apparently not," Fey said. "The victim has as many lives as a cat and more identities than a check-kiter."

A night's sleep had not given Fey any new angles on the case.

"Any suspects?" Jake asked.

"We're not even sure who the victim is. The files San Francisco is sending may provide answers."

"Life is never dull."

"Not in this town."

"How about the Hansen case? Is our victim available?" Jake asked, changing the subject.

"I've got her stashed in a women's shelter. She's safe and getting counseling. She'll be ready when we need her."

The case Jake was referencing was the third arrest of Ned Hansen for spousal battery. Twice before his wife had backed out of testifying. This time around, though, Fey felt they stood a chance.

"Good," Jake paused. "How about dinner tonight?"

"Great," Fey said. "But it depends on how the case breaks today. I'll call you."

"I miss you."

"Ditto," Fey said, and hung up.

Jake Travers was a good man, she thought as Brentwood rubbed around her ankles. She bent to stroke the white bundle of fur. There weren't many good men around who weren't married, weren't gay, and could put together sentences with words of more than two syllables. She considered herself lucky.

As she made the bed, she touched the pillow on which Yank had slept.

She considered herself very lucky.

CHAPTER ELEVEN

When Fey entered the squad bay in the morning, Hatch and Monk were already busy at the homicide unit's desks. Hatch was sitting in Fey's chair with a short stack of reports in front of him. He was wearing a white nylon long-sleeved shirt even an FBI agent wouldn't be caught wearing. The shirt was stuffed haphazardly into black Sansabelt pants over scuffed black slip-ons. One of the shoes had the tassels missing. His tie was a wide orange and black abstract of the kind five-year-olds buy for Father's Day.

"Anything hot?" Fey asked him, referring to the stack of new crime reports.

"A couple of ADWs need some follow-up. In one, the victim took fifty-eight stitches to seal up the gash in his head."

Fey gave a theatrical flinch. "What did he get hit with?"

"A jack handle. The fight took place in the parking lot of the Armory. The suspect didn't like the way the victim talked to one of the waitresses."

"Typical," Fey said. "What about the other?"

Hatch nodded toward his partner. "Monk's talking to the victim. It's probably a *sign-off*."

"Victim doesn't want to prosecute?"

"It's a roommate squabble between alternate lifestyles. One threw a glass at the other. The victim was mad last night, but they made up over the telephone when the suspect called from jail. The victim was calling us first thing. He wants his buddy sprung."

"Fine by me," Fey said. "Get the victim to sign off the report and have Monk to run it by the city attorney for a reject."

Hatch nodded at Fey's retreating back as she headed for the coffee room. When she came back with a steaming mug in her hand, Hatch had moved over to his own desk. Fey sat down.

"Anything else?" she asked.

"The other reports are twos or threes," Hatch said.

Reports fell into three classifications. Those with clues or named suspects were *category one* and had to be investigated and handled within fifteen days. *Category two* reports were those with no solid leads – a partial license plate or the description of an unknown suspect. For a *cat-two*, the detective needed to contact the victim within thirty days making sure there was no further information. Reports where there was no suspect information were *category three*—filed and forgotten.

Fey would never say anything to Hatch about the way he dressed. He was a good detective and an excellent right-hand man. He kept the unit's paperwork flowing and was a fountain of experience and information. Having him in the unit made Fey's job easier. If Hatch wanted to dress like a reject from a thrift store, Fey had no problem cutting him slack.

"Where's Colby?" she asked.

"In the jail doing the paperwork on the glass-throwing ADW suspect."

At the next desk, Monk hung up the phone. Hatch and Fey looked over at him expectantly.

"The victim is on the way to sign-off."

Hatch told him to run the sign-off past the CA for a formal reject.

"Why?" Monk asked.

"You know all domestic violence cases need formal rejects," Hatch said.

"Domestic violence cases, sure. But this is two guys living together."

"Are they roommates or lovers?"

"Lovers apparently."

"Then it's domestic violence and needs a formal reject. This is the age of nondiscrimination."

Monk didn't argue. He looked at Fey. "Cahill wants to see you as soon as you come in."

Fey rolled her eyes. "Stand by, ladies," she said. "Here comes the pressure." She took a gulp of coffee and headed toward the lieutenant's office.

Cahill's door was open. Fey stepped through, rapping twice on the doorjamb. At one end of the large office was a round conference table with several chairs. At the other end, Cahill sat behind a large desk. Mementos of the Marine Corps decorated the walls along with a blowup of Cahill and three police academy classmates. The office seemed larger than it was, due to the wall of mini-blinded windows looking out to the squad bay.

"You wanted to see me?" Fey asked.

Cahill looked up from his desk.

"Nice of you to grace us with your presence," he said.

Fey felt a chill run through her. Cahill was not his normal self.

Fey looked at her watch. It was eight-fifteen. She

didn't usually start work till eight-thirty. She sat down in the chair in front of Cahill's desk.

"What are you complaining about, Mike?" she asked. "I was here until ten o'clock last night."

"Colby spent the night here. Caught a couple of hours sleep in the cot room and was back on the job."

"Good for him," Fey said. She could see Colby making a big production out of his sacrifice.

"This case is close to getting out of hand. We can't afford another unsolved."

"Who said this case is an unsolved? We've been on it less than twenty-four hours."

"Let me put it another way," Cahill interrupted. "You can't afford another unsolved."

"What's going on?" Fey was perplexed by Cahill's change in attitude. "First you act like you're behind me all the way. Now you're making veiled threats."

Cahill hung his head wearily. "There's backlash from the brass," he said quietly. "The chief is playing *smile and grovel* with the mayor and the police commission. They're screaming about crime as usual. Our stats are making the big chief come down on our bureau little chief. Stuff is rolling downhill from there. They don't care why we have four unsolveds in a row. They want cases cleared."

"Should I make them all suicides?"

"If you can."

"Mike!"

Cahill put up his hand to stop further outburst. "I know you're doing your best. I believe you're the right cop for our homicide unit. However, the department has become more political than ever. None of us have protection. I don't want to go back to patrol as a morning watch lieutenant. Neither of us can afford to have another unsolved."

"We may have a break on the Bradshaw case."

"Colby filled me in," Cahill interrupted.

I bet he did, Fey fumed.

"But," Cahill continued, "it isn't going to be enough if we get stuck with another whodunit."

"You're the boss," Fey said. All the stress Yank had helped her relieve was back on her shoulders. "We'll work this until we break it." She stood to walk out.

"One more thing," Cahill said, stopping her.

"Yes?"

"Colby is doing a good job. You need to give him some room. He might surprise you and catch a killer for us."

"Pardon me, Mike," Fey said evenly. "I don't have time for any more of this crap."

Cahill looked like he'd been slapped.

"If you'll excuse me," Fey said in the same even tone, "I've got crime to fight." She turned and walked out of the office.

CHAPTER TWELVE

The look on Fey's face when she blew past her desk, grabbing her purse as she went, almost made Vance Hatcher dive for cover. Neither he nor Monk said a word as Fey stormed by them, nor did they look up from their desks until she was out of the squad bay.

"She is pissed-off," Monk said.

"Glad Colby wasn't up here," Hatch said. "One word out of him would have set her off like an A-bomb."

Monk looked at the rear exit from the squad bay through which Fey had disappeared. "So much repressed rage makes you understand why they used to name hurricanes after women."

"Amen, partner."

Leaving the squad room, Fey walked down a short corridor with bathrooms on one side and the irony of the vice unit's office on the other. At the end of the corridor was a heavy door giving access to a small roof area extending over the slightly larger first floor. The station's generators were gathered together in the center of the area surrounded by a ridiculously small running track.

Fey pulled the door open with a vengeance, stepped

through, and slammed it behind her. On the roof, the generators were working noisily. So angry she was having trouble getting her breath, Fey fumbled in her purse for a battered packet of cigarettes and a chewed-up pack of matches. This time, she didn't hesitate. Old habits die hard, and all reformed smokers have an emergency stash. She tore off the pack's cellophane wrapper as if the secret of life was inside.

Her hands shook. She had to use three matches before she got the tip of the cigarette glowing. She inhaled and felt the orgasmic pleasure of nicotine flushing through her system. She took a second drag, but the smoke caught in her throat and she began to cough. She tried to control it, but eventually doubled over with the hacking.

The purse, which was slung over her left shoulder, slipped and dropped to the rooftop. Still hacking, she threw the cigarette away as if casting out a demon. The pack was still in her left hand, squeezed into an unusable squish.

When she recovered her breath, she switched the pack into her right hand. She wound up like a pitcher to throw the hated thing over the low wall at the edge of the roof. Letting it fly, she watched it fall short. Fey's chin dropped to her chest. Throwing was another thing they never taught girls.

After a few seconds, she walked over, picked up the pack, and calmly dropped it over the low wall. She hoped somebody important was walking below. She looked over. No such luck.

Taking a deep breath, she looked across the street at the police garage and on to the courthouses contained in the next block.

I'm forty-three years old, she thought, *and I still let things get to me as if I were a twelve-year-old who'd been told she couldn't shave her legs. When am I going to grow up? Come on, girl, get a grip. You know how the game is played. You can't take your ball and go home. There are crimes to solve.*

She mentally shook herself and turned to go back inside.

Hatcher was the first to see Fey walk back into the squad bay.

"Stand by," he said quietly to Monk.

"Is she still mad?"

"She hasn't sprouted horns or a tail."

Fey tossed her purse onto her desk with a crash. It landed next to several Express Mail envelopes. Monk and Hatch looked at her.

She shrugged. "I lost it. Sue me."

"It happens to all of us," Hatch said.

"You have an excuse," Fey said.

"I do?"

"You're a male."

Monk laughed, and the tension was broken.

Fey smiled at the two detectives. "Let me get another cup of caffeine," she said. "Then we'll get down to business."

In the coffee room, she filled her cup with the cinnamon coffee some brave soul had brewed. She looked at a group of candid photos pinned to the bulletin board. They had been taken at a promotion party a week before.

Various rude comic captions had been added. There was one of Mike Cahill caught looking down the scooped neckline of a cocktail waitress. The caption read, *Dr. Mike checks for plastic surgery scars.*

Another photo showed a drunken Vance Hatcher with his arm around the newly promoted male detective. A comic balloon pointing to Hatch read, *Now you're a real detective, you're part of the Tee-Hee Club. Meetings are twice weekly in the locker room.*

There was also a group photo of Fey and three female detectives squished around a table to get in the picture. The anonymous caption read, *The Crack Squad.*

Fey shook her head, but she didn't make any move to take it down. There would be those who found it funny, but if the caption was taken down, something worse would be put in its place.

There was also a photo of Colby sitting alone at a table. The camera had captured a fleeting look of confused vulnerability on his face. Fey took out a black felt pen and added the words, *So much time. So few friends.*

Turnabout was fair play.

Colby was back at his desk next to Monk's when Fey returned. He had his head down finishing a 5.10 form for the felony package of the wife beater booked overnight.

"Did the victim turn up?" Fey asked.

"She's signing off the report now. I'll run the paperwork by the CA and we'll have the case out of our hair."

"Until the next time he hits her."

Colby shrugged. "Or she slips a knife between his ribs."

Grunting her agreement, Fey sat down and pulled over the stack of Express Mail envelopes. She took her glasses out of her purse, slipping them into place.

"These are the reports from San Francisco on the Miriam Cordell case," she said, seeing the contents of the first envelope.

Colby stood up and walked behind Fey, looking over her shoulder.

"Easy, boy," Fey said, but without rancor. "I know you're anxious, but my butt is riding on this caper. I'll pass these over when I finish reading."

For a second, Colby looked for a challenge in Fey's words. Not finding any, he returned to his desk. Before sitting down, he carefully adjusted the fabric of his dark okra-colored slacks so the knees wouldn't bag.

Fey watched the ritual, but bit back a sharp-tongued comment. She needed Colby working with her, not against her.

Fey dug into the SFPD reports. Contained within the dry jargon and unusual abbreviations—which made up the mass of police and court narratives—was the story of terrific police work resulting in a successful conviction in a tough, fifty-fifty, win-or-lose court case.

By all appearances, Isaac Cordell had been a successful businessman who enjoyed the fruits of his labors to the fullest. At thirty years old, he owned a string of furniture stores with his partner, Adam Roark. He had a home along the shore of wealthy Sausalito—the other side of the Golden Gate Bridge from San Francisco. He drove a new Cadillac and docked a thirty-eight-foot Bayliner with twin diesels at the local marina.

He also had a beautiful wife—Miriam Cordell née Curtis.

However, all wasn't bliss and roses for the lucky couple. A year after they were married, Miriam—newly anointed to the rich and bored—was arrested for shoplifting. Two years after they were married, Isaac, with his business floundering, wrapped his wife in an anchor chain and threw her off their boat in a bid for the million-dollar insurance policy he'd taken out in her name.

The arson report attached to the case dealt with the burning down of one of Cordell's furniture stores prior to the murder. It had been a clear-cut arson job. The insurance company's refusal to pay off forced Cordell to pursue more desperate measures to raise capital. Measures like murdering his wife.

The detectives had done a great job putting the case together, but their evidence was mostly circumstantial—

the body was never recovered from the bottom of San Francisco Bay. Nevertheless, Isaac Cordell was quickly found guilty and shipped off to prison for the murder of his wife. The case set a number of legal precedents, but these soon became nothing more than discussion points or trick questions to be used by lazy law school professors.

Case closed.

Fey was reading through the reports again when the Homicide Unit's direct phone line rang. She scooped it up a split second before Colby could get to it.

"West Los Angeles Homicide, Croaker."

The voice on the wire was tinged with a soft Scottish burr.

"This is Card MacGregor. I'm a retired detective from SFPD. I have a message here to call a Detective Colby. Seems he doesn't have enough work down there, so he's dug up one of my old bodies."

"This is Fey Croaker. I head our divisional Homicide Unit. Colby works for me." From the corner of her eye, Fey caught Colby's look of thinly veiled animosity. "Hold on," she said to MacGregor. "Let me get him on the line."

She covered the phone's mouthpiece with one hand and gestured at Colby with the other. "Pick up the phone," she told him. "It's Card MacGregor, the detective who handled the Cordell case in San Francisco." Fey figured having Colby listen in was easier than repeating everything later.

Colby's fist swallowed the receiver of his extension. He punched himself into the line with the forefinger.

"I'm on board," Colby said.

"Good," MacGregor said.

"We understand you retired a couple of years ago," Fey said.

"From the department," MacGregor told her. "But I

was still too young to quit working altogether. I got a cushy job freelancing for insurance companies."

"How's the pay?"

"Keeps the wolf from the door," MacGregor told her. "What's all this nonsense about one of my old homicide victims being found dead again?"

"Do you remember a case from ten years ago—Isaac Cordell?" Fey asked.

"Sure," MacGregor said. "It caused a stir because it was the first time anyone in this jurisdiction had been convicted of murder without the body being recovered."

"It seems the reason your body was never recovered was because the victim wasn't dead."

"Come again..."

"If fingerprints are to be believed," Fey explained, "your victim, Miriam Cordell, survived her ordeal at sea only to be murdered again, ten years later, down here in our neck of the woods. This time under the name Miranda Goodwinter."

A rusty chuckle rumbled down the phone lines. "Crazy," MacGregor said. "I've had nightmares about the case ever since it went down. We put it all together, but it never did set easy with me. I knew something wasn't right."

"I've skimmed the official reports," Fey said. "Can you add the color commentary?"

"It was a strange case from the beginning," MacGregor said. "The harbor police had original jurisdiction because the murder occurred within the bay. If you'll excuse the pun, they quickly found themselves out of their depth and asked us to take over."

"You didn't have a problem?"

"Not really. The harbor police do a good job keeping weekend boaters in line, chasing speeders, and investigating illegal dumping, but murder is out of their league.

Since Cordell's boat was berthed in Sausalito there was some discussion if the Marin County Sheriff's Office or SFPD was going to handle the case, but the crime took place on the city side of the bay, so we got stuck with it."

"Handling a floating crime scene must have been a new experience," Fey said.

"It definitely had its challenges," MacGregor agreed, in the happy voice of a grandfather about to tell a bedtime story. "The boat was a beauty called *The Missy*, after the owner's mother. Not his wife or a lover, his mother."

"The owner was Isaac Cordell?"

"Yeah. A strange bird. Cordell was the kind of guy who knew how to spend money but had no idea how to make it."

"What about his chain of furniture stores?" Colby asked.

"His old man, Sam Cordell, started the stores and made them successful," MacGregor said. It was clear he didn't like being interrupted. Fey shot Colby a glance with *shut up* written all over it.

"Isaac had no business sense," MacGregor continued. "He took over the stores when he was twenty-five going on sixteen. There were three Cordell's Furniture stores in the Bay area. Within two years, he was on the brink of bankruptcy. Had to take on a partner, I think his name was Roark."

"Did the infusion of cash help?" Fey prompted.

"For a while. Roark helped to run things, but Isaac was still the majority shareholder. Problems started again a year later when Isaac decided to get himself hitched to an older woman."

"How much older?"

"There was really nothing in it. Isaac was twenty-eight and Miriam was thirty-three. But when we were investigating the case, a lot of people were casting aspersions on her for being a cradle robber."

"Why?"

Fey could almost see MacGregor's shrug over the phone line.

"Not sure, never having met the woman," the retired detective said. "I think it was down to the fact she was viewed as a gold digger. Isaac was considered the most eligible bachelor in the area. He didn't appear to be gay. He had money in the bank. A lot of mothers would have liked to see their daughters settle him down. However, Isaac was tied tight to his mother's apron strings. She was a demanding old bitch, who was probably the main reason behind Sam Cordell jumping into an early grave."

"She's the Missy for whom who Cordell named his boat?"

"The same. Missy had less money sense than Isaac, and no interest in running the business. Trying to keep her happy was probably why Isaac had so many business problems when he took over from his father.

"Missy, however, stuck around long enough to suck all the profits out of the business before she stroked out. Low and behold there Miriam was, out of nowhere, to sweep Isaac off his feet and give him another female anchor to cling on. There was a short courtship, a civil ceremony, then she settled in to spend any of the money Missy had left behind. There were a lot of noses out of joint."

"You remember a lot about this stuff," Colby said.

"It was the most high-profile case of my mediocre career. I researched the whole setup to make sure I wasn't missing anything to come back and haunt me later. I never figured on the victim still being alive, though."

"Isaac had to start borrowing against the business to

keep his new wife in bubbles and Brie?" Fey asked, hoping to get MacGregor rolling again.

"Familiar story?"

"I've run across it," Fey said. "Did Roark—the business partner—know about the new money problems?"

"Claimed he didn't, but it's hard to tell. A year and a half after the marriage, the Cordell's Furniture store down in the Tenderloin district burned down. It was well insured, but the insurance company was screaming about paying up."

"There was an arson report in the package sent to us."

"It was arson, all right. The problem was proving Cordell or his partner did it. They both denied the charges vehemently, but the motive was obvious. They needed the insurance money to keep the other two stores running. Both men, however, had alibis. The arson squad squeezed a few of the local firebugs, but none of them coughed."

"A dead end."

"For the arson squad. But we were able to get the case introduced in court as evidence to show a pattern of monetary desperation."

"How did you slip it by his lawyer?"

"Wasn't hard. By the time the case got to court, Cordell was so broke, he had a public defender. It was the PD's first murder case. She didn't know whether she was coming or going. I wouldn't want to try it now, though. From what I hear, the woman has turned into a real barracuda."

"What about the murder itself?" Fey asked

"Isaac said he and Miriam had taken *The Missy* out for a chug across the bay."

"How could Cordell afford to run a motor cruiser if his business was going down the tubes?" Colby jumped into the conversation again.

"He was trying to keep up appearances to the end. It was something I didn't like about the case. I think the guy truly loved his wife like he loved his mother. He was wound around her little finger. My gut instinct was murdering her was the furthest thing from his mind. He was trying too hard to hang on to her. The boat was due to be repossessed, his Cadillac was leased, and everything he had was mortgaged to the hilt—the house, the businesses, everything—all to keep Miriam in style."

"The court didn't buy the scenario?"

"No. My partner and the district attorney figured it was a reason to get rid of her. When all the other evidence was in, I had to agree."

"Without the body, it must have been a tough case to prove," Fey said, trying to imagine herself confronted with the same set of circumstances.

"Not as tough as you might expect. The circumstantial evidence was solid."

"Are you talking about the million-dollar insurance policy Cordell had on his wife?" Fey asked, referring to the information she'd picked up from the reports.

"Yeah," MacGregor said. "The policy had been taken out a year earlier and the premiums were up-to-date. Cordell denied any knowledge of the policy. We looked into it, but everything was in order. Miriam had a full medical to qualify for the policy and all the paperwork and premium checks were signed by Cordell. Cordell denied knowing anything about the account the checks to pay the premiums were drawn on, but his signature was all over the paperwork."

"Forgeries," Fey said.

"We didn't think so at the time," MacGregor said. "But if you say the victim was still alive until yesterday, I'd have to agree with you."

"What other evidence did you have?" Colby asked.

"The biggest thing was the SOS Miriam put out over the international distress channel. She and Cordell were on the bay when Miriam sent an interrupted message giving the name of their boat and said her husband was trying to kill her. The Coast Guard and half the boats in the bay converged on the scene. They found Cordell in the middle of a tizzy-fit, claiming his wife had fallen overboard."

"Nobody bought the story?" Fey said.

"Not after the distress message. Things got even blacker for Cordell when the harbor police did an inventory of the boat before impounding it. There was no anchor or anchor chain on board. They also conducted an extensive search for the body, dragging several areas of the bay. Obviously, they had no success." MacGregor paused for a few seconds and there was the sound of a cigarette being lit. Fey felt the urge surge through her body anew.

There was a long exhale before MacGregor picked up his tale. "When the case was turned over to us, we found out about the insurance policy, the arson, the business problems, and the extent of Cordell's financial straits. We had a ton of motive. Then Roark came forward and nailed Cordell's hide."

"Roark was the business partner?" Colby asked, trying to keep everything straight.

"Yeah," MacGregor confirmed. "On the day after we get the case, Roark strolls into the office and tells us Cordell told him he was planning to kill Miriam for the insurance money to save the business. Roark claimed he told Cordell he was crazy, never dreaming he would follow through."

"I imagine Cordell denied it," Fey said.

"Wouldn't you?" MacGregor asked. "The jury didn't buy the denial, and the rest of the evidence was solid. Cordell bought a life sentence, and we moved on to the next case with everyone telling us what a great job we did."

"Cut and dried," Colby said.

"Yeah, but you haven't heard the best part."

"What?" Fey and Colby asked in unison.

"Cordell couldn't get the insurance money, of course, because he'd been done for the murder."

"So?"

"There was a second beneficiary on the policy who walked away with a cool million."

"Let me guess," Fey said, her mind jumping ahead to the various possibilities. "The business partner— Roark."

MacGregor chuckled. "Yep."

"Where is he now?" Fey asked.

"No idea. Sold off the furniture stores, paid off the creditors, and got out of Dodge."

"What about Cordell?" Fey asked. "He's going to be surprised to find the woman he's spent the last ten years in jail for murdering was alive until yesterday."

"Doubt he'll be surprised," MacGregor replied. "He said all along he didn't kill her."

"Where's he doing time?"

There was a pause before MacGregor replied again. "Don't you know?" he asked eventually.

"Know what?"

"It made the papers up here. Some hotshot lawyer started championing his case about a year ago. She did a lot of rabble-rousing, getting people all shook up. Finally managed to get the parole board to review the case."

"And?" The anticipation in Fey's voice was clear.

"Cordell was paroled six weeks ago," MacGregor

said, with the satisfaction of a consummate storyteller bringing his tale to a close. "If I were him, knowing I hadn't killed my wife, I'd be pissed off and looking for the bitch."

CHAPTER THIRTEEN

"This thing is more complicated by the minute," Lieutenant Cahill said with a shake of his head. Fey had finished explaining the details of the San Francisco murder case she'd picked up from Card MacGregor. "What do you think happened in Frisco? Collusion between the wife and the business partner—a twist on *Double Indemnity*?"

"Probably," Fey said. She was sitting in one of the chairs surrounding the circular conference table in Cahill's office. Colby was sitting two chairs away. Cahill was behind his desk. "When you accept his wife didn't die, you can see how the circumstantial evidence could have been manufactured."

Fey had spent another twenty minutes on the phone getting Card MacGregor to fill in more of the details surrounding the investigation, the trial and conviction of Isaac Cordell, and the connections to Adam Roark, Isaac's business partner.

Colby left the conversation and started following up on the information MacGregor had already provided. His first call was to the state parole board. After being shuffled around from extension to extension and listening to seven minutes and fifty-six seconds worth of Muzak, he obtained the information Isaac Cordell had been paroled to the Los Angeles office. His supervising parole agent was Patty Kline.

Kline was out of her office, but Colby forced the issue, convincing the parole office switchboard to contact Kline through her pager. Between computers, cellular phones, pagers, Colby wondered how police work was ever accomplished in an earlier age.

However, he realized bad guys made as much use of modern technology as the police. It was move and counter-move. Every time the bad guys came up with a new scam, the good guys had to find a way to outmaneuver it.

Electronic gizmos only made the scams more complex. They didn't change the face of crime. It was still nothing more than an attempt to get something for nothing, no matter what the cost to someone else. It was the job of the police to turn *nothing* into a very high price.

Cops and robbers. Robbers and cops. It was a balancing game played on a high wire, but the scales were currently weighed in the robbers' favor. If the game didn't turn around soon, civilization would fall off the high wire with no safety net below.

Kline returned Colby's call within five minutes, indicating she was new on the job. Most old-timers would have ignored the page or waited till the second or third call. On the phone, though, Patty Kline was efficient and no-nonsense. She immediately grasped the significance of the situation and swung into action.

As soon as she got to her desk, she would fax Colby the file photos of Cordell, then head to the station to help follow-up. Colby thanked her. He also thanked the gods there were still people who cared about doing a good job.

Cahill sat at his desk, thinking. Colby had filled him

in on the facts of Cordell's parole and current residence in a halfway house in the southeast end of the division known as *The Hood*.

"There's a lot of loose ends," Cahill said after a minute. "We know anything about this lawyer who swung Cordell's parole?"

Fey shrugged. "Not yet. MacGregor said her name is Janice Ryder and put her in her early thirties. She made a name for herself in the San Francisco Public Defender's Office before switching to the District Attorney's Office and finally private practice. MacGregor has been on both sides with her and liked it a lot better when they were both on the same team."

"When did she hook into Cordell's case?"

"A year ago, right after she went into private practice. She did do it *pro bono* because Cordell didn't have anything left. She finally won the parole judgment six weeks ago."

Cahill picked up Fey's thread, "Next thing you know, the wife he supposedly murdered turns up dead under another name not five miles away from the parole halfway house where Cordell is living."

"Stinks, doesn't it?" Fey said.

"Like a wet hound dog." Cahill gave away some of his good-ol'-boy origins. "What about the business partner?"

"We don't have a line on Roark yet. If he's still around and found out about Cordell being paroled, he could have panicked and done the victim in to protect himself."

"What name was she using?"

"Goodwinter."

"If Goodwinter only slipped into this new identity a few weeks ago, she could also have known Cordell was out—changed identities so he couldn't find her."

"Then why didn't she clear out of town?" Colby asked.

Cahill shrugged. "Who knows? Maybe she knew he was paroled and had no idea he'd been relocated to LA."

Fey stood up, gathering the papers in front of her. "We aren't going to solve this by guessing. We better start running down all the loose ends. Is the parole agent here?"

Colby nodded. "Ten minutes ago. She's ready to do an unannounced parole check on Cordell and search his pad. We're invited along."

Fey smiled. "No warrant necessary when a suspect is tied to the parole yo-yo."

"First break since we found the body," agreed Cahill.

There was a knock and Monk Lawson stuck his head into the office. His grin was wide and white.

"Bingo," he said, stepping completely into the room.

He held up the *six-pack* photo lineup with Cordell's picture in the number two position, surrounded by five look-alikes. It was a bleak photo, but good enough for having come off the fax machine.

When Fey had first seen the head-and-shoulders shot, she realized Isaac had picked up some habits in the pen his mother wouldn't have approved. He was a big man, but now he was prison-big—pumped up by empty hours of pushing iron and doses of smuggled steroids. The frame of the photo lineup covered the white-power prison tattoo on Cordell's massive chest, which indicated the choice he made to survive inside.

"I tracked down the condo complex security guards," Monk said. "Unfortunately, none of them were able to identify Cordell."

"Too bad," Fey said. "It would have been nice to come up with a witness who could place Cordell at the scene."

"We have," Monk reported with a smile.

Fey looked confused.

"The guards couldn't identify him, but I found someone who could." Monk smiled again. "I did another door-to-door through the complex and found an old lady neighbor who watches the street like a hawk. She picked Cordell out of the lineup immediately, and she can place him at the scene on the night of the murder."

"Great work," Fey said, beating Cahill to the punch this time.

The three detectives looked expectantly at their lieutenant.

"Pull him in," Cahill said, after a beat. "Take the full team. Wear your vests."

CHAPTER FOURTEEN

When Etta Cinque opened the door of her two-story boardinghouse, she immediately knew it was *the man* standing on the doorstep.

"*Whaa choo wan?*" she asked Colby, breathing whiskey fumes into his face.

Colby hadn't been prepared for the vision of woman-hood standing before him. He figured Etta tipped the scales at close to 350 pounds. At slightly over five foot in height, she was almost as wide as she was tall.

The landlady's skin was a deep, shiny black with dark purple highlights. The tone clashed horribly with her bright orange housecoat. She wore an ill-fitting wig above day-old makeup. She hadn't taken a bath in a week because she hated getting in and out of her showerless tub.

Etta ran the residence as a halfway house for ex-cons trying to readjust to society. The state paid her a monthly fee. Her boarders were also required to make up the remainder of the rent. The situation kept Etta well stocked with microwave dinners, chocolate, and whiskey, but it didn't mean she always felt like cooperating.

"I *ax* you *whaa choo wan*, white boy. *Whaa* the man wan here?"

"Isaac Cordell," Colby said, reading all the trouble signs flowing from Etta's hostile presence. "We understand he rents a room here."

"You can *unnerstan whaaever choo wan*, but you ain't comin' in *witout* no warrant."

"You've been watching too much TV, lady," Colby said coldly. "We don't need a warrant. Mr. Cordell's parole officer is with us. She can search his room any time."

"Colby!" Fey yelled from behind him.

Her shout was unnecessary. As soon as Colby saw Etta start to close the door, he slammed his shoulder into it. The speed of his reaction caught Etta off guard. When the door smashed into her, she staggered back like a wayward bowling ball hunting for the gutter.

"Which room?" Colby demanded.

Patty Kline answered in a shout from behind Fey. "Second floor. Third door on the left." Cordell's parole officer had been to the halfway house twice before.

Fey followed Colby into the residence and was right behind him, pounding up the rickety stairs to the second floor. The house was dank and dark, smelling of greasy food, human sweat, and an overlaying odor of cat piss.

Hatch and Monk remained outside the house—Monk in front, Hatch to the rear. It was a standard setup. They knew they needed to cover all exits because ex-cons were unpredictable. Even if they were clean, they would run on the slightest provocation. It was a survival instinct gained through osmosis while in the pen.

On the hallway landing, Colby moved quickly to one side of Cordell's door. His right hand held his 9-mm in the low-ready position. With his left hand, he tried the door handle.

Locked.

Fey eased past Colby to take a covering position on the other side of the door. Her .38 was out of its shoulder holster, nestled in her left hand. Before leaving the station, she'd changed into jeans, a sweatshirt, tennis shoes, and a police raid jacket. A wide leather belt around her waist supported handcuffs, speedy loaders, a can of tear gas, and her Rover radio.

Knocking sharply on the door with the knuckles of her right hand, she called out, "Cordell! Police officers! Open the door!"

There was a loud scuffing noise from inside. Without waiting, Colby moved in front of the door, raised his knee, and kicked out. His Italian loafer slammed into the door above the lock. The force of the kick tore the sole half off the soft leather shoe while splintering the door-frame as the dead bolt burst loose. The door sprung in two inches before coming to an abrupt halt as it banged against a hidden obstacle.

"It's blocked!" Colby yelled. He hit the door with his shoulder but it only gave another inch. "Crap!" he said as a splinter of wood tore a hole in his jacket.

The sound of breaking glass came from inside the room.

"Don't be an idiot, Cordell!" Colby yelled. "Give it up!"

Fey keyed the transmit button on her Rover. "Hatch! He's coming your way."

Colby hit the door again but it still wouldn't give. Turning, he started back down the stairs, running straight into the awesome bulk of Etta Cinque. This time she was ready for him. Colby bounced off her as if he'd been hit by an entire NFL defensive front line.

"Out of the way!" Colby yelled. He waved his gun, to no effect.

"*Yoo don* be comin' *inoo* my house, Mr. Man, *an thin yoo* can kick stuff *aron an* get away *wit* it. Mr. Cordell's a decent man. *Yoo* got no cause to be messin' *wit*..."

Colby sunk his fist into the fat woman's stomach. The whiskey fumes almost blew him off his feet as air belched out of Etta's mouth.

Etta whooped for oxygen but didn't move.

Colby hit her again, but she smiled viciously before smacking him backward with a swipe of a fleshy arm. Colby went ass over teakettle and crumpled on the stairs.

Fey saw the start of the confrontation but had left Colby to it. There wasn't room enough on the stairway for three of them. Meanwhile, Cordell was getting away.

She quickly turned and ran to the door of the next room. It was unlocked, and she entered on the run, gun up and ready.

The stale smell of sweat and marijuana was an overpowering physical force. A thin body was flopped on a camp bed, oblivious to the commotion. Fey spared the body a quick glance before moving to the rear window. It was painted shut.

The Rover, back in its belt holder, crackled with Hatch's agitated voice. "He got by me. Running southbound. I'm cut by falling glass...need an ambulance."

Fey swore. The body on the bed didn't move. Incongruously, Fey wondered if they had another dead body on their hands. Pulling the Rover from her belt, she keyed the mike. "Monk!" she said, trying to make her voice calm and in command. "Get a broadcast out and get to Hatch. Do it now!"

She didn't wait for a reply. Instead, she threw a disgusting pile of clothing off a metal folding chair in a corner of the room. She swung the chair into the window, shattering glass. She realized she was raining more glass down on Hatch, but it couldn't be helped.

Clearing glass shards from the window frame, she internally gathered her nerve. If Cordell could survive the jump, so could she. Without thinking further, Fey put one foot on the windowsill and launched into air.

The ten-foot drop came to a jarring halt, which sent spasms through her knees she would feel for weeks. Using momentum, Fey rolled onto her right shoulder and came up into a limping run.

Her .38 was in her hand and fire in her heart.

A quick glance revealed Hatch on the ground under Cordell's window. He was holding a bloody arm. There was a gash down his face pouring blood.

"Looks worse than it is," Hatch said. He could tell Fey didn't believe him and changed tacks. "I'll survive," he said grimly. "Get the bastard!" With a bloody finger, he pointed in the direction Cordell had gone. "Be careful. He's a big mutha."

"Screw careful!" Fey said, moving into a shambling run.

After a hundred yards, her breath was rasping, and her legs felt like jelly. She rode her horses three or four times a week, but it didn't keep her in the physical shape demanded by a foot pursuit.

The alleyway behind the boardinghouse was a rabbit warren of carports, apartment back entrances, and cross-alleys. A dog barked hysterically somewhere to Fey's left. She cut between two buildings in the direction of the noise.

Trash and rotting garbage were strewn everywhere. Above her, the buildings folded in as if ravaged by some kind of internal cancer. The daylight diminished and the world rapidly became a strange gray color. Several black children stared as she ran past. Their mothers, sensing danger from the white man's world, yelled at the children to get inside.

A cat screeched and flew out of nowhere to skitter across Fey's path and disappear. Fey almost capped off a round, her heart leaping.

As she ran, adrenaline pumped through her body, sharpening her brain, slowing down the world around her, putting her into the zone - a natural danger high more addictive than any drug. The only sound she could hear was the pounding of her own biological pulses.

Breath wheezed in and out of her lungs as if she were an ancient crone with a four-pack-a-day habit. But her gun was up and ready, and her peripheral vision was working at maximum.

She caught movement to her left.

A garbage can crashing toward her.

Throwing up her gun hand, she deflected the blow. The impact still drove her to her knees and numbed her arm. Her gun exploded from her grasp like a startled hawk taking flight.

She rolled to her right but wasn't quick enough to escape a kick smashing into her ribs. She grunted, kept rolling, eventually coming to her knees with her arms held out defensively.

"You're a woman. They sent a woman after me."

Fey shook her head, trying to focus on the speaker.

Isaac Cordell.

He was bigger than his mug photos indicated. His naked chest rippled with smuggled steroid and jail-built muscles above a pair of jeans on slim hips. His feet were bare. A wide belt looped around the jeans a large buckle cinched at the center.

Cordell stopped his advance, giving Fey time to stagger to her feet.

"They sent a woman after me," Cordell said again.

Fey ignored his outrage. "Give it up, Cordell," she

said, shakily. "Turn around and put your hands behind your back."

Cordell laughed. "I'm not letting a woman take me in."

He lashed out an apelike arm, connecting solidly with the side of Fey's head.

Her body dropped to the ground, her head feeling it had been turned around on her neck. What happened to the mama's boy Card MacGregor had described? Cordell was a maniac.

Sluggishly, she scrambled for her gun, yelling out abuse lost in the drone from the police helicopter doing a low pass overhead.

She felt herself punched in the back and dropped flat on her stomach again. Cordell started to work her over with his feet. If he had been wearing boots or shoes, he probably would have killed her.

Forgetting the gun, Fey went into survival mode. If she could hold on, help would arrive quickly.

Quickly, however, might not be quick enough to save her life.

Fey rolled away from the kicks and kept rolling until she slammed into the wall of a surrounding building. Calling on every nuance of strength she had left, she pushed herself upright and turned to face Cordell with the building wall behind her.

"Come on, you mother," she said, tasting blood at the back of her throat.

"Feisty, ain't you?" Cordell said, an evil smile turning up the corners of his mouth. He was advancing toward her, a hulking mass of brawn on the move. His short, red brush cut capped a melon face full of malice and prison carbohydrates. The body of an ape God had decided to turn into a man at the last moment.

Fey noticed the police helicopter had moved away. It

was still circling, but it had moved away from the air space directly above.

Cordell had noticed as well.

"Stupid halfwits don't know where you are," he said. His voice was calm, tinged with amusement.

Fey felt for the rover on her belt. Pulling it out, she saw the battery pack on the bottom had twisted off during one of her violent meetings with the ground. The thing was useless. Less than useless as she couldn't even think of a way to use it as a weapon.

She thought of bluffing, key the mike and request help as though the rover still worked. The idea, though, was abandoned while only half-formed. It was clear from Cordell's expression and laughter he knew the score.

Fey also realized Cordell was no longer running away. His demeanor had changed from flight to fight. Somehow, her being a woman had triggered a violent response in Cordell.

"I thought you cops ran in packs," Cordell said, still not advancing toward her.

Fey was breathing heavily and didn't bother to respond. She watched Cordell cock his head sideways to look at her as if he were a curious cocker spaniel. "Yet here you are, all on your little lonesome."

Fey knew she'd been stupid to run after Cordell alone, but she'd thought Colby would soon be on her trail. Etta must have proved more of an obstacle than anticipated.

"Screw you," Fey said. She tried to move along the wall but stopped as Cordell moved to shadow her.

The big man's face clouded over. "Watch your mouth. I'm not going to take crap from yo, or anybody. Cops railroaded me. Now, I'm going to maim as many cops as I can. If you're lucky, I may let you live."

Fey kept trying to think of ways to stall. If she could

keep Cordell talking help would arrive. She listened for the police helicopter, but it seemed even further away.

"If you don't give it up, Cordell, you're going to make things much worse."

"Things can't get any worse," Cordell said. He took a step toward Fey. "Boo!" he said, flinging his arms at her without making contact. She flinched backward.

Cordell laughed. "I'm through listening to women. Women have screwed me over my whole life—my mother, my wife, my parole agent, all of 'em. It's time I screwed back."

"What about your lawyer? The one who got you paroled?"

"Screw her too!" Cordell yelled.

He charged at Fey. She tried to sidestep, but her legs and feet wouldn't coordinate. Cordell slammed his shoulder into her and drove her back into the wall of the building. Consciousness started to fade as Fey slipped down to her knees.

From far away she heard Cordell talking to her. "The perfect pose, like the love canal boys in prison. I'm going to start with your pretty mouth. Then I'm going to break you open like a shotgun and do to you what they did to me in prison—only there was seven of them for my initiation."

Fey felt a huge hand take the top of her head in a solid grip. She heard the sound of a zipper being pulled down and opened her eyes to see the length of Cordell's erect penis in front of her face. It bobbed up and down.

She looked up, suddenly feeling she was ten years old again. Through the fog in her brain she saw her father's face transposed over Cordell's features.

She clearly heard her father's voice. "You're a bad, filthy little girl. You're making Daddy punish you again. You'll do what I tell you and like it. And if you tell anyone, I'll cut your little brother's privates off. You wouldn't want that to happen, would you?" The harsh voice would then gradually soften. "Come on. Show Daddy you're his favorite little girl."

The male stench of Cordell's unwashed crotch swept into Fey's nostrils. She felt sick to her stomach.

"You're going to do what I tell you and like it." The words were her father's, but the voice was Cordell's.

Rage overflowed from deep in the primeval recesses of Fey's soul. Anger exploded through her veins as if it had burst through a dam.

Fear...Frustration...Confusion...Pain...Hatred.

Fey remembered the vow she'd said every time her father had violated her—*never again, never again.*

She'd been too small and helpless to keep her vow when she was ten. But the years had made her stronger. She had survived and, eventually, her determination to never again be abused, debased, or shamed became an unbreakable vow.

Never again. Never again. The words filled her being as Cordell pushed his penis toward her face again.

"Open your mouth or I'll kill you right now!"

With a power born of sheer determination, Fey stiffened the thumb of her left hand, took a deep breath, and drove its sharpened nail deep into the base of Cordell's scrotum. The big man's scream matched the decibel count of Fey's own explosion of sound as she brought forth a scream from the center of her childhood pain.

As Cordell doubled over, Fey smashed the palm of her other hand into the center of his face. His nose splattered flat and blood spewed in a long arc across the ground. The attacker had suddenly become the attacked. Cordell had no idea how to get away from the helpless rabbit turned wildcat.

Coming to her feet, Fey viciously kicked the side of

Cordell's left knee. Ligaments tore and the knee buckled like a tree snapped in a hurricane.

Giving no respite, Fey slammed a palm into Cordell's shoulder and spun him around. Knowing her next action would be considered deadly force, she didn't hesitate before wrapping her right elbow under Cordell's chin and then locking up the carotid choke hold by placing her left arm behind Cordell's neck. As she squeezed her arms together, the carotid artery on the side of Cordell's neck was shut down, stopping the flow of blood to his brain. Within seconds, the big man was flopping around like a dying fish. His bowels evacuated as his eyes rolled up in his head and consciousness fled.

When she was sure Cordell was out, Fey released the hold, rolled her prisoner over on his stomach, pulled the handcuffs from the back of her belt, and used them to secure his hands in the small of his back. When she finished, her strength deserted her, and she slumped onto her knees beside Cordell.

Where the hell was Colby? Where the hell was anybody in a blue uniform?

She swore a bitterly, but inside her soul a little ten-year-old girl was smiling.

Her vow remained unbroken. *Never again. Never again.*

CHAPTER FIFTEEN

Colby came running full pelt around the corner of the building nearest to Fey. His gun in his hand, his face pale except for an ugly welt over one eye. His usually immaculate hair was mussed, his sartorial elegance a thing of the past. The sole of one Italian loafer flapped up and down as he ran, like something borrowed from a circus clown.

He slowed as soon as he saw Fey. Finally stopping next to her, he bent over at the waist to put his hands on his knees and catch his breath.

"You look like hell," he said. His voice casual.

"You don't look much better." Fey's tone held the same casual note as Colby's, but there was no underlying malice in their exchange.

Colby took a closer look at Fey, seeing the extent of her condition. "You okay?" he asked.

Fey tried to stand up and grunted before staying slumped down on top of Cordell. "I don't know," she said. "More of me hurts than doesn't."

Colby pulled the Rover off his belt and spoke rapidly

into it. Almost immediately, the sound of the police helicopter increased as it pinpointed Fey's position.

Colby continued talking into the rover until a black-and-white unit arrived on the scene, followed rapidly by an ambulance. The uniformed officers took custody of Cordell, throwing him none too easily in the back of the patrol car. The ambulance attendants took custody of Fey.

A detective car pulled up containing Monk Lawson and Patty Kline. They both exited the vehicle and walked to where Fey was being attended by a paramedic.

"How's Hatch?" Fey asked.

"Fine," Monk said. "They took him to the hospital for stitches, but the ambulance crew think he'll be okay."

"Great...Ouch! Watch it," Fey said to the paramedic who was poking her in the ribs. "Who trained you? Quasimodo?"

"Yeah, but I could never get used to wearing a hump," the paramedic replied, continuing to probe.

"Just what I need," Fey said, "a comedian."

The paramedic finished taking her vital signs and pulled the stethoscope out of his ears. "We're going to put you on a stretcher and take you to the hospital," he said, waving his partner over.

"Like hell," Fey said. "I hate hospitals."

"Don't be stupid. You may have internal injuries and a couple of ribs are cracked or broken."

Fey grunted. "Tape me up. I'll survive. I'm not going to the hospital."

"Fey..." Colby started in to change her mind.

He was sorry Fey had been hurt, if only because someone might question why he hadn't been around to back her up, but he figured she deserved what she got. She was the one who took off by herself, trying to do a man's job. And if she was made to stay in the hospital, it would certainly get her out of his hair.

"Shut up, Colby," Fey cut him off. "I don't need a wet nurse. I caught him, and I'll clean him." Fey could already hear the gears turning in Colby's mind. If she was in the hospital, he'd quickly find a way to make everyone think he'd made the arrest.

"Come on, partner," Colby said, consciously not using his favorite Frog Lady tag. "Nobody is going to look down on you for going to the hospital."

"Would you go?" Fey asked him. She was having trouble keeping the pain and anger out of her voice.

Colby opened his mouth and then closed it. He didn't have a comeback. Fey was staring at him, so he answered her with a shrug.

"Case closed," Fey said. She turned back to the paramedic "Tape me up. If things get too rough, I promise I'll check myself into the hospital."

The paramedic surprised Fey by sticking a needle in her arm.

"Ouch!" she said again. Seconds later, she was out cold.

"Another bad case of macho cured," the paramedic said calmly.

Colby shook his head. "She is going to be pissed when she wakes up."

"At least she'll wake up," the paramedic said. "She's in a lot of pain. She needs X rays, and I want a doctor to confirm she isn't in any danger. Cops always think they're immortal."

"Being immortal is a prerequisite to get on the department," Colby said. The way he felt, he wished he was on the stretcher.

———

The following morning Fey was in the office when Monk and Hatch arrived. Even with her ribs taped up, she felt sore and agitated. A yellow bruise ran down the left side of her face, emphasized by a purple shiner.

"What are you doing here?" Hatch asked. "You look like you've been dragged through a hedge backward."

"Don't give me a bad time," Fey said. "You look as bad as me, and you're here."

Fey had winced when she looked at Hatch. There was a large white plaster on his right cheek and his right sleeve was rolled up, exposing the long line of stiches on his arm.

"How many stitches in your cheek?" she asked.

"Eighteen," Hatch said. The plaster made his mouth move awkwardly when he talked.

"You going to need plastic surgery?"

"Nah." Hatch shrugged. "Lorraine says scars are sexy. She's always wanted to be married to a pirate."

Lorraine was Hatch's third wife. Ten years younger than him and a sexual dynamo. Rumor was, she left him wrung out—but happy—six nights a week. Sundays, apparently, were a day of rest. Nobody thought the union would last, but the honeymoon had been going on for three years with no cracks in sight.

"Did you get Cordell booked without problems?" Fey asked, turning toward Monk.

"Colby booked him, and I did the reports."

Fey nodded. "Colby interrogate him?" The thought frustrated Fey. She had wanted the first shot at Cordell.

"Tried, but Cordell immediately yelled lawyer. Refused to waive his rights before they were read to him."

"Did he ask why he was being arrested?"

Monk thought for a moment. "I don't think so."

"Interesting," Fey said. She firmly believed things suspects didn't say were as important as what they did.

"However, we don't need Cordell's statement," Monk said.

Fey raised her eyebrows. "Why not?"

Stretched out the suspense, Monk looked at Hatch with a huge smile.

"Give," Fey demanded. "I'm not up to playing games."

"We recovered the murder weapon in Cordell's room," Monk told her.

"Serious?" Fey said.

"Serious. We went back to his pad with Kline, the parole agent. We did a search under her authority. Colby was poking around in the closet and found a flat-head screwdriver caked with blood and skin."

"You're yanking my chain," said Fey in disbelief.

"I'm not," said Monk with a laugh.

"How could anybody be so stupid?"

"You don't need to be a rocket scientist to commit murder," Hatch said. "He obviously didn't kill the woman the first time. Maybe finding her again was coincidence and he killed her in a fit of rage."

"I don't like coincidence," Fey replied thoughtfully. "It could have happened, but I don't like the feel of it."

"If criminals didn't mess up, we wouldn't catch them."

"I know. But keeping the murder weapon in your room…"

Hatch and Monk both shrugged.

"Did the lab find anything positive on the screwdriver?"

"You're kidding," Hatch said. "Even with a rush request, the earliest we'll hear is this afternoon."

"Let's hope its good news when it comes."

There was a clattering on the back stairwell preceding Colby breezing into the squad room.

"Hey, Frog Lady," he said when he spotted Fey. "You made parole."

"Not quite," Fey said. "They took my clothes away, but I stole a nurse's uniform and discharged myself."

Colby laughed. "How you feeling?"

"Like a dog trying to poop in the rain—miserable. How about you?"

"About the same," he said. "The landlady sure could punch. My clothing bill will be astronomical."

"My heart bleeds," Fey said.

"Nice to see things back to normal," Monk said to Hatch.

Lieutenant Cahill stuck his head into the squad room from the outer lobby. "If you're done comparing war wounds, you have a customer at the front counter."

She stood up slowly, trying not to wince. She knew it wouldn't be good news this early in the morning.

Standing at the lobby counter was a petite blonde—all legs and California good looks. Her fine golden hair was pulled back from her face, secured in a ponytail dropping to her waist. Her high cheekbones were sharp enough to cut glass, and her perfect nose was complemented by piercing blue eyes.

The entire package was poured into a hand-tailored skirt and jacket ensemble, completed by a scoop-necked silk blouse and a glitter of diamonds at ears, neck, and wrist.

Fey took one look and wanted to bury herself under a rock. The woman hadn't said a word, but Fey felt she was entering a battle of wits unarmed.

Men would die for this one.

Colby's hormones would do themselves an injury when he saw her. The woman was big trouble.

"Detective Croaker?" the woman asked, before Fey had a chance to introduce herself. "I'm Janice Ryder... Isaac Cordell's lawyer."

Oh crap, Fey thought, *here we go*!

CHAPTER SIXTEEN

Fey poured herself a cup of coffee, trying to gather her thoughts.

Colby sauntered into the coffee room and refilled his own cup. "Who's the good-looking spinner?" he asked. He'd seen Fey walk Janice Ryder down the hall to a private interview room.

"Cordell's lawyer."

"Wow," said Colby. "If I could get her to handle my case, it might be worth getting arrested."

"She would chew you up and spit out the pit before you got to first base."

Colby laughed. "Glad Cordell didn't damage your sarcastic streak."

"It's the only thing he didn't damage."

Needing time to think, Fey had abandoned Janice Ryder in the interview room. She was determined to get the upper hand, knowing first blood had already gone to Ryder.

"You booked Cordell on the open murder charge?" she asked Colby.

"Along with charges for *resisting arrest* and *battery on a police officer*. We took the package to Judge Taylor. He gave us a *no bail* deviation. Kline also slapped on a parole hold. He's not going anywhere."

"I'm not so sure," Fey said. "I think his lawyer has something up her sleeve."

"It's what's up her leg I'm interested in."

Fey shook her head in disgust. "Don't you ever give it a rest?"

When Colby and the others arrived on the scene of Cordell's arrest, Fey didn't say anything about the sexual attack. She justified the omission in her mind by convincing herself they had enough charges without further complicating the case.

However, the truth was, she couldn't face the inevitable comments. Colby would have a field day. Experience had proven the other males she worked with would have gone along.

Nobody would mean to be malicious – except maybe Colby – but she would have felt tainted. She had hidden the abuses by her father for years. Even though she had been victorious over Cordell, she was not going to let the acceptance she had achieved be destroyed.

When she choked Cordell into unconsciousness, his penis shrunk and slipped back into his pants. If anyone noticed his trousers were unbuttoned and unzipped, they didn't say anything. They probably figured it was a result of his hurried exit from the boardinghouse, or they'd come undone in the altercation.

In some ways, the situation created a strange bond between Cordell and Fey. If he kept his mouth shut, so would she. Her silence now made it impossible to throw around charges later.

Anyway, what charges could she bring? *Forced oral copulation*? The intention had been there, but the act was never completed. *Assault with intent to commit forced oral copulation*? Maybe, but it was still her word against his. It would be hard to prove without any corroborating evidence. *Attempted rape*? The facts wouldn't support the charge. *Lewd conduct* or *indecent exposure*? Again maybe, but who cared about misdemeanors? All in all, Fey felt she was better off keeping her mouth shut. A conspiracy of silence plaguing women since Adam chased Eve around the garden.

Fey drank her full-strength brew slowly, leaning against the wall of the small coffee room. She didn't feel up to confronting the ice queen who was waiting for her in the interview room, but it had to be done.

"Do me a favor," she said to Colby. "Set a tape running for the big interview room. I want a record of the conversation."

Colby went without argument. Fey wondered why, then realized she'd given him the perfect opportunity to sit in the recording room listening. She'd not only have to be careful about letting Janice Ryder gain the upper hand, but also be sure not to give Colby something to use to his own advantage. She was tired of having to constantly protect herself.

She poured a cup of coffee into a Styrofoam container, threw in a dash of powdered creamer and a package of Sweet & Low. She knew Cordell's lawyer would never let real sugar cross her lips.

When Fey entered the interview room with her peace offering, Janice Ryder was pacing around in a snit.

"Have my heels cooled enough for you, *Officer* Croaker?"

Fey looked at Ryder and smiled. She set Ryder's coffee on the table. "My demotion from *detective* to *officer* is duly noted," Fey said calmly. "It's a good tactic, but like keeping you waiting, it's basically a waste of time. Can we cut to the nitty gritty? What do you want?"

Janice Ryder sat down in a hard, straight-backed chair across from Fey. The stark interview room had urine yellow walls. Gang graffiti was scratched into the back of the door, the top of the table, and the two chairs.

For a moment, Janice Ryder didn't answer. She looked around, focusing on the room's only decoration – a cross-stitched sampler jury-rigged to one of the acoustic metal walls. The homily read: *No man has a good enough memory to be a successful liar*.

Fey followed Janice's gaze. She thought the saying was appropriate for the setting, but her favorite was a carved wooden sign over the interrogation room in an Air Force MP station: *You came in here with information and a pretty face. You can't leave with both*.

"Well?" Fey said.

Janice Ryder looked at her. It was as if she had been having an out-of-body experience and returned to reclaim her physical form. Fey wondered where the other woman's mind had been and felt a shiver run down her spine.

"Is this conversation being recorded?" Ryder asked.

"Absolutely," Fey told her.

"Why?"

"For my protection. This is a high-profile case. I want a record in the event there are questions later."

"Are you always this careful?"

"Always," Fey said. "Thanks to your client, I feel like hell. What can I do for you?"

Ryder picked up her coffee and sipped. She made an unladylike face, setting the cup down.

"You develop a taste for it," Fey said, watching the reaction. She knew Ryder was using delaying tactics but decided not to be drawn.

"What I want," Ryder said eventually, "is my client's

immediate release from police custody with all charges dropped."

Fey couldn't help a laugh escaping. "And I want to be the queen of Sheba," she said. "You must think I'm a few fries short of a Happy Meal."

"I'm serious."

"Then you earned your law degree on another planet. No way is your client walking away. The case is open, closed, and wrapped in Christmas ribbon. Dead bang."

"The problem with dead-bang cases is they're often dead in the water."

"What's your point?"

"A man can't be tried for the same crime twice. You are accusing my client of murdering a woman who was once his wife. A woman whose murder he was convicted for ten years ago. My client's years in prison have paid his debt for the crime. You can't convict him again for murdering the same woman. It's double jeopardy. On this planet, detective, double jeopardy is against the law."

CHAPTER SEVENTEEN

Fey looked shocked. "Ridiculous."

"Consider the facts." Janice Ryder confidently overrode Fey's protest. "Isaac Cordell has been tried, convicted, and served time for the murder of Miranda Goodwinter, aka Miriam Cordell. Even if he did murder her this time – and I'm not indicating he did – it would be double jeopardy. You can't murder someone twice."

"How do you know about the connection between Miranda Goodwinter and Miriam Cordell? The information hasn't been made public."

"Guess again, detective." Janice Ryder slid her slim calfskin briefcase onto the tabletop and flipped open the catches. From inside, she removed a copy of the front page of the *Los Angeles Tribune*. She dropped the newsprint on the table and swiveled it toward Fey.

Fey held Janice's eyes for a second then dropped her gaze to the newspaper. She scanned the headlines. She sighed, picking up the pages.

The banner headline dealt with another Middle East crisis, but a secondary headline carried the message, *murder done twice! Woman Believed Murdered Ten Years Ago Found Dead Again.*

There was a grainy black-and-white photo of Miriam Cordell, obviously taken years earlier. Next to it was a photo of Miranda Goodwinter being taken out of her home in a body bag. The caption read simply, *Miranda Goodwinter or Miriam Cordell?*

The accompanying article contained little factual information, but ghoulishly rehashed the details from the San Francisco case, Cordell's conviction, and speculation concerning his current arrest.

Fey felt deflated. How had the paper latched on to the story so quickly? She realized there must be a leak in the division. She also knew the most likely suspect. It would explain where Colby got the money for his flashy lifestyle.

Fey sighed again. "Counselor, you assume you throw me off by dropping this bomb. However, your client will stay under arrest for murder until the court decides differently."

Ryder jumped into the middle of Fey's narrative. "I'd think twice before you take this case to court. Not only is my client innocent, but it's clear Miriam Cordell was alive until two days ago. My client should never have been convicted. The state's liability over Isaac Cordell's false imprisonment is outrageous. Further blunders will only result in the civil suit increasing in magnitude."

"Isaac Cordell is guilty. We have an eyewitness placing him at the scene."

"Eyewitnesses are as reliable as a toilet tissue in a rainstorm."

Fey held up her hand. "The murder weapon was recovered at your client's residence."

"Frame-up," Janice Ryder interrupted again. "Same as ten years ago. You want to wrap this murder up fast and cover past mistakes. Isaac Cordell makes a perfect patsy. It's not going to happen. Cordell was framed once for the murder of his wife. You're not doing it again." Janice Ryder's voice rose passionately.

Fey leaned back in her chair, waiting for Ryder to wind down. "A pretty speech, counselor, but it's not going to wash," she said, eventually. "I'm in no position to release your client. The district attorney or the court will decide."

"Neither serve my client's best interests." Ryder was still heated.

"Quit busting my chops," Fey said. She leaned into Ryder's personal space. "Tougher nuts than you have tried and failed. As *civil liability* is such a big deal, I'm doing everything by the book."

"I want my client released."

"Grow up, counselor."

Janice Ryder snapped her briefcase closed. "When will my client be arraigned?"

"The sooner I get back to doing my job, the sooner Cordell gets arraigned." Fey stepped over and opened the door to the interrogation room. "Counselor," she said, with an ushering gesture toward the opening.

Janice Ryder stood and walked out of the room.

"This is far from over," she said as she passed Fey. "Before this is done, I'll have your ass on a platter."

"Take your best shot." Silently, Fey finished the sentence with *bitch*.

———

"She's a piranha, Jake," Fey said, sitting in the deputy district attorney's small office.

Jake Travers was a tall, slim man. He looked more like a hard-bitten saddle tramp than the DA's head filing deputy. His thick black hair came to a widow's peak low on his forehead before sweeping straight back to tickle his collar. His tanned face had enough wrinkles and crow's-feet to give him *character*. On a woman they would have been considered ugly.

At thirty-eight, he was still considered a rising star, and possibly a strong candidate for DA during the next election year. He had divorced four years earlier, his world revolving around his job, golf, and fishing.

Having been friends for years, and intermittent lovers for five, Jake and Fey were happy with their relationship. It suited their needs, asking no commitments beyond friendship and bed. They knew they couldn't remain static forever. Sooner or later, the relationship would have to evolve or die.

"You let her get to you," Jake said. His deep voice held a note of amusement. It wasn't often someone got the better of Fey Croaker.

"Stuff it," Fey said with resignation. "What about this double jeopardy stuff?"

Jake shrugged and stroked his chin. "I don't know."

"You don't know?"

"She may have a point. I can see a definite constitutional argument. Whether it will hold up is another question."

"Are you considering dropping this case? The bastard slit a woman's throat. What difference does it make if he did it ten years ago or two days ago?"

"All I said is she may have a point. We're going to have to find a way to blunt it."

After getting rid of Janice Ryder, Fey had gone back to the squad room with her head spinning. She wanted to believe Ryder's argument was all bluster, but there was a gnawing grain of doubt.

She needed this case wrapped up tight to secure her

position as the Homicide Unit supervisor. If it got screwed up, she could find herself handling a Juvenile Unit – the traditional home for female detective supervisors.

It wouldn't be a demotion, but it would be a large drop in prestige, and there was nothing she would be able to do about it. She could hear the divisional sharks feeding, "Put her in charge of juvenile. If she messes up there, nobody will care."

The attitude wasn't right. There were good people who dedicated their careers to working Juvenile. Officers and detectives who made a difference in young people's lives. However, the assignment didn't carry the promise of glory cases.

On her desk were a stack of phone messages from reporters following up the *Tribune* scoop. Fey chose to ignore her suspicions about Colby and the leak. She also chose to ignore the messages and the insistent ringing of the homicide unit's direct phone line.

"What are you telling reporters?" she asked Hatcher and Monk, who were processing paperwork.

"We're referring them to you," Monk said. "They are not happy."

"Tough," Fey said. She dropped the messages in a trashcan. "Keep taking messages, then file them with these," she said. "When we know more, we'll do a press conference. Till then, screw 'em."

"Will do," Hatch said. "Your shiner is going to look great on television."

"It would get my sympathy vote," Monk said.

"Shut up," Fey said without heat. There was nothing behind the gentle ribbing. "You should both be doing stand-up." She glanced around the squad room. "Speaking of clowns, where's Colby?"

"Court. He's got the prelim on Mason Dunnet today."

Fey nodded, remembering. "Should keep him busy for a while."

The Dunnet case had been a *self-solver*. Neighbors reported gunshots from inside the Dunnet residence. When patrol officers arrived, they found Dunnet standing over the rapidly cooling body of his wife. He was literally holding the smoking gun. Dunnet had happily confessed, but now a public defender was grandstanding. Using a male version of the *burning bed* defense, the PD maintained Dunnet had been forced to kill his wife before she killed him through ongoing physical and mental abuse.

At her desk, Fey gathered up the reports pertaining to Miranda Goodwinter's murder and Cordell's arrest. Car keys in hand, she signed herself out to the District Attorney's Office in Santa Monica. It was time to file the case and get Cordell arraigned.

"Cases like Cordell's convince me God is a man," she said to Monk and Hatcher as she was leaving.

"Why?" asked Hatch, ever willing to play the straight man.

"Because if God was a woman, she wouldn't have screwed things up this badly."

———

Fey drove the short distance to the DA's office on autopilot. Her conscious mind filled with the possibilities Janice Ryder had brought to the surface. There was no telling what a jury or a judge would do with the double jeopardy situation.

Fey remembered a well-publicized case where patrol officers arrested a burglar inside a residence while the owners were on vacation. It seemed dead-bang until it went to court. In front of the judge, it was revealed the arresting officers had been overzealous, putting a parking ticket on the defendant's car parked in front of a fire hydrant for a quick getaway.

While out on bail, the defendant appeared in traffic court. He pled guilty to the parking infraction, receiving a fifty-dollar fine. When the burglary charges came to court, the defense attorney argued his client already pled guilty to a charge stemming from the case and been punished by paying a fine. To try him on further charges would place his client in double jeopardy. The judge agreed. Instead of going up the river for five years, the defendant was immediately released to return to his chosen profession.

In a court of law, anything was possible.

Janice Ryder was right on one point – *dead bang* didn't mean squat.

There were also a ton of things demanding attention before the case would be ready for court. There were unanswered questions from the first case in San Francisco, plus unknowns related directly to the victim.

Before this point, Fey and the other homicide detectives had been scrambling to beat the magical seventy-two-hour deadline when the chances of solving a case drop dramatically. In accomplishing the feat, they had burned through a lot of mental and physical energy. The fast and loose part of the case was over. It was time for the grunt work of making sure the case held up. A tough task, especially with a firecracker like Janice Ryder trying to thwart their every move.

Now, sitting across from Jake Travers, Fey felt overwhelmed by the magnitude of things still to be accomplished. "Can you handle this from the arraignment on down?" Fey asked. "I don't know what Ryder is going to throw at us, but I'd feel better with you there to handle it."

"I haven't said I'm going to file the case."

"You'll file it," Fey told him.

"Because why?"

"Because you can't resist a challenge, and because you won't be able to resist taking on Janice Ryder."

"You mean personally or in the courtroom?"

Fey gave Jake a sly smile full of open sexuality. "In the courtroom, of course. If you take this on, I promise you won't have energy left to deal with her personally."

Jake Travers looked suitably shocked. "Promises, promises," he said.

Fey knew she was playing dirty pool, but when life got tough, you used whatever weapons were in your arsenal. Sex was constantly used against women. Sometimes it was nice to turn the tables to your advantage.

She also knew she enjoyed sex a lot more when she controlled the reins.

CHAPTER EIGHTEEN

Isaac Cordell's arraignment was to be held in Division 90, located in the court buildings across the street from the West Los Angeles Area police station. Fey managed to get the complaint filed and typed in time for afternoon court.

This required her to walk Cordell from the station jail – where he had been held overnight – to the sheriff's lockup at the back of the court building. If the *no bail* status held during the arraignment, he would be transported from the courthouse to County Jail, a facility run by the sheriff's department. He would remain there until his preliminary hearing.

Colby was back from morning court when Fey returned to the station. She collared him to assist in escorting Cordell across the street. Going into the station jail to take custody of the prisoner, Fey felt her guts begin to churn. Every ache and pain in her body seemed to intensify. She had taken a couple of painkillers, but she felt exhausted. She knew she had to get through the afternoon before she could collapse.

Cordell stood up from his bunk when he saw Fey and Colby approaching the bars of his cell. The jailer unlocked the cell door, and Fey moved to stand in front of it. Her eyes locked with Cordell's, but the big man didn't move or say anything.

"We're here to take you to court," Fey told him. Her mouth was dry. She struggled to keep her voice even. "Turn around so I can put the handcuffs on you."

Cordell didn't move.

Fey shrugged. "Don't screw with me, Cordell. Don't make me come in there and kick your butt again."

Cordell stared at her. "You're one tough dyke." His statement held a curious note of respect.

"I'm old and tired and I ache everywhere. Now, turn around."

Cordell slowly turned his back to her.

"Put your hands behind your back, palms together as if you're praying."

Cordell complied. Fey moved into the cell with her handcuffs in her hand. It was one of the toughest things she had ever done. She realized she was scared of this man. It made her angry.

His presence brought out all the childlike insecurities she thought she had conquered long ago. She realized, not for the first time, it was impossible to escape your childhood. Its dark edges and hidden frights were always waiting to ambush you at any given moment.

As she got closer to Cordell, the smell of the man's stale sweat filled her nostrils. She saw the tension ripple across his shoulders, but she did not hesitate to firmly grab his left wrist and secure the first cuff around it. Holding on to the second cuff, so Cordell couldn't pull it away from her if he decided to go off, she waited for a second before securing the other wrist. The small wait between the handcuffing of the hands sent a very strong message. It told Cordell if he wanted to go for it, she was willing to go up against him again. The second ticked past, and with it, Fey achieved psychological dominance.

The short trip to the sheriff's lockup was done in silence. Fey walked on one side of Cordell, Colby on the other. The weight of Fey's .38 revolver, which Colby had recovered from the arrest scene, hung heavily under Fey's arm. It was as if the inanimate object was fanning the embers of her anger toward what Cordell tried to do to her. Their hidden secret.

The gun seemed to be whispering in Fey's ear – the words echoing over and over – *Shoot him. Kill him. Make him pay. Put him out of your misery.* Fey struggled to shove the thoughts away, grateful when they reached the back door to the lockup.

A uniformed sheriff's deputy took custody of Cordell.

"He's for afternoon arraignment," Fey said, handing over the prisoner and the transfer paperwork.

"No problem," the deputy said. He knew Fey slightly and looked pointedly at the bruising on her face. "Somebody put you through the ringer."

"You should see the other guy," she told him, and pointed her chin toward Cordell.

"Really?" the deputy said in surprise. He took in Cordell's size with a brief, impressed, glance then hefted his baton from the ring on his belt. "You want us to teach him a few manners?"

"Things are pretty even right now," Fey said. "No lessons are necessary."

"Too bad," the deputy said. Fey, the deputy, and even Cordell knew the exchange was merely a ritual, not a legitimate threat.

The deputy removed the cuffs from Cordell's wrists, handing them to Fey.

"Thanks," she said. Cordell still had his back to them as she and Colby turned to walk away.

Another deputy used a key to open the lockup door for the detectives to exit. They nodded to him and stepped through.

"She's one tough woman," Fey heard Cordell say as the deputy slammed the lockup door behind them.

Colby turned to look at her. "From *tough dyke* to *tough woman*," he said. "Progress."

Division 90 was on the ground floor of the court building. At one-thirty, Fey met Jake Travers at the front doors, entering with him.

Bill Swanson, the regular arraignment DA, was surprised to see Travers. He was relieved when Travers explained why he was there.

"Only this case," Travers told the younger DA. "The defense lawyer is full of tricks. I want to handle any surprises."

"No problem," Swanson said. He considered himself a climber. He didn't want a problem case rocking his boat. If there were fireworks, he was more than happy to have Travers take the heat.

Looking around the courtroom, Fey saw a handful of people scattered through the visitors' chairs in various states of anxiety. An empty jury box lined the left wall. The traditionally high judge's bench stood imposingly in front of the counsel table, which was piled high with briefs.

The doors to the courtroom opened and Janice Ryder stepped in. She had changed her outfit since her morning confrontation with Fey. She looked stunning in a pale blue sheath with pearls at ears and neck. Her hair fell attractively over her shoulders in soft curls. Her calfskin briefcase had been switched for a white leather model matching her pearls.

"Is she the piranha?" Jake asked softly.

Fey nudged him hard with her elbow. "Stop

drooling."

There was the sound of a buzzer and the bailiff stood up announcing, "Please remain seated. Division 90 is now in session, the Honorable Judge Martin Beckworth presiding."

The level of noise in the room dropped to a low murmur as the judge exited his chambers while still zipping up his robe – an action revealing a T-shirt and jeans underneath. He took his seat behind the bench and reached for the docket the court clerk held out.

Putting on a pair of cheap reading glasses, Beckworth peered at the notation on the docket. "Call *People v. Isaac Cordell*. Case number SA-zero-four-seven-one-five."

Jake and Fey sat next to Bill Swanson at the counsel table. Travers stood up to speak. "Jake Travers for the people, Your Honor."

Janice Ryder pushed open the wooden swinging gate separating the gallery and the courtroom's working area. She stepped to the counsel table and placed her briefcase on top. "Janice Ryder for Isaac Cordell, Your Honor," she said, flashing perfect teeth.

"What have you got me into?" Travers asked Fey in a murmer.

"Where is the defendant?" Beckworth asked.

As if waiting for the perfect cue, there was a knock at the back door of the courtroom. The bailiff opened it to admit Isaac Cordell and an accompanying deputy. The bailiff took custody of Cordell, walking him over to sit next to Janice Ryder. The bailiff removed the cuff from Cordell's left hand and secured it around the right arm of the chair.

Beckworth peered over his reading glasses at Cordell. "Sir, is Isaac Cordell your true name?"

Cordell stood up, trailing his still-cuffed arm behind him. "Yes, Your Honor."

"You may be seated," Beckworth told him. He shifted his gaze to the much prettier Janice Ryder. "Counsel, is your client ready for arraignment?"

Janice stood up. "No, Your Honor. There is a jeopardy issue here. My client has already been tried on these charges. Any further prosecution is barred by my client's Fifth Amendment right precluding double jeopardy."

Beckworth looked surprised. Arraignments were almost always routine. He didn't like to be in the middle of a problem situation – it was why he was in the arraignment court. Janice Ryder didn't look so attractive anymore. "Mr. Travers?" he asked the DA, looking for clarification.

"Your Honor, I'm not sure what counsel is alleging. Since the *people* have had no formal notice of such a motion, I feel it would be inappropriate to litigate at this time. I believe any question of jeopardy would be better handled during a preliminary hearing."

Janice Ryder came to her feet. "Excuse me, Your Honor. This is a fundamental right. Neither the *people* nor the court have jurisdiction to proceed as jeopardy prevents further prosecution."

Beckworth was not happy. He looked at the tower of dockets for the afternoon session, thinking about the eighteen holes of golf he wanted to play before dark. All things considered, especially his golf game, his decision was easy – pass the buck.

Beckworth looked at Janice Ryder. "Counsel, this is a calendar court. I am not in a position to litigate this issue. The appropriate forum is Judge Grant's court before the prelim."

"Your Honor..." Janice Ryder attempted to interrupt.

Beckworth forestalled her, holding up his hand. "I'm sorry, Counsel. I have made my decision."

He shifted his focus to Cordell. "Mr. Cordell, you are

charged in complaint number SA-zero-four-seven-one-five, one count alleging a violation of Penal Code section one-eighty-seven – murder. Counsel, do you waive further reading of the complaint and charges?"

"Yes, Your Honor," Janice Ryder said. Her jaws were visibly tight.

Fey smiled, loving every second of it.

Beckworth continued. "I am therefore going to enter a plea of not guilty for your client. I am putting it on the record this arraignment will not affect your ability to pursue the matter in Judge Grant's court."

Beckworth turned to his clerk, an older woman with an orange flower-print dress, a bun of flyaway gray hair, and steely intelligent eyes. "Becky, what's the matrix day on this case?"

Becky shuffled a stack of papers on her desk to consult her calendar. "Your Honor," she said after a moment, "the ninth day is Wednesday, the eighteenth."

"Fine," Beckworth said, making a notation on the docket. "This matter is set for prelim on Wednesday, the eighteenth of January, in Municipal Court Division Ninety-six."

He flipped to a page in the docket, peering at it briefly. "I see the defendant is being held without bail. There is also a parole hold. This seems appropriate. Counsel, do you wish to be heard?"

"Your Honor, if the facts surrounding this case were known, it would be clear there should be no parole hold or charges against my client..."

"Ms. Ryder," Beckworth interrupted. "I have ruled on this issue. I am not going to waste time repeating myself. Do you have anything pertinent to the question of bail?"

Janice Ryder's cheeks glowed from the rebuke. She had a tough time getting her next words out through her teeth. "No, Your Honor. The defense would request an *own recognizance* report be prepared before prelim."

"So ordered." Beckworth happily banged his gavel. "Next case."

The bailiff handcuffed Cordell again, releasing him back to the custody deputy. Janice Ryder picked up her briefcase and stalked out of the courtroom without a backward glance.

"Whew," Jake said. "She is wound tight enough to explode."

Fey agreed. "She went all out to fight for Cordell's parole. But now he's blown everything."

"You think she's pissed because Cordell turned on her?"

Jake and Fey moved out of the courtroom behind Ryder. They watched her through the building's glass wall as she walked quickly through the civic center.

"Could be," Fey replied. "She's a crusader, but there's more to it."

"Find out," Jake said. "We don't want her exploding all over us."

CHAPTER NINETEEN

Isaac Cordell sat on a bench in the lockup chained between a Mexican junkie and a black robbery suspect. He tried to calm himself. He had survived this before –

thrived actually. He would survive again.

His head hurt. The throbbing came from the center of his brain. It wasn't a new pain. He'd lived with it for two years. The prison doctor told him what it was but hadn't offered hope for a cure. Cordell knew what caused the pain, and it made him angry. He hadn't deserved to go to prison. But because of what happened to him there, he had the relentless pain in his brain.

He'd been innocent when they convicted him. But it hadn't done him any good. The law didn't care about innocence or guilt, right or wrong, justice or injustice. The law twisted only to the advantage of those who controlled it.

He had hoped Janice Ryder knew how to control the law. She had done it before. Somehow, she had convinced the prison board to grant him parole. If she stayed with him, she might be able to do it again.

If she stayed with him.

All the women that Isaac Cordell knew had used him and abandoned him. It didn't matter he would have done anything to please them. Love, like the law, was twisted by those in control.

He had loved his mother, for all the good it did him. Like his father, nothing he did pleased her. He'd been tied to her by an emotional umbilical cord tough enough to resist the sharpest scalpel. Despite his physical size, he had never been strong enough to break away from his mother's demanding presence.

Living at home, he had watched in silent agony as his mother drove nail after nail into his father's coffin. The Cordell's Furniture stores were a testament to how much a desperate man can achieve, yet still fall short of expectations. Finally, Isaac's father had swallowed a .22-caliber bullet on a rainy Saturday afternoon. Even then, he'd tried to accommodate his wife by committing suicide in the shower stall with a small-caliber bullet so there wouldn't be much mess.

Isaac had repressed his feelings for twenty years before his father ate his gun for dessert. He blamed his father for his mother's spoiled disposition. If his worm of a father had stood up and smacked her in the mouth, life might have been different for all of them.

Taking over the running of the family business was a nightmare. Cordell's people skills were learned from his mother. He began to lose employees, customers, and money at an astonishing rate. His mother, however, insisted on still living in high style, while demanding more and more. Cordell found himself as trapped as his father.

When his mother was killed by a hit-and-run driver, Isaac felt guilty relief, but also an overwhelming sense of abandonment. His tormentor was gone, but also the rock to which he'd been tethered.

Miriam was there to rescue him.

Sweet, divine, loving Miriam. A surrogate mother in the body of a temptress. She swept him off his feet. He bought her diamonds and rings. In return, she filled the void left by his mother. She gave direction...driving him to achieve despite his incompetence.

When he thought about it later—and he had a lot of time to think about it later—he realized there was only one difference between Miriam and his mother—his mother led him around by his nose, while Miriam led him around by his cock.

One woman repressed his sexuality while the other exploited it. Both women savaged his emotions for their own gain. Over the years he spent in prison, the love he'd had for them turned to the white-hot hatred now droving his every waking hour.

In prison, he had learned to hate. He had learned to fight, to stomp, and to destroy. He had discovered inside himself what he liked to think of as his *feminine side* – the same greedy, selfish, controlling traits of his mother's character.

He had also learned to wait. Prison had given him a lot of practice. Ten years' worth of waiting, until another woman had appeared to tell him she was going to get him paroled.

Isaac hadn't believed Janice Ryder. He'd applied for parole twice and been turned down. But Ryder fought for him, spent hours going over and over the circumstances of the case with him until she knew each aspect more clearly than he did.

Cordell knew he hadn't murdered his wife. He knew she must have gone over the side of the boat of her own free will, probably wearing scuba gear she'd put on after making her phony distress call. After Roark, his supposed business partner, had told the police Isaac planned to murder Miriam for the insurance money, it was clear Roark must have been waiting in a boat to pick Miriam up.

After those revelations, more became clear to Isaac concerning the insurance policy he knew nothing about— the insurance policy condemning him and making Roark rich.

Miriam liked rich men.

Janice Ryder, on the other hand, didn't seem to care about money. She never asked him to pay for the effort she put into getting him paroled. He still had no idea why she had championed him. He asked her once, but she had ignored the question and distracted him with further talk of getting him released. He didn't understand it, but he didn't care. All he'd cared about was getting out.

But it hadn't done much good.

He'd spent ten years in prison, while somebody else enjoyed life outside with a million dollars in his pockets. For ten years, Isaac dreamt about having the money and the freedom to spend it. He wanted the money and he wanted revenge. But first, he needed to be free. Janice Ryder won his freedom, so he didn't care what her motives were.

Circumstances, however, were now following a familiar sequence. Sitting in the lockup, Cordell wondered if Janice Ryder would stay with him, or would she abandon him like every other woman in his life.

Chained to the men on either side of him, he waited, churning half in anger and half in fear.

A deputy, his gut hanging over his belt, walked along the line of prisoners. The name on his grubby shirt identified him as Deputy Booker. His partner, a tall, sleek model wearing wraparound sunglasses was Taggert. Holding a clipboard, he followed Booker down the row.

As Booker read the name on each prisoner's wristband, Taggert ticked the corresponding name on his clipboard.

When Booker checked Cordell's wristband, he recognized the name.

"Lookit here," he said to his partner. "A celebrity."

"Who?" Taggert worked the transportation detail because it gave him three hours every shift to work out on-duty. However, this benefit was often outweighed by having to deal with Booker and the idiots who were chained together.

"This here's Isaac Cordell," Booker announced loudly.

"Never heard of him," Taggert said. "What show is he on?"

"He ain't on no show," Booker told him. "He's a criminal celebrity."

"A mob guy?"

"Better. I read about in the newspaper. He figured out a way to kill his old lady twice. Can you believe it? Wacked her ten years ago, but then she comes back to life. He has to get himself out of jail and whack her again." Booker's big oval face grinned into Cordell's.

The challenge was there, unspoken, but with a physical life of its own. Booker had the upper hand. He could do or say whatever he wanted, and Cordell had to take it.

"Broads," Booker projected fake sympathy. "Can't even trust 'em to stay dead." He laughed, dropping Cordell's wrist to move on to the next man.

When the line was checked and approved, Booker led the chained men outside to a transportation bus. Getting everyone situated on the bus as they fought with the confusion of being attached was like a Keystone Kops caper. Eventually, an awkward truce was struck between comfort and security, and Taggert eased himself into the driver's seat.

Booker stood at the front of the bus his baton held easy in his hand. "Listen up. There ain't no emergency exits and no emergency oxygen masks, barf bags, toilets, beverage service, or in-flight movies. If we crash while driving over water, there ain't no flotation devices, so you might as well bend over and kiss your butts good-bye." He paused for an appreciation of his humor, but there were no takers.

"We'll be driving at approximately fifty-five miles an hour at an altitude of five feet," he said, flogging a dead horse. "Our arrival time at county jail will be forty-five minutes. So sit quietly like good boys, and we'll get you de-loused in time for dinner. Don't piss me off and we'll all get along fine. On behalf of the pilot and myself, we hope you enjoy your flight and will join us again real soon." He guffawed and sat down behind Taggert, patting him sharply on the shoulder.

Taggert, who had heard it innumerable times before, shoved the bus into gear and pulled into traffic. One day, he'd enjoy taking his baton to Booker and shoving it where the sun doesn't shine.

At the back of the bus, Cordell's bulk was squeezed in next to the Mexican junkie. The Mexican needed a fix and was fighting hard for control. Snot ran out his nose and dripped from the ends of his gunfighter's mustache. He looked at Cordell with fearful interest.

"Are you really the guy Booker was talking about?" he asked quietly. "I read about it myself. I read good, man, you know? I'm teaching my kids."

Cordell looked at the pathetic prisoner. "You ain't going to be teaching them much from jail," he said.

"It's not my fault, you know? It's this screwed-up society. A guy like me don't got a chance, you know?"

Cordell swiveled his head forward. "Yeah. I know."

Encouraged by this response, the junkie pushed on.

"Are you really him? You know, the guy who killed his wife again?"

Cordell grunted.

"The paper said you got arrested by Detective Croaker, right? She's a real ball-breaker. She arrested me twice last year. She's bad news, you know?"

Cordell was silent. He'd been thinking a lot about Fey Croaker. Every time he moved, his testicles felt as if they had been snapped off. He thought about how good his fist felt smashing into her face. He thought about how bad it felt when the helpless kitten turned into a lioness. There wasn't much he wouldn't give for a second crack at her.

"Did you know she put her own brother in jail?" The Mexican's question caught Cordell's attention. He turned his head to look at his seat companion again.

"What do you mean?"

The Mexican looked happy he was able to provide this big man with information. The protection of having a friend the size of Cordell went a long way in the jail system. "They sent me up to Wayside to do my ninety last time I got arrested."

"What's Wayside?" Cordell interrupted.

"It's the county's honor ranch. They got medium and maximum sections up there, but almost everybody is in the minimum-security section. You can almost walk away from the place, but it's not worth it, since most people there a short-timers."

"What about Croaker's brother?"

"Who? Oh, yeah. His name is Tommy Croaker, you know?"

"What was he in jail for?"

The junkie smiled. "He got a habit takes a bigger bite than mine. Ripped his sister off one too many times. She did him like a dog. Sent him up on a county lid for burglary, you know? Can you believe it? Her own brother?"

"Is he still there?"

"Should be. I got out a week ago after doing forty-five of my ninety. He still had six months. Croaker fixed it so he had to do the full stretch."

Cordell's brain started to churn. He'd learned the ins and outs of the jail system the hard way. He knew with the right moves he might get himself out to Wayside. There, he could make use of Croaker's brother. Junkies were easy to use. They'd do anything for a little dope.

Cordell had not been a bad man when he'd gone to prison, but prison had made him bad. He'd made his bones within a month—getting away with murder in prison while being in prison for a murder he didn't commit.

Now, they were trying to send him back to prison. But this time, they weren't going to send him down for a crime he didn't commit. Since they were charging him with murder, he'd have to get free long enough to kill someone.

And he knew the perfect victim.

CHAPTER TWENTY

It was late again when Fey stumbled through the front door to her house and collapsed in a heap on her living room couch. She felt nauseous. Every bone and muscle in her body ached with fatigue.

Things had gone to hell after she'd left Cordell's arraignment. The pressure from the press had been turned on full blast, and she'd worked with Mike Cahill to prepare a news release and hold a press conference.

During the course of handling the press, another dead-body call had come in to the unit. This one turned out to be a suicide, but Fey still had to roll out with Colby to deal with while Monk and Hatch handled another spousal abuse arrest.

Suicides didn't add to the homicide stats. There were a number of homicide dicks who were aces at turning triple murders into double murder suicides. Not only did it keep your body count down, but it also solved the cases in the process. The paperwork was shuffled, the families of the victims were kissed off, and the cases were marked closed. Everybody was happy, including the murderer.

This case had been a straight-out overdose with no real possibility of foul play. It was an easy case, but it was far from pleasant. It worked out but took its toll on Fey's time and energy. She felt like seven kinds of hell.

She knew she could have taken the day off. She'd fought to get released from the hospital. But leaving the Goodwinter/Cordell case to Colby had galled her. He would have reveled in taking the credit for breaking the unit's unsolved streak, and she would have been out in the cold. The day's events and confrontations, however, left her wishing she'd stuck her head in the sand and hid.

Groaning, she rolled off the couch and made her way to the bathroom. From the medicine cabinet, she took a bottle of prescription-strength Motrin, shook two of the eight-hundred-milligram caplets into her hand, and swallowed them dry. She turned on the shower water as hot as she could stand and soaked her troubles for twenty minutes under the heavy spray.

When she exited the shower, Brentwood was sitting on the bathroom's tiled floor looking at her with disapproval. The cat's tail swished from side to side in obvious irritation.

"Ooops," Fey said when she saw the animal. She'd forgotten about picking up cat food. Wrapping a towel around herself, she went to the kitchen to open another can of tuna. She was surprised, however, when she noticed a new set of cat dishes on the floor filled with water and dry food. The freaking cat was pretty self-sufficient, Fey thought.

Looking around, she noticed a note from Peter Dent, the neighbor who took care of her horses, attached by a magnet to the door of her refrigerator. Peter's cramped handwriting let her know he'd taken over the responsibility for the care of Brentwood and the horses.

He'd read about her case in the paper and knew she

would be overworked. Fey sent up a prayer of thanks to the patron saint of good neighbors. She made a mental note to do something nice for Peter.

Brentwood sauntered toward the new feed bowls. She ignored Fey, as if letting her know she hadn't been fulfilling her responsibilities.

"All right, all right," Fey said to the cat. "I get your point."

She knew she should check on the horses, but she trusted Peter. The horses wouldn't react the same as Brentwood, but the cat had put her off stride.

Back in the bathroom, Fey exchanged towel for terry cloth robe. She knew she should have shaved her legs in the shower, but she'd been too tired. Shuffling into the bedroom, she saw the two messages on the answering machine she'd ignored two nights ago had been joined by two others. The other machine was empty.

Sitting on the corner of her bed, she stared at the first answering machine's flashing light. Four messages. Four hate-filled missives of confusion and despair. She knew they would be from her brother.

She wanted to reach out and wipe them clean. She wanted to throw the machine through the window and never be slave to it again, but there was always a shred of hope her brother would change.

In her heart, she knew he never would. It was impossible, though, for her to admit. She spent too many years and spilled tears protecting her brother from the world. Now, she was faced with constantly helping somebody who refused to help himself.

As the eldest child in their abusive home, Fey let her father abuse her over and over to protect Tommy.

At school, she was always intervening between Tommy and bullies or teachers. Later, when Tommy began committing petty crimes, she got him off the hook. He was never grateful.

Fey told herself Tommy was her brother, her blood, her kin. But when he turned to drugs there was nothing she could do. She felt like a failed parent. Taking care of Tommy had become an obsession, a fixation, causing trouble in both her early marriages.

Her mother died from cancer. Her father eventually drank himself to death. Fey felt minimal emotion over both outcomes. But Tommy's drug habit had turned him into a living corpse, and Fey felt the blame heavy on her shoulders.

The final straw came, however, when Tommy broke into Fey's house, ransacking it for anything to pawn for his next fix. After years of abuse, Fey's outrage exploded. She did everything she could to get him locked up.

Since then, she had severed her ties with Tommy except for the answering machine. He had the number and called often from Wayside Honor Rancho, where he was serving his time. The calls were of two types— obscene and threatening or pleading and pathetic.

The latter was designed to play on Fey's guilt feelings. Tommy would whine and cry, beg for forgiveness, plead for another chance, or at least a visit. He would swear he would never touch drugs again. He would do anything, if Fey would help him get out.

Fey knew better.

The obscene calls were far worse. Tommy's voice, pitched at the same tone as their father's, would spill vitriolic hatred down the phone lines. Sexual obscenities and threats of bodily harm crashed out in jagged waves. Fey never knew her brother to have such a vivid imagination before being put away.

As exhausted as she was, Fey was so low, listening to

the messages couldn't make her feel worse. She punched the machine's replay button leaving the volume on low.

The first two messages were *pleaders*. Nothing unusual. The third message was filled with Tommy's anger, hate, and frustration. Again, nothing new. But the fourth call was a deadly new twist. As soon as she heard the voice, Fey pushed up the volume.

"Hello, Croaker." The voice was an iced chill. Fey was rooted to the floor. She felt lightheaded, almost missing what Isaac Cordell said next.

"I turned your little brother into a squealing little girl. Did you know he likes man love?"

Fey collapsed to a sitting position on the floor. Her heart slammed around in her chest like a terrified animal.

"Tommy was so grateful he gave me your number and your address. I'll be there soon, but don't feel you have to wait up. I'll let myself in."

There was a short silence then the click of disconnection.

The tape ran on.

"Nine fifty-five p.m." Fey flinched involuntarily as the machine's mechanical voice kicked in. "That was your last message."

CHAPTER TWENTY-ONE

For three long seconds, Fey sat motionless—a wildcat gathering strength for a killing charge. When she moved into action, it was at top speed with no time wasted on deliberation or worry.

Coming to her feet, she stepped to the side of her bed, bent down, and pulled out an Ithaca shotgun from behind the dust ruffle. Cradling the shotgun, she crawled across the bedspread to remove a .38 Smith & Wesson Chief with a two-inch barrel from between the mattress and box springs on the other side.

A woman living alone, Fey never took safety for granted. She didn't need to check the loads in either weapon. She knew they were hot. Every month, she removed the weapons from their hiding places, cleaned them. Every six months, she replaced the ammunition.

Putting the revolver in the pocket of her robe, she held the shotgun in one hand and picked up the phone with the other. Raised on B-movies as a form of escapist entertainment, she half expected the phone line to be dead and the house lights to be cut any second, but the dial tone buzzed reassuringly.

Fey didn't know how Isaac Cordell had made the switch from county jail to Wayside. It was something to worry about later. Right now, there were more important considerations. She punched the phone's speed-dial button for LAPD's Devonshire station.

A voice picked up on the third ring. "Los Angeles Police Department, Officer Stokes. Can I help you?"

"This is Detective Fey Croaker. I need to speak to the watch commander immediately."

"Yes, sir." The excitement in Stokes' voice betrayed his rookie stature.

Fey had called the watch commander's office direct. If she'd dialed 911, chances were, she'd get a recording saying all emergency lines were busy.

Another, more mature voice came on the phone line. "Fey? Gene Mallet. What's up?"

Fey was relieved. She and Mallet had ridden in a patrol car together.

"I've got a problem at my house." Fey gave him the address. "Can you get a patrol car here *code three*?"

"On its way. Tell me all about it later?"

"Promise." She hung up, blessing Gene Mallet not wasting time with questions. Mallet would immediately use the ACC control center to send the closest unit racing to her location. She figured backup would be there within five to six minutes.

Moving quickly, she threw off her robe and slipped into jeans and a sweatshirt. She stepped into tennis shoes and pulled her hair back in a ponytail. The shotgun was never out of her immediate reach.

When she was ready, she hit another of the phone's speed-dial buttons. The phone rang five times before a sleepy voice answered.

"Hello."

"Jake, wake up."

"Fey? What's the matter?" Jake's voice came instantly awake.

"Isaac Cordell left a nasty message on my answering machine. I don't know how, but it seems he's managed to escape. Claims he's on his way here."

"Get out, now!"

"A unit is on the way. I'm staying armed to the teeth until it gets here. Then I'm going to the station."

"Come to my place."

"Later. I've got to find out what's going on. For all I know, Cordell is outside

waiting to follow me some place I feel safe putting down my guard."

"Which station—Devonshire or West L.A.?"

"West L.A."

"I'll meet you there in forty minutes."

"Thanks."

As Fey hung up, she could hear a wailing police siren coming down her street.

Eventually, six police units pulled up outside Fey's house. Four of them were black-and-white patrol units. The other two were unmarked cars used by the division's special problems unit. Fey knew two of the patrol cops and quickly filled them in.

She was grateful for the quick response, even if the noise and lights woke most of her neighbors, bringing them into the street to see what was happening.

Within a few minutes, two of the patrol units and the two unmarked units returned to their duties. The other units waited as Fey threw a change of clothes and overnight necessities into a suitcase and locked up the house.

Fey had been hoping Peter Dent would have been roused by the noise, but she hadn't seen him. She tried calling but was only able to leave a message requesting he continue caring for her animals. She apologized, promising to make it up to him.

Before leaving the house, she searched everywhere for Brentwood. The cat was not to be found. With no more time to waste, Fey put down fresh water and refilled the dry cat food dish.

Throwing her shotgun on the front seat of her car, she headed for West Los Angeles Division. One of the police units followed her to the freeway, making sure her tail was clean. The other pulled back into a secluded spot near her house in case Cordell had the audacity to turn up.

Fey realized the phone call had simply been a terror tactic, but she refused to speculate on the circumstances of the call. She was almost positive Cordell wouldn't turn up at her house.

If he had really been coming, he wouldn't have called. By announcing his intentions, he had short-circuited his chances. Fey figured Cordell was either delighting in a game of cat and mouse, or he had something else in mind entirely.

The morning watch desk officers were not surprised to see Fey. Homicide detectives showed up at all hours due to the nature of their work. She nodded to them then turned to go up the stairs to the squad room.

Automatically, she turned on lights and set coffee brewing. She felt safe in the deserted room. The station becomes an extension of cop's lives, a place they spend more time in than their homes. It becomes a haven, a place filled with a large, squabbling, loving cop family. Ties ran deep.

With a cup of coffee, Fey took a deep breath and picked up the phone. Driving to the station, she had plotted a course of action beyond her initial self-protection reflexes. She had no idea if Cordell was on the loose, or if some jailhouse hophead had given him enough information to play out a sick joke.

Before she sounded the alarm, she needed to verify her information. It wouldn't look good if she had everyone spinning their wheels while Cordell was snug in his bunk.

Her call to county jail was picked up on the first ring. She asked for Intake and Detention Control. She identified herself to the deputy, confirming Isaac Cordell, booking number 3194788, was in custody according to the computer.

"Can you do a visual check?" Fey asked.

"Why?" The deputy's voice had a nasal whine. "If he's in the computer, he's locked down in his cell."

Fey tried to keep her exasperation in check. She knew she would run into this kind of resistance. "Are you saying your computer never makes mistakes?"

"Not since I've been here."

"How long? Two months? Three?"

"Six."

"I'm sure you think you've seen everything after six months of working custody, but you've never seen me pissed off." Fey made her voice rock-hard. "I am a homicide supervisor. I started on this job when you were an itch in your daddy's pants. If I drive down there to do my own visual check, and he's not where he should be, your rapidly spreading butt is going to become a piece of raw meat. Are you going to do a visual check, or do I start sharpening my incisors?"

"I'll check." The voice was subdued. "But it will take a while. Do you want to call back?"

"Not on your life, cowboy. I'll hold."

The phone line muted in her ear. Fey took a long swallow of coffee. She played with a pencil on her desk, turning it over and over, finally doodling little moons and stars on scrap paper. Her heart was pounding harder than normal. The acid in her stomach was an Atlantic storm. Fatigue and an overdose of caffeine were working their combined demonic magic.

A noise from the stairwell made her jump. She pulled the short-barreled .38 from her waistband.

"Easy," said Jake Travers, identifying the movement. "I'm one of the good guys."

Fey held her hand up as the custody deputy came back on the line.

"You still there?" the deputy asked. His voice held a cocky note.

"I'm still here."

"Well, so is Cordell. Sleeping like a baby."

"You checked his wristband?"

"Yep."

Fey felt a relief run through her. She didn't have an explanation for the phone call yet, but it would come later.

"Is everyone in county jail still as innocent and pure as the driven snow?" she asked, attempting through ritual humor to lighten her relationship with the deputy.

"Everyone except the deputies," he replied easily enough.

"Thanks for checking. I appreciate it. I'm sorry for getting uppity."

"No problem. These skinny hypes all look alike. I'm sure mistakes get made occasionally."

Fey's heart rate went ballistic. "Did you say Cordell is a skinny hype?"

"Yeah. Mexican guy with a droopy mustache."

Fey hung her head down.

"Satan wept," she said softly.

CHAPTER TWENTY-TWO

Tommy Croaker sat on a hard-back chair in the middle of an interrogation room otherwise empty of furniture. Fey stood behind him, arms crossed, leaning against the white rubberized wall. She was wearing a wine-colored blouse over black slacks and sensible flats. Her shoulder holster was empty, her gun placed in a lockbox before she entered Wayside Honor Rancho's security area.

Colby was resplendent in a new blazer, and pleated wool slacks. Fey thought he was pushing his fashion statement too far when she caught a flash of bare ankles above another beautiful pair of calfskin moccasins.

He was also leaning against an interrogation room wall. He had the good sense to keep his mouth shut while Fey interrogated her brother.

After verifying Isaac Cordell had escaped from county jail, Fey put out an all-points bulletin. She then contacted Wayside to check on Tommy.

At first it appeared Tommy had also escaped from Wayside. However, an enterprising deputy found Tommy in a clump of bushes outside the minimum-security barracks—doped to the eyeballs.

There was no sign of Cordell.

The sequence of events was eventually established. Cordell had managed to switch wristbands with the Mexican hype, Manny Sesteros, on the prison bus. Manny was later found in the bunk assigned to Cordell at county jail. Manny had been on his way to Wayside to serve another ninety-day stretch. He hadn't seen any reason not to screw with the system. It had screwed him long enough.

At county jail, Booker and Taggert had turned their charges over to two other deputies to process. The two new deputies didn't question the wristband switch, not recognizing Isaac Cordell as Booker had done. Through bureaucratic faith in the infallibility of the wristband system, Manny had been left at county jail, and Cordell transported to Wayside in his place.

As an extra bonus, Cordell had a hit of tar heroin hidden behind his upper lip. The small, brown lump was covered with plastic cling-wrap, a gift from Manny—who was found to have a whole string hidden in his mouth.

The final destination of Cordell's tar heroin stash was the veins of Tommy Croaker. But only after an exchange of valuable information. As Manny Sesteros, Cordell had been placed in Wayside's minimum-security compound. He located Tommy during the recreation hour. Gaining the information he needed in exchange for the dope was easy. The only thing easier was walking away from Wayside's minimum security.

A car was reported stolen close to Wayside. It was recovered near Devonshire Division station, which served the area where Fey lived. Fey didn't doubt Cordell used the car until he found something better.

While this information was being discovered, Fey notified Lieutenant Cahill of the situation. She then woke up Colby and arranged to meet him at Wayside at noon.

She then let Jake Travers take her home and put her to bed. With the sheets covering her naked form, and Jake's arms tightly around her, she fell into an exhausted sleep.

When Fey awoke to the smell of coffee and sizzling bacon, she didn't want to disturb the happy bachelor routine going on in the kitchen.

She stretched on the bed, realizing how much she liked Jake's bedroom. It was part of a small, two-story house along one of the canals running through the Venice beach area. Jake had renovated it, along with the residences on either side, which he also owned. Using the middle of the three houses gave Jake the luxury of choosing his neighbors. The residents working through a realty company, had no idea Jake was their landlord. Another plus in Jake's estimation.

Jake's first wife had fleeced him for a chunk of change, but he had enough family money to live in Beverly Hills or any of the ritzy areas of L.A. Jake, however, preferred the Bohemian lifestyle of Venice Beach—gangs, hippies, and homeless aside.

Jake had decorated the house himself, using dark tones and rough-textured fabrics to distance him from female influences. His ornaments, pictures, and knickknacks reflected his interests in maps and architecture. His books filled several wall-to-wall fixtures, spilling onto other scattered surfaces with random abandon. The titles were a mix of law books, *Golden Age* detective stories, with a selection of sailing and nonfiction adventure titles.

Jake appeared in the bedroom doorway wearing a smile and an apron. He held a glass of orange juice in one hand and the morning paper in the other.

Fey burst out laughing. "You look like a butler in a French film farce," she said through a fit of giggles.

"I thought it had a rather macho appeal," he said,

with a mock pout. Thick black hair grew rampant across his chest and arms, covering a wiry musculature. His stomach was flat and hard, and Fey always thought he had a nice butt.

"You thought wrong," she told him.

"Aren't you a bright ray of sunshine this morning?"

He put the orange juice on the bedside table. "Come on, lazybones," he said. "Breakfast in five minutes." He turned his back and twitched his butt as he went through the doorway.

Fey threw a pillow at him, still chuckling.

The healing power of sleep had worked. Fey sat at the breakfast table wearing one of Jake's white work shirts. She ate ravenously through pancakes, bacon, and fluffy scrambled eggs.

"If I'd known a pig would be snuffling through the trough this morning," Jake said, sipping coffee as he watched her, "I would have stocked the larder higher."

"Shut up," Fey said, scooping a dribble of syrup from her chin. "It's not often I have a man around who cooks for me. I'm showing appreciation by eating everything on my plate."

"And mine," said Jake, as Fey snatched a half-eaten rasher of bacon and popped it in her mouth.

"What's the agenda?" he asked.

Fey swallowed a last bite of pancake and pushed her plate away. She made a face. "I'm meeting Colby at Wayside to speak to Tommy at noon."

"Gonna be a load of chuckles."

"It has to be done. I doubt he can tell us anything about Cordell, but I have to cover the bases."

"And afterward?"

Fey shrugged. "I see if I can plan a way to track Cordell. I can't be constantly looking over my shoulder. I also need to go back to square one with this investigation.

The pieces seem to fit together, but the picture is bizarre. I'm missing something." She drained her coffee cup and poured a refill. "How about you?" she asked.

Jake raised his eyebrows. "The day's regular contingent of filings and problems. I don't have anything in court for a few days, so I'll dig into the double jeopardy question."

"Can Ryder really use it as a defense? Especially now Cordell's an escaped felon."

"The escape isn't going to have any bearing. If Ryder can pull off the double jeopardy defense, the murder charge will be dropped. Then the escape and resisting-arrest charges are going to become moot. Vanderwald is not going to want the press turning this into a *Les Misérables* situation, which is what I would expect Janice Ryder to pursue."

Fey nodded her reluctant agreement. Janice Ryder wouldn't let an opportunity to exploit public outcry. Jake's boss, Simon Vanderwald, was a savvy political animal. Janice Ryder would scare him like a force-ten gale. There would be no support from him.

Fey wondered how far Jake would push the case. Jake had a great chance of ousting Simon Vanderwald in the next election. His backers wouldn't want him to jeopardize their interests by taking chances.

Fey gave a mental shrug, glancing at the digital clock on Jake's microwave. She still had time.

"Come here," she said to Jake.

He had changed out of his apron into a short kimono robe. He looked at her in surprise, recognizing her tone of voice. One eyebrow crawled up his forehead in a questioning gesture.

"Don't go coy on me," she said.

"Are you accusing me of being shy?"

"Until you prove differently."

Jake pushed his chair back, took two steps to Fey's side of the large kitchen table, and pulled her to her feet. He put his arms around her and kissed her gently, very aware of the livid line of bruises on her face. Most of the swelling was gone, but the kaleidoscope of colors was still evident.

"Mmmmm...nice," Fey said. She kissed him back, wrapping a bare leg around him.

"Are you sure?" he asked, concerned for her aches and pains.

She pushed a hand between their bodies and inside his kimono. She grasped him with her fingers and kissed him again, excited by his heat "Does this answer your question?"

Jake kissed her, their tongues inflamed serpents, and made to move toward the bedroom.

"Uh-uh," Fey said, stopping him with a seductive smile. "I want it right here, right now." She turned from him and quickly pushed the dirty dishes to one side.

"You're joking," Jake said. His voice had thickened. His robe hung open, exposing his excitement.

Fey perched her naked backside on the edge of the table. She leaned back on her arms, Jake's shirt riding high on her hips. She pulled her knees back and opened herself to him.

There weren't any other answers or questions needed.

———

Colby had been waiting when Fey arrived at Wayside at twelve-thirty.

"You're late," he said.

"A master of the obvious," Fey replied.

"What were you doing? Catch up on your beauty sleep?"

"I was boinking my brains out," Fey told him nonchalantly. "I'd do it to you, but it's obvious somebody beat me to it."

"You should be so lucky."

Fey shook her head. "Not even if you were the last man on the planet."

"Proves my theory about you being a lesbian."

"Eat your heart out," Fey said, twitching her hips as she moved toward the security building.

She didn't understand why Colby was constantly riding her sexually. With his looks and flash, he could pull women who were far younger and better looking than she was. But she'd met men like him before. It frustrated them when a woman wouldn't lay down for them. They didn't realize they were obnoxious asshats. Therefore, the woman must be a dyke.

Fey learned over the years the only way to handle men like Colby was to never let them see they bothered you. If they saw you were upset, it gave them a sense of power. If they couldn't screw your body, they wanted to screw with your mind.

To keep them in line, they had to be slapped down. You insult them right back and kept the upper hand. Eventually, they would back off to lick their wounded egos, waiting for a chance to stab you in the back.

There was no way to earn their respect or become friends. You were either a notch on their bedpost or you were a lesbian. Fey, like many other women, preferred the mislabeling. Sleeping with asshats certainly didn't accomplish anything.

Inside Wayside, Fey and Colby placed their guns in the lockers along one wall. They introduced themselves to the watch commander, who took them to an interrogation room before sending for Tommy.

Another deputy brought Tommy into the room, sitting

him in the single chair. He was a frightened rabbit. Fey expected his nose to start twitching.

"Hello, Tommy," she said.

"I got nothing to say," Tommy whined, in the aggressive manner of a man trying to show he isn't scared to death.

The eyes of the scrawny inmate darted around the room. In his mid-thirties, Tommy's body was soft and anemic from years of drug abuse and malnutrition.

"Why did you do it, Tommy?"

"Why did you put me in this hellhole?" Tommy retorted. "I'm your brother and you sent me to jail."

Colby saw where the conversation was going and kept his mouth shut. Fey had filled him in on the background between Tommy and herself. He read between the lines, realizing there was more baggage than she was admitting. Being an only child, Colby only understood enough about the semantics of siblings to be glad he didn't have any.

"We've been over the reasons a thousand times, Tommy." Fey's voice was unnaturally calm. "I didn't put you in here. You put yourself in here."

"Sure. It was me who talked to the judge and asked for the maximum sentence."

"You gave Isaac Cordell my phone number and address because you were angry?"

"Hell no," Tommy said. "I gave it to him because he offered me dope in exchange for the information."

Fey hung her head. Colby realized she was on the verge of tears. He recognized it would have been easier if Tommy had given up the information simply because he was pissed off. The emotion would have been easier to accept and rectify than the real monkey on Tommy's back.

When Fey remained silent, Colby chipped in for the

first time. "Tommy, there's a good chance Cordell is out to hurt or kill your sister. Is there anything you can tell us to help catch him?"

"You got any dope?" Tommy asked. "No? Then go screw yourself with a broom handle. Cordell can kill her for all I care."

Colby looked at Fey.

"Let's get out of here," she said, and pushed herself off the wall by her shoulders.

"Wait! I'm sorry," Tommy said, turning in his chair to face Fey as she reached the interrogation room door. His voice was a whine, the bravado now nonexistent. "I really didn't mean to tell him. I mean...you know...and then he offered me the dope..."

"Shut up, Tommy," Fey said, and pulled the door open. "It's too late."

"No! No! Wait!" Tommy's voice was imploring. "Don't leave me here. Get me out. I didn't mean to tell him anything. He made me take the dope!"

Fey turned around to face her brother, making no attempt to hide the tear running down her cheek. "Don't call anymore, Tommy. I'm going to disconnect the number."

"You can't!"

Fey walked out of the room, followed by Colby. She twisted the lock on the outside as she heard Tommy fling himself against the door. She wiped her eye. "He's ready to go back," she told the deputy waiting outside. He gave her a strange look, never having seen a detective cry during an interrogation before.

When Fey turned to walk away, Colby followed close on her heels. They retrieved their guns and walked out to the parking lot.

Fey had told Colby about the answering machine on which her brother left messages. He understood her reference to disconnecting the number. "Are you really going to shut down the number?" he asked, thinking about the emotions of the situation.

"Not for a while," she said. "Cordell may use it again. We should get a tap in place."

"You think he's going to come after you? Wouldn't it make more sense to take off for the boonies and hide out?"

Fey reached her car and turned to Colby. "You weren't there in the alley when he and I were rolling around in the garbage. He stopped running when he realized it was a woman chasing him. He enjoyed hitting me. I was able to stop him, and he won't be able to live with it."

"You must have a high opinion of yourself to think he'll stick around to take you out."

"You're wrong. I have a low opinion of men who enjoy hitting women. I was there. I saw his eyes when he was hitting me. I heard his voice when he called. He isn't going to run and hide."

Fey unlocked her car and slid into the driving seat. "I'll tell you something else for free. I'm not going to run and hide either."

CHAPTER TWENTY-THREE

"Any luck?" Mike Cahill came out of his office when he saw Fey and Colby returning.

Fey, still fighting to rein in her emotions, shook her head, moving on to her desk. Behind her, Colby shrugged his shoulders and rolled his eyes in the lieutenant's direction. "Anything new on this end?"

"Nothing specific to Cordell," Cahill said. "Hatch and Monk went to roll call here and in Devonshire with photos and info-bulletins, so patrol is aware he's out there. They also had a judge sign the warrant paperwork and placed it in the system."

Colby stepped into the lieutenant's office as the two men talked.

"How's Fey doing?" Cahill inquired.

"She had a tough time handling the situation with her brother."

Cahill disregarded the statement. Anybody would have trouble handling the family dynamics.

"Think Cordell is a real threat to her?"

Colby shrugged. "I don't buy it. The guy is probably running for the border if he isn't across already." Colby sat in an office chair. "What does he gain by sticking around to mess with Fey? I think she's running scared."

Cahill knew Fey never ran scared.

"I think she has more on her plate than she can handle," Colby continued. "The unit needs shaking-up or this string of unsolveds will continue."

"Remains to be seen," Cahill said. His tone was cool, letting Colby know he was dangerously close to stepping over the line. If Cahill reassigned Fey, it would be a black mark on his own judgment for putting her in charge. "She wrapped this case up quick. Cordell escaping is not on her."

"This case was a self-solver from the get-go. Nothing tricky about it. We found a witness who placed Cordell at the scene. We found the murder weapon in his room. He ran when we went to talk to him. It wasn't exactly great detective work."

Cahill shook his head. "Careful. You're in no position to buck for her job. Remember it only takes one *ah-crap* to wipe out every *atta-boy* you've ever earned."

"Shut my mouth and write the president," Colby said in a fake feminine, southern accent as he briefly covered his lips with his palm. "I don't know what gets into me sometimes, but it do make me twitter on."

Cahill couldn't help laughing. "Twitter out of my office and make us both look good by recapturing this jerk."

Colby looked put out. "Can I wait until he carries out his threats?"

———

Fey planned to take Colby with her when she started backtracking the case, but seeing him come out of Mike Cahill's office, her paranoia kicked into overdrive. Feeling

Colby's knife in her back, she retaliated by dumping the day's paperwork on him.

"Dig in," she said when Colby opened his mouth to complain. Seeing Fey's expression, he wisely relented.

"Where are you going?" he asked.

"I've got to make my apologies to Harry Carter for missing the autopsy. Then I'm going to SID—see if they have anything further from the crime scene."

"Let me come with you," Colby said. His voice sounded strained.

Fey shot him an odd look.

"You think I need protection?" Her voice held a dangerous edge.

Colby felt his face flush.

Fey saw the rising crimson tide. She smiled as she grabbed her purse and briefcase. "Take care of the stuff already on your plate. Let me worry about the stuff on mine."

Heading downtown in her unmarked detective sedan, Fey thought about the idea of protection. She glanced at the shotgun on the passenger floorboard, wondering if her precautions were necessary. Was Cordell stupid enough to make a run at her while she was on duty? Then again, Cordell might figure it was the best time to take her by surprise.

What about when she wasn't on duty? She had told Jake she wasn't going to constantly be looking over her shoulder for the rest of her life. She'd also told Colby she wasn't going to run and hide—even if it was what she felt like doing. There had to be a solution. Her mind chewed over options as she drove.

Harry Carter was in his office filling out paperwork when Fey arrived. It was a small, cluttered space, but Harry was comfortable in it, refusing to move despite being chief coroner. His face came alive when he stood up to greet Fey.

"You've been busy," he said, giving her a genuine smile and shaking hands.

"Wasn't anything I couldn't handle."

Harry reached out to gently touch her chin, examining the bruises on her face. "Interesting battle scars."

Fey chuckled. "I prefer to think of them as war paint."

Harry took his hand away. "If you were the winner, how bad did the other guy look?"

"His testicles are probably still in orbit."

"Ouch." Harry winced. "Ever considered fighting fair?"

"*Fighting fair*? There's an oxymoron if I ever heard one."

"Like jumbo shrimp?"

"Or military intelligence."

Harry laughed. "Coffee?" he asked. He turned toward an old-fashioned plug-in pot on a back counter.

Harry poured brown liquid into two glass measuring beakers. He added cream from a jug in a refrigerator holding various samples.

"Sorry I didn't make the autopsy," Fey said when they were settled.

Autopsies were a curse, but a necessary evil. Fey knew two detectives who enjoyed going to autopsies. She suspected both were serial killers in a previous life.

"Didn't miss much," Harry said, waving off her apology. "It was routine. Nothing startling or case-breaking."

He pulled a file from beneath a stack of papers. The stack tilted but held. He pulled glasses down from the top of his head to read.

"Female, Caucasian, approximately forty-five to fifty years old. Sixty-six inches tall, one hundred and thirty pounds. She was in good shape for her age. Must have worked out like crazy." He flipped over a couple of pages.

Fey knew Harry Carter well enough to realize he was using the file as a prop. He could have told her everything in it without referring to a single page. His memory was virtually photographic, but he enjoyed the role of absentminded professor.

"Time of death approximately two a.m.," Harry continued. "There was semen in the vagina vault. From the condition of the sperm, she'd had intercourse around three hours before death. There were no physical indications of force."

Harry checked his notes. "The victim ate a salad for dinner the previous evening. From her colon, I'd say she was a vegetarian. Her liver showed no alcohol or drug damage. She didn't smoke, had a strong heart, and a good set of lungs. From the way she took care of herself, I'd say she was planning to live forever."

"Until she ran into somebody specializing in throat slashing."

"True," Harry said. He closed the file. "The carotid was slashed, and she bled out quickly. I'd said the weapon was a screwdriver, but closer examination showed it to be a wider blade."

"But we've recovered the murder weapon," Fey told him. "It was a flat-head screwdriver as you originally said. The lab hasn't confirmed, but there was blood on the tip and handle. I've no doubt it was the victim's."

"Hmmmm," said Harry, raising his eyebrows. "I'm surprised. I won't dispute the fact in court. It could have been a screwdriver, but I still favor something slightly different."

This bothered Fey. She had never known Harry to be wrong.

"I'll keep it in mind," she said. "Things have

happened so rapidly I haven't had a chance to think straight about the evidence. I'm not really comfortable with the way everything has come together. On the surface, it has been handed to us on a plate. But something is missing."

"Like who the victim really was?"

"Exactly," Fey said. "Who was she before she was Miriam Cordell? Who was she between being Miriam Cordell and Miranda Goodwinter?"

"Good point."

Fey sighed. "Need to go back to the beginning."

Harry tossed the file back on his desk. "What are you going to do about Cordell now he's escaped?"

Fey swigged a last swallow of coffee from her beaker. "One thing at a time, Harry."

Fey called ahead from the coroner's office arranging to meet Annie Thaw at a sandwich shop across from Parker Center. The afternoon was waning, but Annie had put off eating lunch until Fey arrived. The two women sat eating sandwiches and chips at a tiny outdoor table.

"How's life?" Fey asked Annie as they munched.

"Those fairy tales our mothers told us are crap," Annie said sourly.

"No happily ever after part?"

"When was the last time you came across a Prince Charming? Men are slime."

Annie and Fey were firm friends. Annie started work in the Scientific Investigation Division's lab the same time Fey entered the police academy. Over the years Fey had found Annie's scientific expertise to be invaluable. She could, however, live without Annie's bleak view of the world.

"I take it Danny is not keeping up with alimony and child support?"

"When has he ever been up-to-date?"

Danny Thaw was Annie's ex-husband, the father of her two sons. He wasn't as bad as Annie made out, but he could be a bastard when he wanted. Fey also knew life with Annie wouldn't be easy.

"What about the results on the Goodwinter case?" Fey asked, cutting to the chase.

"Another prime example of why men should be nuked," Annie replied. "A woman would never do something like this to another woman."

Arguing with Annie when she was in this kind of mood was fruitless. Feminism was one thing, man-hating another. Fey knew women did awful things to other women. She'd seen the evidence—shootings, stabbings, bludgeonings, poisonings, arsons. If anything, women were more vicious than men when it came to murder and physical child abuse.

Sex crimes, however, were another matter, but this case did not appear to qualify. There were no indications of deviant sex acts or forms of torture. The style of the murder was more consistent with an act of anger. Just because the victim engaged in intercourse before being murdered did not mean she'd had sex with the murderer. Nor did it mean she didn't. As usual, sex only complicated matters.

"I hear you. Men are slime," Fey said, agreeing simply to move on. "Now, what do you have for me?"

Annie took a bite of sandwich. She chewed while talking, spraying crumbs. "Not much."

Why did the evidence in this case keep coming up empty Fey wondered. She needed something more than *not much*. She needed something solid to stand on.

"This is me, Annie. You can do better."

"Not this time. There were no prints in the room matching your suspect. What's his name?"

"Cordell."

"Yeah, Cordell. Anyway, you're out of luck when it comes to his prints."

"What about the murder weapon?"

"Zippo, baby. Clean. No prints."

"Crap,"

"Exactly."

"What about the blood on the murder weapon?"

"There you score some points. The blood is A-positive same the victim's. The first level of DNA testing indicates the blood could belong to your girl. It will take a couple of weeks for long-term testing, but I don't think there's any doubt."

"Anything else?" Fey pushed her plate away and fought the urge for a cigarette.

Annie was silent.

"Annie?"

"You're not going to like it."

Fey rolled her eyes. "What else is new?"

"Most of the prints recovered at the scene belonged to the victim, but there were two other prints still unidentified."

"Not Cordell's?"

"Not even close. Best I can tell, we have prints from a thumb and an index finger. Both have nicks and scars indicating someone who does hard work with their hands."

"Construction?"

Annie shrugged. "Perhaps. The thumbprint came off of the bedroom door handle. The index finger was only a partial caught in a smear of blood on the sheet."

Fey gave an excited start. "So, it was left after the killing blow was delivered."

"I agree, but it adds to your problems."

Fey stopped to think. "It means somebody else was there after Cordell."

Annie gave her friend a condescending look. "Get your head screwed on straight, Fey. The print may be a lot more significant."

"Don't say it."

Annie did anyway. "It may also mean Cordell isn't your murderer."

Fey's heart was pounding in her chest. "Again," she said quietly.

CHAPTER TWENTY-FOUR

Things were going from bad to worse.

Fey was sitting in the comfortable living room of Mrs. Kathleen Bridges, having another piece of evidence against Isaac Cordell blown out the window.

After finishing her late lunch with Annie, Fey knew she had to go back to the foundations of the investigation, rebuild the case from scratch. She felt sure there had to be some kind of trace evidence to tie Cordell to the crime scene.

His connection to the victim was logical, motive abounding, but far more was needed for successful prosecution. Getting twelve straights on a jury to agree on anything beyond a reasonable doubt was always tricky. When the charge was murder, you needed to hit them over the head repeatedly with the evidence to win a conviction. You had to remember you were dealing with twelve people too stupid to get out of jury duty.

Reviewing the evidence, the motive had originally been provided by Card MacGregor via the prior case in San Francisco. Then Cordell was placed at the scene, identified by the witness who lived across the street.

When Monk Lawson came back with the positive ID, everyone was convinced Cordell was responsible. The only thing needed was to get him in custody.

Wrong.

Their solid evidence turned porous.

Eyewitness identifications were notoriously unreliable. Driving back from Parker Center, Fey determined to pay her own visit to Mrs. Kathleen Bridges—the woman who had so conveniently dumped Cordell in the crap. Even though she was prepared for the worst, Fey was still surprised by Kathleen Bridges.

A stern-looking woman answered the door to Fey's knock. She managed to appear confused and intrigued when Fey identified herself.

"Are you Kathleen Bridges?" Fey asked, slipping her badge back in her purse.

"Yes." The woman's voice held a suppressed south Texas drawl. "Is this about the murder?"

Through the partially open door, Fey could see the woman was in her early sixties with the wrinkled face of a lifetime smoker. Judging by her expensive designer sweats, the condition of her nails, and her stylish hairdo, she had money to pamper herself. A single strand of pearls hung over the crew neck of her black velvet sweat top.

"I'm sorry to bother you again," Fey said. "I have a few more questions."

The woman looked confused but opened the door to admit her guest. The inside of the town home was tastefully furnished, but it was clear most of the pictures and antiques used as decorating highlights had been in place for a long time. It was definitely a home where the woman was comfortable with her memories. Fey instinctively felt the woman was a widow. When she stopped to admire a particularly riveting painting, her judgment was confirmed.

"Musashi," the woman said, referring to the Japanese samurai depicted in stunning detail on the canvas. "My late husband was fascinated by the samurai code of Bushido. Musashi is the most famous of the Japanese swordsmen. My husband found the painting on a business trip. Personally, I find it a little terrifying, but now Edgar is gone, I can't take it down."

"Musashi wrote the *Book of Five Rings*," Fey said. She was friends with a retired policeman who was heavily into samurai philosophy. He'd given her the book as a gift.

"You're familiar with the work?" The woman looked impressed.

"Slightly."

Fey was ushered to a nondescript couch.

"I want to talk to you about the identification you made yesterday," Fey said, thinking about how much had happened since.

The woman looked confused again. "I don't understand," she said. "What identification?"

"The man you saw on the night of the murder."

The woman shook her head. "I'm sorry…"

Fey paused. "You are Mrs. Kathleen Bridges?"

"Yes."

"You talked to a detective yesterday who showed you some photographs." Fey held up the photo lineup Monk had used for the identification.

"No. I didn't."

It was Fey's turn to look confused. The woman appeared normal, but you could never tell.

"I'm sorry, Mrs. Bridges. I was told Detective Monk talked with you yesterday."

The woman looked amused. "I would have remembered if he had. The murder is the talk of the neighborhood. A visit from a detective would have made a good piece of gossip."

Fey didn't know what to do or say next. She was floundering for words when she was saved by a sharp voice from the second level of the residence.

"Kathy! Kathy! Who's here?"

Kathleen Bridges shifted her gaze to an open hallway running across the second floor of the townhouse. "It's a detective, Mother Bridges." The woman's eyes came back to meet Fey's, then rolled in exasperation. "My mother-in-law," she said in explanation.

There was a series of noises from the second floor. Kathleen Bridges jumped to her feet. "It's all right, Mother Bridges," she said, moving toward the stairway. "You don't have to come downstairs." She turned her head back to Fey. "She's a dear, but it takes forever to get her back up the stairs."

Fey wondered why the woman didn't have a bedroom on the ground floor. As if reading her thoughts, Kathleen Bridges gave her an answer. "We tried giving her a room downstairs, but she was always underfoot. Before he died, Edgar and I could never get a minute to ourselves. Even now he's gone, it's best to keep her out of the way."

"Hello," said the older woman as her daughter-in-law failed to stop her determined descent. "How nice it is to have visitors."

The woman was slight and stooped, fifteen to twenty years older than her daughter-in-law. Her eyes still sparkled, giving her the appearance of a retired fairy godmother. She took small steps in a pair of fuzzy mules and a cotton housecoat. She held out a liver-spotted hand. Fey shook it, feeling the frail bones beneath the parchment-dry skin.

"You're a police detective?" she asked Fey.

Fey smiled. "I am."

"How exciting for a woman to be doing your job." The eyes twinkled. "In my day, we had police matrons. They took care of the children and the woman prisoners. Now look."

Kathleen Bridges put her hands gently on the woman's shoulders and guided her to a seat. The woman went willingly, sitting down while staring at Fey.

"I'm sorry," Kathleen Bridges said.

"It's fine," Fey told her. "It's a pleasure to meet your mother."

"Mother-in-law," Kathleen Bridges said.

Fey held up the photo lineup. "Are you sure you've never seen these photos before?"

"Positive," Kathleen Bridges said.

Fey sighed.

"I've seen them," Mother Bridges said from her chair.

Fey looked at her sharply.

"Don't be ridiculous, Mother Bridges." Kathleen Bridges moved to her mother-in-law's side and patted her on the shoulder.

"I've seen them. It was like on TV."

"What are you talking about?" Kathleen Bridges' voice was rapidly filling with impatience.

Fey leaned forward in her chair. "What is your mother-in-law's first name?"

The woman stopped her patting movements in mid-action. "It's Kathleen, the same as mine...Oh, my...I never thought...I always call her Mother Bridges. Edgar and I laughed about the coincidence when we were first married." She shifted her look from Fey to her mother-in-law.

"Do you ever leave Mother Bridges home alone?"

"Sometimes. She's okay if she doesn't have to make any meals."

"Did you leave her alone yesterday?"

The woman thought. "I ran errands in the morning. I was gone for maybe an hour. She doesn't answer the door when I'm gone, so I'm sure she didn't talk to anyone."

Fey stood up and walked over to crouch in front of the older woman. "Can I call you Mother Bridges?" she asked.

"Of course, my dear."

"Did you answer the door while your daughter-in-law was out yesterday?"

"I did," the old woman said smugly.

"Mother," Kathleen Bridges said, with a heavy dose of exasperation.

"Stop fussing," the older woman said. "I was bored, and he was very handsome."

"Was he a black man? A detective?" Fey asked.

"Yes. Polite and nicely dressed."

"Did he ask about seeing somebody enter the house across the street the night the woman was murdered?"

"Yes. I told him what I saw from my bedroom upstairs. So exciting talking to a real detective—like on TV."

"Did the detective show you some photographs?"

"Yes."

"These photographs?" Fey asked. She handed Mother Bridges the photo lineup.

Mother Bridges took the lineup and squinted at it. "I picked this one," she said, pointing to the picture of Cordell. "Your detective was very excited. I was glad I picked the right one. I didn't want to disappoint him. He was so nice."

"Is this your signature?" Fey pointed to the name scrawled under the picture.

"Yes."

Thank goodness, Fey thought. Mother Bridges seemed pretty sharp. Her identification of Cordell would probably hold up. Her sparkling eyes alone would convince a jury.

"Mother Bridges," her daughter-in-law broke in. "How could you possibly see anyone across the street? You can hardly see across the room even with your glasses." Kathleen Bridges turned her head to speak to Fey. "Her eyesight is so bad she can't read anymore. I bring her books on tape from the library. We also put drops in her eyes since her cataract operation. The drops make her vision blurry."

Fey looked closely at the old woman's eyes. What she had taken to be a sparkle was light reflecting off the medicine drops.

"Mother Bridges." Fey took the old woman's hand. "This is important. Can you honestly identify this man?"

The old woman looked stubborn for a moment and then shrugged. "I didn't want to disappoint your detective. I didn't see anyone across the street. I only wanted company and he was so nice."

I bet he was, thought Fey. Monk believed he'd found a witness who could break the case. What detective wouldn't be nice?

"When he showed me the pictures," Mother Bridges continued, "I picked one. I didn't like the looks of this character." She pointed again to Cordell's picture. "Your detective was so pleased. He said he'd come back, but now I guess he won't." Mother Bridges sounded disappointed. "Am I going to be in trouble?" Her lower lip trembled.

With an effort, Fey patted the old woman's hand and struggled to reassure her. "Thank you for being honest, Mother Bridges." She forced a smile. "You're not in trouble."

But I am, thought Fey. *Right along with this case.*

CHAPTER TWENTY-FIVE

Fey and Monk were alone in Mike Cahill's office, sitting
across from each other at the round conference table.

"I'm sorry, boss. I had no idea."

Fey waved her hand and sighed.

"I expected more from a veteran detective. Hell, I
would have expected more from Colby."

Monk hung his head.

Fey felt bad. She was trying to keep the butt-chewing
low key, but Monk had earned it. He'd shown the original
lineup to Mother Bridges. Everyone took his word the
identification was righteous.

"I know you thought you had this nailed down,"
she said, in a softer voice. "The old lady could have
fooled a lot of people. Sometimes we get caught up in
what we want to hear—not what is really being said.
However, you know how easily identifications can fall
apart."

"I still can't believe it." Monk shook his head in
amazement. "She was so freaking convincing."

Fey fought a chuckle. Mother Bridges had almost
sucked her in.

"Those twinkling eyes," Monk said. The chagrin in his voice was so genuine, Fey couldn't hold in her laughter.

Monk's eyes flashed, but realized she held no malice. He let his own deep chuckle leak out.

The two detectives got a grip, then looked at each other and started laughing again until they had tears in their eyes. The laughter was cathartic, releasing the stress of the situation as well as the pent-up anticipation Fey had been carrying since hearing Cordell's phone message.

When they calmed down, Fey wiped her eyes and tried to get back on track. "The case against Cordell is collapsing. We need to find a hammer and nail the bastard down."

"You still believe Cordell is the best suspect?"

"At the moment. The murder weapon was recovered in his crib."

"What about a frame-up?"

Fey's interest sharpened "Talk to me."

Monk shrugged. He didn't want to look foolish again.

"Out with it," Fey encouraged.

"What's his lawyer's stake in this? The guy was bankrupt when he went to prison. He didn't get rich on the inside. So why is Ryder working so hard?"

"You don't believe in altruism?"

"No. And I don't believe she's on a quest to right a judicial wrong."

"Maybe she has a movie deal?"

"Anything is possible, but I don't think so."

"Me either," said Fey.

"There's other points bothering me."

"Like what?"

"How did Cordell get paroled in San Francisco and immediately move into a half-way house within a mile of his supposedly dead wife?"

"Coincidence?" Fey said, lightly.

"Not in this line of work."

Fey nodded. "You want to do some digging?"

"Absolutely." Monk was eager to repair the damage to his reputation.

"We also need to backtrack the victim. This change of identity stuff is nonsense. I want to know who she really is, what her story is, and who else might have wanted her dead."

"I'm on it," Monk said.

Through the window of Cahill's office, Fey saw Hatch holding up a phone and pointing toward her.

"I'm being paged," Fey said, standing up.

"Boss," Monk said, stopping Fey at the door. "I'm sorry I let you down."

Fey smiled. "I know. It's what makes you a valuable friend." She jerked a thumb toward the squad room. "Others would be sorry for screwing up, but not care how it affected me. I appreciate you." The two detectives nodded at each other.

Fey went to handle the next crisis.

"What do you have?" she asked, approaching Hatch.

"I'm screening press calls, but this might be different. The guy has called three times. He insists on talking directly to you."

"Is he a flake?"

Hatch shrugged. Fey sometimes wondered if it was a habit he'd picked up from Monk or the other way around.

"I don't think so," Hatch said. "He's a straight, but he sounds squared away."

Fey walked to her desk. "What line?"

"Eighty-four-ten."

She pulled a clip earring off her left ear and picked up

the phone. "Detective Croaker," she said into the mouthpiece.

"My name is Longley, Myron Longley," said an assured male voice. "I manage the Wilshire Boulevard branch of Beverly Hills Savings Bank."

"What can I do for you?"

There was a slight hesitation, then Longley asked, "You are in charge of the Miranda Goodwinter murder investigation?"

"I am."

Seemingly reassured, Longley continued. "I saw the picture of Miriam Cordell in the paper yesterday. Also, the photo of the police taking her body out of the house after she'd been murdered. The news reports indicate Miriam Cordell and Miranda Goodwinter might be the same person..." Longley's voice trailed off.

"Yes," said Fey, rapidly losing patience.

"I think I recognized the photo of Miriam Cordell as a customer who recently closed out her accounts with a large withdrawal. The problem is, I knew the customer as a Mrs. Monica Blake..."

Bingo thought Fey. "Don't move, Mr. Longley. I'll be right there."

————

Fey checked her watch as she and Colby approached the front doors of the Beverly Hills Savings Bank. It was after six o'clock. Fey realized the bank was closed to customers.

The front door was locked. Fey tapped on it, displaying her badge to a uniformed guard on the other side of the glass. The guard nodded, made a *wait a moment* gesture, and walked away. He returned in a few seconds trailed by a dapper-looking man brandishing a key.

The man was short with slicked-back hair almost as shiny as his patent leather brogans. Through myopic lenses in fashionable black frames, the man scrutinized Fey's badge and identification before unlocking the door.

"Mr. Longley?" Fey asked as soon as verbal communication was possible.

"Yes."

The man hustled the two detectives inside before rapidly re-locking the door. His actions were of a fastidious man expecting bank robbers any second.

There were several tellers in the bank closing out their cash drawers. Longley gave a set of keys to a nicely dressed woman, whom Fey took to be the assistant manager. Longley told her to secure the vault and deal with the tellers. She nodded solemnly, entrusted with a great responsibility, then went to do the manager's bidding.

Approaching a large black desk, Longley ushered Fey and Colby into chairs set on a Chinese carpet. He then took his *rightful* position behind the desk. He even smoothed his pants over his backside before planting himself down. He adjusted the precise position of his desk blotter. Fey realized Longley was having trouble parting with bank secrets.

"We appreciate you contacting us, Mr. Longley," she said, broaching the awkwardness. "It isn't often we have a financial institution offer us information without demanding court orders."

Longley smiled. It transformed his face from banker's blank to naughty little boy. "Banks want everyone to believe they treat their customers' confidences as sacrosanct. In reality, it is only a manager's petty power."

"A refreshing point of view," Fey said, not sure what Longley was driving toward.

"My attitude results from having a brother and a son in law enforcement."

"The picture becomes clearer."

"Quite," said Longley, "But there are other factors."

"And they are?" Fey asked.

Longley turned his attention toward her. "Whenever a customer withdraws a large sum of money from their account—I'm talking in excess of half a million dollars—or closes an account with a similar amount, a manager takes it as a personal affront and wants to know the reason. First, because it hurts the assets of the branch. Second, because managers come to think the bank's money is theirs. We begrudge giving it up."

Fey laughed. "How did you wangle your way into a manager's position?"

"My uncle owns the bank," Longley said. The corners of his mouth turned up slightly. "Nepotism is a wondrous thing, don't you agree?"

Fey and Colby realized the question was rhetorical and waited for Longley to go on.

"Under normal circumstances, perhaps I wouldn't have thought to call you. I'm still not sure my Monica Blake is the same woman as in the photo. They look alike, however, and I have been unable to contact Mrs. Blake since she withdrew her funds. She has disappeared." Longley checked his watch.

Fey shifted in her chair. Longley might be willing to cooperate, but it was going to be on his own time schedule. "You mentioned other circumstances surrounding the case?" she asked.

Longley looked up as the uniformed guard approached and signaled him.

Longley raised his hand in acknowledgment, then returned his attention to Fey. "Please excuse me. A circumstance has come to meet you."

He walked away from his desk, fishing the front door key from the depths of his trouser pocket.

Fey looked at Colby and made a perplexed face. Colby shrugged. Their silent consensus was to await developments.

Longley returned in less than a minute with another man in tow. The second man was tall and thin. His gaunt face was ravaged with the pockmarks of traumatic teenage acne. Dark, hooded eyes gave him the appearance of a half-asleep bird of prey. He wore a good quality, but ill-fitting gray suit, a starched white shirt, an expensive blue tie, and black wing tips.

Colby figured there were initials monogrammed somewhere on the cuffs or pocket of the starched shirt. He had no problem categorizing the guy as some kind of federal agent. Even without saying a word, the walking stick figure practically screamed his occupation.

Longley brought over another chair. "This is Mr. Kyle Craven," he said. "He's an IRS investigator."

Fey and Colby felt fear move in their bowels. Neither knew any law enforcement agency in the country with more power and less oversight than the investigative arm of the Internal Revenue Service. Without effort, an IRS investigator could even scare hell out of agents from the government's ultrasecret National Security Agency.

IRS agents were God unto themselves. If you didn't want to find yourself at the wrong end of an audit, you meekly did whatever they asked and got out from under as quick as you could.

Craven's slow smile would have done credit to a corpse. He could smell the fear in the air and found it invigorating—a Hannibal Lector of the CPA set.

"I'm from the government," he said in a deep voice. "I'm here to help." He sat down without offering his hand.

A comedian, Fey thought as she cringed inwardly. Colby had visibly paled at the disclaimer. Even Longley seemed affected by Craven's presence. He scuttled back to the minimal protection offered by the far side of his desk.

Craven produced his rictus grin again, enjoying the effect he was having. It was the effect he had on anyone with an inkling of the power of the IRS—an unconstitutional organization condoned by the government as a necessary evil.

"I really am here to help you," the stick figure said, knowing no one would believe him. "No pressures, no hassles. If Monica Blake, Miriam Cordell, and Miranda Goodwinter are the same person, I've been tracking the woman and her financial dealings for twelve years."

"Can we start from the beginning?" Fey asked. "I'm getting out of my depth."

Longley sat forward, leaning his arms on his desk. "I'm sorry. I know all of this must be confusing."

"Most cops do have IQs higher than Nerf balls," Colby said, resorting to natural sarcasm when confronted by an awkward situation. "If you use words of three syllables or less, we can get on with things."

A look from Craven almost froze Colby in midsentence, but he managed to get the words out. Fey was proud of the effort.

"I apologize," said Longley. "From what Mr. Craven has told me, I can hardly believe it myself."

"Please, Mr. Longley," said Fey forcefully.

"Sorry." Longley took a pause to compose himself. "Whenever a customer extracts a large amount of cash, there are forms to be filled out for the IRS and other entities. The forms filled out on Monica Blake alerted Mr. Craven, who then contacted me."

"How long ago?" Fey asked.

"Five weeks."

Cordell had been paroled six weeks ago. It looked as if Monica Blake—aka Cordell, aka Goodwinter—put on her running shoes as soon as she found out. "What was so strange about Monica Blake's withdrawal it came to your personal attention?" she asked Longley.

"You mean besides the amount?"

"Yes. But for the record, how much did she withdraw?"

Longley cleared his throat and pulled a sheet of paper from under his blotter and consulted it. "Three million, five hundred, and seven thousand dollars."

"Holy cow!" Colby said.

"Ditto," said Fey, slightly stunned by the amount. She remembered the new checkbook from another bank, which was at the crime scene. There had been a freshly deposited two hundred dollars added to the one thousand dollars used to open the account. She also remembered the million dollars in cash in the dryer.

Either amount was a long way short of three million.

"The problem was," Longley continued, "Mrs. Blake's account was minimal by our standards. Rarely did she have a balance in excess of five thousand dollars."

"How did she expect to withdraw three million dollars?" Colby asked.

"On the day before, we received a three-million-dollar wire transfer to her account."

"From where?"

"The Cayman Islands."

"Hello, offshore banking," Fey said.

"Exactly," Craven chipped in, and then went silent.

Colby and Fey glanced at him then returned their attention to Longley.

"As Mr. Craven says, *exactly*. When a bank receives a deposit of over ten thousand dollars, they are required to fill out a form notifying the IRS. There are large fines and penalties for noncompliance."

"Did the transfer surprise you?" Fey asked.

"Mildly, until Mrs. Blake requested to close out her account the following day. She requested two million transferred to a brokerage house to purchase bearer bonds. She took the rest in cash."

"Bearer bonds?"

"Yes. Basically, a monetary draft payable to anybody who has the bonds in their possession. As good as cash, only in far higher denominations for easier transport."

Fey and Colby exchanged glances. There was a million dollars in cash in Miranda Goodwinter's dryer, but no bearer bonds. The bonds hadn't surfaced at Cordell's crib either. If he'd been stupid enough to bring the murder weapon back to his room, why not the bearer bonds, if he had taken them?

Fey shifted in her chair to get a better look at Craven. "How do you fit into this scenario?" she asked.

"I've been chasing this woman for over twelve years. I've tracked her forward through six different personalities—seven if you count Miranda Goodwinter—and backward through at least four identities. Much to the irritation of my professional pride, I have never established her true identity. Now, somebody else caught up to her before I did."

"How can you be so sure this woman you've been tracking is the same person as Miranda Goodwinter?" Fey asked.

"You have established Miranda Goodwinter and Miriam Cordell were the same person?"

"Yes."

"Miriam Cordell was an identity assumed by the woman who plagued me."

"How did you tie all of these women together?"

"Money and murder, Detective Croaker. One makes the world go 'round and the other stops it."

CHAPTER TWENTY-SIX

"Nobody likes the IRS because everybody cheats on their taxes," Craven said, stating the obvious in his oddly modulated style of speech. "Even people who don't think they're cheating on their taxes always fudge a bit. It's the American way."

"Are you expecting sympathy?" Fey asked, showing surprise. "The role of poor misunderstood Internal Revenue Service investigator doesn't suit you."

Craven laughed. Threw back his head, opened his mouth, and guffawed. Fey liked him better when he was serious. He was more menacing when amused.

Craven got a grip and wiped his eyes with the tip of an index finger. "Detective Croaker," he said, "I enjoy my job."

"Really?" Colby said softly, but everybody ignored him.

"However," Craven continued, "it doesn't reduce the necessity of my job."

"What is your job?"

Craven paused before replying. "My job is tracking down individuals who seek to avoid paying any taxes. In doing so, they show contempt for other citizens who do pay despite their petty attempts at cheating."

"What about organized tax protest groups?" Colby asked.

Craven winced. "Spare me. Fanatics are not my bailiwick. They are misguided scum. My quest is the individual, the criminal with no political agenda, the man or woman who holds up their middle finger to society as they rob us blind."

Fey wanted to cut to the chase. Craven was having too much fun atop his high horse. "How does this apply to Miranda Goodwinter?"

Craven's features darkened. "A pariah with no conscience and an insatiable greed for money."

Craven described how he tracked Miranda Goodwinter for years. He was always an identity behind her, able only to use her paper trail to another identity after she moved on. In each shed identity, she left behind a chaos of murder and financial gain.

"Are you saying Miranda Goodwinter was some kind of black widow killer?" Fey asked, the scenario becoming clear.

"Exactly," Craven said. "Twenty-two years ago, as Marsha Wallace, she picked up a tidy sum of fifty thousand dollars when her first husband fell down a flight of stairs and broke his neck. She also inherited his minor estate and disappeared without a trace.

"Next, we switch to twenty years ago when, as Madeline Fletcher, she picked up a hundred thousand dollars when her new husband was killed in a drunk driving accident. This time she plundered the estate before leaving behind a penniless thirteen-year-old stepdaughter to be raised by impoverished grandparents."

"Sweet lady," Fey commented as Craven plowed on.

"Fifteen years ago, as Mavis Curtis, she cops a cool

five hundred thousand when yet another husband has a sailing accident and drowns. The poor guy couldn't swim. He didn't even sail before she came into his life and insisted on buying the boat." Craven paused briefly for breath.

"Then there's the Miriam Cordell identity, with which you're already familiar. She picked up her first million-dollar payoff in the scam, although it ran a little differently than her usual MO."

Craven reached into a slim valise and withdrew several computer printouts. He checked them quickly.

"Our lady went underground after the Cordell affair. My theory is the high profile of the case threatened to tip over her apple cart. Still, I bought the scam—believing she'd pushed things too hard and was sleeping with the fishes—until six years later."

"I'll bite," said Fey. "What changed your mind?"

"I inherited a case from another investigator involving a female suspect whose first name started with *M*—May Wellington—and the chase was on again."

"You knew she was alive, but didn't do anything to clear Isaac Cordell?" Fey asked.

"I couldn't prove she was alive. Anyway, Isaac Cordell's father had a history of delinquent tax payments. Having the son behind bars for the debts of the father had ironic appeal." The death's-head grin came and went with startling speed.

Please, Fey thought, *save me from the self-righteous.*

Craven looked at his printout again. "After May Wellington there was Mona Ford. After Mona there was Maxine Trent. With each identity, *Lady M* put a husband six foot under. Each husband had provided for her in advance should they die unexpectedly. The cycle was an obsession with her. Men kill for sex—women for money."

Fey had a headache. "The trail eventually led you to Monica Blake?"

"Except something spooked her before I got there."

"Spooked—because there was no dead husband left behind."

"Yes. Frustrating..."

Colby saw the trend playing out. "Then the Miranda Goodwinter persona was killed before she had the chance to get established."

Fey was bothered. "How does Miriam Cordell's scam fit the pattern—it's not the same MO?"

"Consider the situation objectively. On the surface, Isaac Cordell was the perfect candidate for a *black widow*. I believe she bumped off Cordell's mother to gain access before realizing the estate was already drained—not enough left even to buy a good-sized life insurance policy on Cordell."

Fey's mind was racing. "Instead, she took a policy out on herself..."

Craven picked up the thread. "Using money from prior scams."

Fey took the ball back. "Seducing Cordell's business partner into helping fake her own death. Then the business partner—as the second beneficiary—picks up the million secondhand when Cordell gets convicted on manufactured evidence."

"Top marks," Craven agreed.

"Where is Roark, the business partner, today?" Fey asked, still trying to absorb all the implications. asked.

"Disappeared, never to file a tax return again," Craven told her.

"How did you come by all this information?" Colby asked.

Craven looked at Colby as if he'd urinated on his shoe. "Taxes are my life. I use numbers, forms, and obscure rules and regulations to tie people up in knots too tight to wriggle free. I scan thousands of computer printouts a day to make sure Uncle Sam gets his fair share out of your pocket." He waved his hand around the bank's interior. "I've tracked drug dealers, money launderers, and organized crime racketeers until the thrill is lost. But occasionally, someone like Lady M puts meaning back into the chase. When it happens, I pay attention. I savor the case..." He held up a hand and squeezed it into a fist. "Until I squash them!" Craven's voice hopped an octave, and he realized his mask of civility was slipping. With effort, he stabilized.

"Apparently, this one got away," Fey said.

"In this life," came the stoic reply.

CHAPTER TWENTY-SEVEN

By the time Fey and Colby arrived, the promotion party at Two-Step Tilly's was in full swing. Tilly's was a country-western club on the border of Pacific Division and West L.A., frequented by coppers from both areas. It wasn't the traditional cop bar—run by a retired blue-suit with an all-gun-toting clientele—but an eighties urban cowboy version providing a safe haven for cops to let loose.

The party was in honor of Paul Trotweiler, a young P-III Detective Trainee who had been promoted to full detective. The upgrade unfortunately came with a transfer to the ghettos of Southwest Division. In a year or two, he could get a transfer out, leaving a bad billet for another promotion chaser.

In the euphoria new promotions bring before the reality sets in, Trotweiler coughed up six hundred bucks to Two-Step Tilly's bartender. The beer and liquor would flow until the tab ran out. Everyone would then leave except for a hard-core group of serious drinkers.

Sponsoring your own promotion party was a tradition as important as bringing doughnuts on your first day in a new division. You weren't forced to do it, but life became socially awkward if you didn't. Anyway, you owed for the free drinks and *fat pills* supplied by others.

Fey waved at the raucous group of detectives sequestered in a corner near the dance floor. Colby moved toward the men's room. Fey headed for the bar.

On the way, they had chewed through Craven's information dump. Ultimately, it was interesting, but they couldn't see how it got them closer to Miranda Goodwinter's killer.

Craven's input defined and confirmed motive for Cordell, but it didn't add anything new. The sordid history of Miranda Goodwinter didn't stop the current evidence from evaporating. New clues or leads were still evasive.

Fey's head spun with the implications. Her subconscious needed time to process the input. Meanwhile, getting mildly drunk had definite appeal.

Vance Hatcher made room and Fey sat down with relief. She raised her glass to Jake Travers, who was at another table. He winked back. People knew about their relationship, but they played it cool in public.

"Any word on Cordell?" Cahill asked from across the table.

Fey shook her head. She'd put Cordell being loose out of her mind while listening to Craven. Thinking about it now, she decided she would get more than mildly drunk.

"Any good stuff from the bank manager?" Hatch asked.

"Maybe," Fey said. "But there's too much to recap tonight." She finished off the second half of her beer while waving to a waitress. "Let me have more beer and talk about something else."

"I agree," said Monk from her other side. He took a fresh beer for himself from the waitress's tray.

The jukebox was cranked up and the voice of Clint Black boomed from ceiling speakers. Couples headed for the dance floor, including several pairings from the gathered detectives. Slacks, ties, and shoulder holsters had been exchanged for Wranglers, cowboy boots, and hidden backup guns.

Fey took in the scene. The chatter rose to compete with the music. Mike Cahill's thigh was being massaged under the table by one of the station's record clerks. If his wife found out, she would skin them alive. At another table, a robbery detective had a lip-lock going with a female burglary detective. Fey figured their spouses wouldn't be happy either.

Colby came back from the bathroom and pulled another chair into the group. To catch up, he quickly knocked back two beers and started a third.

The promotion party sported thirty detectives, a dozen faces from uniformed patrol, four off-duty record clerks, and couple of well-liked DAs. Several younger station volunteers were prowling for husbands—even if they currently belonged to someone else. There were also the requisite cop groupies who knew there was a price for inclusion.

A couple were hard-core *cop whores* who only wanted to get it fast and dirty in a patrol car. Most groupies, however, were good-hearted straights who enjoyed flirting with a world outside their staid existence. They gained fringe access by providing cops a variety of services cost or gratis—meals at restaurants, computer equipment or service to cops who didn't know a RAM from a byte, private vehicle mechanic work. These were valuable barter for cops stretching paychecks to cover alimony-hungry spouses and L.A. area mortgages.

En masse, the gathering was large enough to take over the bar. Tilly's regulars tolerated this because management liked the free—if inebriated—security. For their part, cops could let their defenses down due to the safety of numbers. At Tilly's they were the biggest fish in a small pond. If anybody challenged them, there was instant backup. Gang mentality as applied by the *good guys*.

Jake came over and whirled Fey out onto the dance floor. With five beers under her belt and no food to speak of since breakfast, she was feeling a slight buzz and was glad for the movement. They joined the circle of dancers and broke into a fairly smooth Texas two-step.

"You doing okay?" Jake asked.

"Ask me again after another couple of beers."

After one turn around the dance floor, Jake felt a tap on his shoulder and turned to see Colby standing behind him. Colby's eyes were bright with too much alcohol consumed too fast.

"Do you mind?" Colby asked. The challenge was clear in his voice.

Jake stepped back with a shrug to Fey, letting Colby cut in. He knew Fey could fend for herself.

"This is a surprise," Fey said as Colby guided her away. "Are all the groupies on to you already?"

"This was the easiest way I could get my arms around you."

"Get off it, Colby. I'm a fat old broad."

"You're not fat and you're not old."

Fey sneered. "The only reason you want me is because the unattainable is always desirable."

"Are you unattainable?" Colby ran a hand lightly across Fey's breasts.

"Where you're concerned." Fey twirled out of Colby's grasp, shot him a mocking look, and walked off the dance floor.

Taking another beer off the bar, she sat down next to Jake.

"You've developed a fan club," Jake said, teasing her.

"Colby is a walking hormone with an asshole. He thinks he can stab me in the back and get me into bed."

Jake laughed.

"I'm serious," Fey said. "It's typical warped male logic. He knows I'm his boss, but because I'm a woman, he figures if he can find a way into my shorts, he can control me."

"One good tumble and you'll be jelly at his feet." Jake was still laughing.

Fey threw a pretzel at Jake.

"It worked for me," Jake teased.

"Screw you, counselor. You can sleep alone tonight." Fey sat back and crossed her arms over her breasts.

"Hey, let's not go overboard."

Fey shook her head in resignation. "What is it with men? It's bonding stuff, right? Something to do with Monday night football and beer commercials?"

"Right," Jake agreed. "Also, lots of tree hugging and chanting. Rediscovering our essential maleness squelched by years of sensitivity training."

"Good-bye, Alan Alda. Welcome back, Grog the Caveman."

"Ugg...Ogga ogga..."

"Scrape your knuckles over to the bar, Grog, and get me another drink before dragging me by the hair back to your cave."

"Beer?"

"No. It's time to switch to the real stuff."

Fey watched Jake move off carrying their empty glasses. The West L.A. lightweights were all gone. The station brass had left before Fey and Colby arrived – paying their respects, sipping one drink, and then leaving the troops to enjoy themselves. It was the politically correct thing to do. Also, if the party got out of hand, they wouldn't be hit by anything the fan threw off.

Still, a number of coppers remained. Even though Paul Trotweiler's money was long gone, the liquor was still flowing. A mixed group of males and females anchored a corner booth. There were no sexual overtones beyond one-liners and innuendoes, with everyone giggling like naughty schoolchildren.

The single male-and-female matchups had moved into darkened corners or the intimacy of the dance floor. These couplings were noted, but the sanctity of the open secret would not extend beyond the group to outsiders or spouses. What went on within the police family stayed within the family.

The unspoken justification for infidelity was only a cop could truly understand another cop—a conspiracy of blue silence and acceptance, a bonding beyond marriage vows, church commitments, or blood relations. If you were a cop, you were in. If you weren't a cop, you were out. Volunteers, attached civilians, and groupies could only penetrate so far. The rules were the rules. In or out. Cut and dried. Simple.

Good cop or bad cop, you took the mark of the badge with you to the grave. You weren't one of God's children, or one of God's sheep. The mark of the badge made you a wolf. God's wolves.

Or it could be cops were genetically unfaithful.

Colby sauntered over and leaned on the table next to Fey. He looked at Jake's retreating back.

"What's with you and the counselor? Screwing your way into another promotion?" His voice was loud enough to be overheard. Across the table, Monk started to stand and intervene before trouble broke out, but Fey's look stuck him to his chair.

Several female officers sitting, were watching intently, as if some secret communication had passed silently and invisibly between them.

Fey smiled at Colby. "You really are pretty good-looking," Fey said. "Perhaps you're right." She stood and swayed her body into Colby's, turning him so his back was to the table.

She kissed him full on the mouth as the cops gathered around the table hooted and hollered.

Colby was completely caught off balance. Leaning back against the table, pinned by Fey's substantial weight, left him no way to maneuver. Through an alcohol haze, he realized he was in trouble.

He tried to brazen his way out.

"Why don't we go somewhere more comfortable?" he asked, his voice husky. Despite himself, he could feel an erection building as Fey straddled his thigh and rubbed against him.

"Smooth talker," she said. She kissed him again, all tongue and spit, grinding her body into him, pressing her breasts into his chest. She'd learned very early how to turn a man on—about the power it could give her over him. The group at the table roared their approval. They knew Fey had Colby on the hook.

When Fey broke the kiss, she continued to press herself against Colby. She kept one hand wrapped behind his neck, controlling his movements as she would those of a strong stallion she was riding.

"You're heating up, partner," she said in a sultry bedroom voice full of lust and teasing. Fey waggled her free hand behind Colby's back. One of the other women at the table, sensing what Fey wanted, placed a freshly opened bottle of beer in her hand.

Fey kissed Colby again, her mouth wide and open on his, her tongue flying between his lips to entwine with his. She brought the hand with the bottle around and rubbed it over the obvious bulge in Colby's groin.

"My, my," she said admiringly. Staying close to him as she broke the kiss, she took her hand from Colby's neck and grabbed the waist of his loose-cut slacks. She pulled the fabric forward.

Colby struggled slightly, thinking Fey was going to reach her other hand down to grope him, but he was trapped by the table and Fey's weight.

"Not here," he said, his voice thick.

"Why not?" Fey asked. Still using her body to hide her actions, she placed the open mouth of the beer bottle inside Colby's pants, letting the liquid pour out, "I can't think of a better place to cool your jets."

"What?" Colby said, sounding confused. Then the icy cold wet of the beer hit his skin. "Crap!" he said, trying to push Fey away.

She buried her face in his shoulder and leaned into him, bending him across the table. Colby struggled until his back was flat on the table. Beer glasses, chips, salsa, and ash trays scattered everywhere. The other detectives and their companions stood up, jumping clear of the debris and laughing at the spectacle.

Leaving the beer bottle to empty down his pants, Fey backed off and stood laughing with her hands on her hips. Colby cursed, struggling to pull the bottle out. He eventually removed it by standing up and shaking it down one leg of his pants like a slap-stick comedian. The groin and one leg of his pants were soaked with the beer. Everyone fell into convulsions of laughter.

"You cow," he said to Fey, looking down at himself. "You'll pay for this."

"I wouldn't pay you for anything," Fey said, still laughing. "Especially, not a beer flavored erection."

The crowd of detectives hooted at the slashing remark.

Colby grabbed a napkin from the floor and began rubbing ineffectually at the stains. He knew everyone was delighted by his discomfort. It pissed him off. All his life, he'd never been able to keep friends. He couldn't understand what turned people against him.

In school he'd been a top athlete, but he could never rally a team behind him. Somebody else was always voted the captain, even when they weren't as talented as Colby. He could never understand why being the best wasn't good enough.

As a detective, his arrest and conviction record was one of the highest on the department, yet nobody cared. They refused to give him credit, ready to jump at any chance to see him flounder. They were jealous.

"Go ahead, laugh," he said, storming out of the bar.

"Cute butt," one of the other female detectives called out loudly. It tripped everyone's laughter button again. Even in the dimmed lighting it was possible to see the flush of red flare up the back of Colby's neck. He turned around and gave everyone the finger.

Fey watched him go. Her initial pleasure was slowly being replaced by a feeling she'd carried the joke too far. She'd fought fire with fire, but she should have risen above schoolyard tactics. Why had she let him make her so mad?

Jake returned to the table. "Did I miss something?" he asked casually, setting off laughter again.

CHAPTER TWENTY-EIGHT

The party at Tilly's wound down around eleven p.m. A few stragglers hung on until midnight, but Jake and Fey split arm in arm around ten-thirty.

Going home to the threat of Cordell lying in wait did not appeal to Fey. Despite her tough talk, Fey wasn't ready to act as bait. There were things she needed in place before becoming a staked goat. Another night in Jake's bed sounded like a better idea.

Or it had at first.

Heavy-headed with exhaustion and alcohol consumption, she barely managed to get undressed before falling face-first into Jake's pillows. Several hours later, she was in a dead sleep when something brought her back to the surface of awareness.

A man stood beside the bed looking down at her, his dark outline nothing more than a darker black against the room's interior. Not fully conscious, Fey sensed the man was naked and aroused. She flinched when he reached out to touch her. Memories exploded from deep inside her psyche.

"Get away!" she screamed, drawing her legs to her chest and flailing her arms.

"Easy. It's me." Jake reached out to grab her wrists as they whirled about.

"Get away! I won't let you! I won't let you!"

"Fey! It's me, Jake." His words fell on deaf ears.

Fey mentally registered it was Jake in the room with her. The thought it might have been Cordell only briefly flitted through her mind, then disappeared under an avalanche of suppressed emotions sprung by a combination of alcohol and déjà vu—the image of her father standing beside her bed, naked and aroused.

When she was thirteen, she had awoken to the same scene. Her father standing over her in the dark, as he had so many times before. Only this time something was different. The male smell of him was the same. The heat emanating from his groin, where it pressed into her side, was the same. But the atmosphere was different. Anger was there as always, but it was raging.

"You little slut!" Her father's angry whisper reached her ears with the force of a shock wave.

Fey sat up in bed, the blankets falling away from newly forming breasts hidden behind a teddy-bear-motif nightshirt. "Daddy? What?"

He smacked her across the mouth. "You keep your voice down, you evil little slut. Wake your mother up, I'll beat her, too."

He hit Fey on the side of the head with his closed fist. Her father had been a policeman in a time when corruption ran rampant. He knew how to hit and cripple without leaving marks.

"Daddy!" The thirteen-year-old Fey kept her plea to a vocal level of a whimper.

"I know what you did with the Higgins kid from down the street."

"No, Daddy. I didn't do anything!"

"Keep your voice down, you filthy little tramp!" Garth Croaker cuffed his daughter roughly across her right ear. Fey's head rocked on her shoulders and she fell back across the bed.

Her father climbed onto the bed, pinning Fey down with his knees. "You let him screw you, didn't you?"

"No, Daddy, no! He only kissed me."

The flat of Garth's hand flashed out, smacking, left, right. "Liar!"

"No!"

Again the slapping, left, right. "Lying, filthy, little bitch. You'll have to be taught a lesson not to do filthy things with every little boy who comes along."

The lesson consisted of all the filthy things Fey had never done with anyone, except when forced to do them with her father.

Then, as usual, there was even more anger after he spent himself.

This time it was worse. Much worse.

The sledgehammer of Garth Croaker's fist smashed time and again into the heart of Fey's wide-spread legs and across the soft flesh of her abdomen.

Again. And again. And again. A never-ending nightmare continuing even after the physical act was finished.

The doctor had been a friend of the family. A tame medic. A known abortionist whom Garth Croaker kept out of jail on more than one occasion. There was always a use for a doctor who could keep his mouth shut.

The doctor stopped the bleeding. Saved the life of the poor thirteen-year-old girl on his operating table.

Good old Doc Martin.

He saved the girl, but he couldn't save everything. Fey would never be able to conceive a child. Her life was saved. Wasn't it enough of a miracle?

Good old Doc Martin.

One of dear old Dad's drinking buddies.

Six months after saving Fey's life, he forced himself on her while her father held her down.

Back in the present, in Jake's bedroom, with the man she loved standing beside her, Fey trembled with the fear of old scars torn open. Images flashed through her mind and scared her half to death. The nightmare had truly never ended.

"Fey? What is it?" Jake's voice reached her from far away.

She flinched again when he touched her arm, drawing herself into a protective ball. She felt the damp of tears on her cheek, the ever-suppressed scream stuck in her throat —because you better not wake Mommy. But Mommy was dead, and so was Daddy. He couldn't hurt her anymore.

He couldn't hurt her anymore...anymore... anymore...

Jake didn't know what was happening but had sense not to push. He'd been returning from the bathroom, pausing beside the bed to watch Fey sleeping. It was a private moment he always found pleasing. When she started to rouse, the thought of making love to her suddenly aroused him. And then she screamed.

He stood back when he saw the effect of his touch and made soothing noises. Calling Fey back from whatever hellish landscape in which her mind was dwelling.

He turned a bedside lamp on and watched as Fey returned to normal. Color seeped back into her face. Her trembling slowed. The visible beating of the carotid artery in her neck subsided. Her eyes focused.

Then she reached out for him. Crushing him to her. Fiercely wrapping her legs tightly around him, as if trying to meld her body with his.

Back in control of the lovemaking, she found the now soft length of him with her hands and stroked him back to erection. With a fevered cry she opened herself and swallowed him into her, tight but determined.

And she rocked. And she cried. And he held her, without asking for explanation. They slept.

CHAPTER TWENTY-NINE

Janice Ryder did not do mornings well. As a result, she was not a happy camper when the phone beside her bed jangled her awake.

"Whatzit?" she inquired, sleep drenching her voice.

"Ms. Ryder, this is Cabo, the night manager. Sorry to disturb you, but an important package has been delivered for you."

"Package?"

"*Si*. A large envelope. It is marked urgent."

"Who delivered it?"

"I don't know. I went into the manager's office to answer the phone. When I came out the envelope was on the reception counter."

"I'm not expecting any packages or envelopes."

"But it is marked urgent."

Janice Ryder looked at her clock and sighed. Six-thirty a.m. "All right, bring it up." She didn't wait for Cabo's reply before hanging up. She rolled over in the bed and closed her eyes again. After a few seconds, she groaned and tossed the covers off before sitting up slowly. She needed coffee. Strong coffee to kick-start her heart.

Sitting on the edge of the bed in naked splendor, she stretched by pulling each knee individually to her chest, wiggling her foot, and then straightening her leg out again. She flexed her torso and rolled her head around on her neck several times. She stood up and slipped on a light robe when she heard the knock on her door.

She chose the exclusive Century City Towers Hotel because of the anonymity and security it offered and easy access to the surrounding Los Angeles area. She had reserved the room for three months but hoped to be checked out sooner if everything went according to her plan. The problem was Isaac Cordell didn't appreciate what she was doing for him. By escaping, he had screwed up her original plan three ways to hell. But Janice Ryder was very good at adapting on the fly.

As long as it wasn't in the morning.

She opened the door on the security chain and peered out. Cabo, a smooth-looking gigolo type, was standing outside with a perky look on his face. He handed her the large manila envelope and stood waiting.

Janice wondered if he expected her to ask him in. If he was, he was in for a big disappointment. She didn't like the smooth and oily types. Then she realized he was expecting a tip.

"Give me a second," she said. Leaving the door open on the chain, she rummaged through her briefcase until she found two crumpled dollar bills. She took them to the door and shoved them through the opening.

"Thanks," she said as Cabo whisked the bills away.

"Is there anything else?" he said, innuendo dripping off every word.

"Sure as hell not at this time of the morning," Janice said, and slammed the door.

How she hated people who were happy in the morning.

She walked toward the bedroom looking more closely at the envelope. On first inspection, it was nothing impressive—an oversize manila envelope with her name printed in black marker, the word *urgent* printed in red marker. The envelope was blank on the back, but the locking flap had been clasped down and then taped.

Janice threw the envelope on the bed and picked up the phone receiver from the night table. She never ate after three in the afternoon, so breakfast was her big meal of the day. When room service came on the line, she ordered fruit; a mushroom, tomato, and bacon omelet; wheat toast; yogurt; and coffee. Lots of coffee.

Hanging up, she looked at the envelope again. She had no idea who it was from, but she could feel the contents were going to be dynamite. She wasn't ready yet to handle dynamite. Ryder's rule number one: Coffee first, then dynamite.

She reached for the envelope, then pulled back again empty-handed. Best to stick by the rules, she decided.

For as long as she could remember, Janice Ryder had been driven. She knew people called her as an ice queen, coldhearted, calculating, frigid, anal-retentive, and many other non-flattering terms the less-driven reserve for the more determined.

Janice agreed with most of the tags except for *frigid*. It was a word she hated, a demeaning and sexist slur. *Frigid* was a handy label her husband threw at her when she refused to engage in sexual games with groups of three or more. The term hadn't gotten him far in the divorce settlement, leaving her easily able to afford staying for three months at the Century City Towers.

She made no argument about being driven. She had specific goals to attain. She'd have plenty of time later to take things easy. Until then, easy going was not one of Janice's personality traits.

She was thirty-one before she found, and was capable of handling the case of Isaac Cordell—a man whose innocence she'd believed in absolutely and positively from the start.

Her peers said she was a fool to take the case—there was nothing in it but certain loss and a smear to her professional reputation. But Janice had five years of hard slog behind her in the public defender's office and the district attorney's office. She'd performed brilliantly but chafed at doing what others told her. When the Cordell case came along, she was in private practice and didn't care what her peers and detractors thought.

The case had been perfect for her purposes. She couldn't have set the situation up any better. And she'd achieved a brilliant opening victory when she'd won parole for her client.

The toughest thing about the whole scenario had not been the legal wrangling, which had been fairly straightforward. The biggest problem she had to overcome had been gaining the confidence of her client. Ten years in jail had not been kind. Physically he was a fine specimen of monster proportions, but survival behind jail walls had twisted and perverted his emotional and mental makeup.

After the time she'd spent with Cordell preparing his case and securing his release, Janice understood what she was releasing into the outside world—a psychotic killer. But he was also the perfect weapon for her purposes. And the cold, calculating, frigid, anal-retentive bitch didn't care. She'd deal with the consequences after her end game had been played.

Room service knocked on the door and wheeled in a cart full of food. Janice signed the check and added a generous tip. Anybody who brought her coffee deserved a generous tip.

She raided the coffeepot. Double strength as

requested, black, no sugar, piping hot. Swallow it down without it touching lips or tongue. Wait for it to hit bottom, and boom, bring on the caffeine rush.

Two cups down. Fruit and yogurt devoured. Omelet and one slice of toast half-eaten. Third cup of coffee in hand. Heart in gear. Eyes open. Time to expose the contents of the envelope.

One long red fingernail slipped under the flap and slit open the top of the envelope. She slid the contents out into her hand. One typed sheet of paper. Double-spaced, half-full. Her eyes rapidly scanned the words. She'd been right, it was dynamite. Absolute dynamite.

She turned the photograph over. It showed two women embracing in a nightclub. Janice stared at the photo dumbfounded.

She'd been wrong.

This wasn't dynamite.

This was a nuclear explosion.

CHAPTER THIRTY

Fey felt rough when she dragged herself out of Jake's bed early in the morning. It would have been nice to spend a few extra minutes next to Jake's comforting form, but Fey had an obligation to fulfill before going to the station.

Moving quietly into the kitchen, she made a cup of instant coffee and buttered two pieces of toast she burnt on purpose. The first time Jake saw Fey eat burnt toast, he couldn't believe it. His surprise did nothing to change her preference for charred bread.

After sleeping briefly in post-coital glow, Fey awoke with Miranda Goodwinter's murder haunting her like a poltergeist whirling around a belfry. The specter of Isaac Cordell spooked her.

Clearly, Cordell had been falsely convicted of murdering his wife in San Francisco. Was it possible he was innocent this time? Not innocent due to double jeopardy, but truly *innocent*—set up as a patsy again?

Fey struggled with the concept. If Cordell was innocence, who had killed Miranda Goodwinter? Was it someone connected to the first case, or someone involved with Goodwinter's more recent life?

Finishing her toast, Fey called the station. She identified herself to the watch commander and requested Colby's home address. She knew he lived with his father, who was some kind of toy maker, but she'd never paid attention to particulars—too busy sparring with Colby to care about his personal life.

Fey wasn't surprised to find Colby lived in Pacific Palisades, an exclusive community splitting its personality between cliff houses overlooking the beach and custom homes hidden within rambling hills. However, the specific address—a street considered exclusive even by Pacific Palisades standards—was unexpected.

Hanging up the phone, Fey slipped into her shoulder rig before grabbing her jacket and briefcase. She wore a light blue blouse, dark blue slacks, and matching shoes. She kept the outfit at Jake's for when she spent a night without going home.

On the short drive to Pacific Palisades, she felt her stomach fluttering with self-recrimination and anticipation. The murder case had not been the only thing plaguing her in the early hours. She was upset by her actions toward Colby at Two-Step's. Being slightly drunk and pissed off were not acceptable excuses.

Sexist actions cut both ways, and Fey cursed herself for acting in a manner she expected from Colby, but not from herself. If she had been the brunt of the joke, she would have been embarrassed beyond belief. Though she had never encouraged Colby's attentions, she should have found a better way to defuse him.

She had been mad, thinking it would be funny to give Colby some of his own back. It had been funny. At the time. In retrospect, she knew she made a bad mistake at Two-Step's and was not sure how to rectify it.

Her own insecurities also played a part. Part of her couldn't help wondering if Colby was right. Perhaps she didn't deserve—or couldn't handle—the job. Logically she knew it wasn't true, but she couldn't help beating herself up emotionally for having screwed up.

She turned off Pacific Coast Highway and wound her way along the hilly residential streets of Pacific Palisades. Parking outside the address scribbled in her notebook, she was taken aback by the imposing residential structure. She checked the street address again. It was correct.

The house was huge, well into the several million-dollar-plus range. Fey considered Colby might be on the take because of his flashy clothes and flashy car, but the type of corruption required for this level of wealth was reserved for politicians. Colby's father's toys must bring in a lot of dollars.

Looking closer, Fey realized the house showed signs of neglect. The front grass and garden were tidy, but not well-tended. The used brick exterior had weathered well, but the shingled roof sagged slightly in need of replacement. The effect was of an ancient, once rich, dowager forced to keep up appearances on a fixed income.

Fey didn't see Colby's car, but there was a long driveway running out of view along the side of the house. She knocked at the imposing front door. Most cops always knock. In a police academy officer safety class, rookies were told about an east coast cop who'd been blown up when he pushed a doorbell buzzer.

The warning always left an impression. It didn't matter no other cops had been killed by an exploding doorbell. One cop dying horribly made every cop who heard the story wary of pressing doorbells. There were so few dangers cops could control, but not pressing doorbells had the same effect of not stepping on sidewalk cracks or walking under ladders on Friday the thirteenth.

When there was no answer to her knock, Fey gathered her courage and played Russian roulette with the doorbell. After a second, the intercom by her elbow crackled with a male voice.

"Hello. Who is it please?"

The voice wasn't Colby's. The butler maybe? Many houses in the area supported maids.

"My name is Fey Croaker. I'm looking for Colby... er...Alan." Colby's first name tasted strange in Fey's mouth.

She didn't want to face this chore, but it was necessary. She was Colby's supervisor. After her actions the previous evening at Two-Step Tilly's, it was her responsibility to address the situation.

"Come on through the house to the workroom in back," the voice from the intercom directed.

An electronic buzz swung the front door open. Fey stepped into a foyer where she had the choice of stairway or hallway. Fey looked up the stairway, but the vast reaches of the second story remained hidden.

The hallway led Fey through living room and formal dining area to a large family room opening on one end to a bright kitchen. The furnishings and decorations were expensive, but old-fashioned—bought years before and never replaced. The color scheme was deep forest greens, reds, and blacks with a touch of gold.

There was a huge sliding glass door giving access to an overgrown garden with a small carriage house standing in the center. The carriage house was the same used brick style as the main house. It had probably been servants' quarters at some time in the long-ago past.

A man waved at Fey from the door to the smaller building. Fey followed a path of wandering stepping-stones through the garden to reach him.

"Hello," the man said. "I'm Arthur Colby, Alan's father." He held out his hand, and Fey shook it. His fingers were strong and rough. "Come in, please," he said, stepping back and ushering Fey into his workshop. "I'm putting the final touches on a new toy design."

Fey looked around in wonder and delight. Everywhere, shelves held beautifully carved and chiseled wooden toys.

"The Square Head toys," she said with delight.

"Humble, but mine own," Arthur Colby said, reveling in Fey's recognition of his work. "My father invented the originals, and I have carried on the tradition."

"I always wanted them as a child, but they were so expensive."

A cloud came over Arthur Colby's face. "The choice of the company who purchased the designs. If it were up to me, I would give them all away—and I do, to children's hospitals and other charities."

"I'm sorry," Fey said, embarrassed. "I didn't mean to imply..."

"Of course, you didn't." Arthur Colby waved away her protests and smiled again. "The toys are expensive. So expensive they priced themselves out of the market. The company who mass-produced the toys discontinued the line five years ago. They couldn't compete with the Japanese."

"I thought you said you were finishing a new design?"

"Business setbacks only curtail sales. They can't stifle the creative spirit. This world around you was created from the residuals on the designs. Now there are no residuals, but there are still collectors willing to pay for individual items of quality work." He moved past Fey. "Come look at this," he said, leading her to a large workbench.

"It's beautiful!" Fey said.

On the workbench—surrounded by wood chisels and chips—was a hand-carved fire engine made completely from different-shaped wood blocks. There were several tiny firemen, their heads proportional square blocks, placed strategically along the length of the toy. The detailing on the fire engine was meticulous, bearing all the signs of a master craftsman.

"This isn't a toy," Fey said. "It's a work of art."

Arthur Colby glowed with the praise. "Thank you. It is too bad more people don't have your appreciation."

Fey looked around at the similar toys on shelves around the room. There were cars and buildings and work machines and houses and schools—all populated by the square-headed people from which the toys took their name.

She gave a slight gasp as she spotted one toy in particular. "The merry-go-round!" She took a step toward the toy, reaching out to push a square-headed horse. The horse and its compatriots obligingly spun silently around.

"The origin of the line. Designed by my father."

"It was always my favorite. I loved horses as a child. Still do. I remember seeing this in a Sears Christmas catalog. I was twelve or thirteen." She gave a sad laugh. "I didn't believe in Santa Claus, but I was willing to believe again if this turned up under my tree. I wished on stars. I said my prayers. I crossed my fingers..."

"And?" Arthur Colby asked gently, after a few seconds of silence.

Fey snapped out of her reverie. "And nothing. Only Democrats believe in Santa Claus." She took a deep breath. "Is Alan here?"

"I'm sorry. He left early this morning."

Fey was puzzled. "Then why..."

"Why did I have you come in?"

"Yes."

"An old man's foolishness. I've heard so much about you from Alan. I wanted to meet you."

Fey gave Arthur Colby an appraising glance. He was not such an *old man*. Somewhere in his late fifties, he had a thick head of salt-and-pepper hair. It was still easy to see where Colby had inherited his movie-star looks. Arthur Colby's features were matured, but he still cut a fine figure.

"I'm sure not much of what Alan told you about me was good."

Arthur Colby bestowed the same brilliantly smile possessed by his son. In the father, however, the smile came without his son's trademark leer. He flapped his hands expressively. "With Alan you have to listen beyond his words. He is full of untested confidence. There isn't much room left for common sense."

Fey figured young Colby was full of something other than untested confidence. Arthur Colby seemed to sense what she was thinking. He held up a hand as if to stop Fey's train of thought.

"Any extra emotional room Alan has is filled with anger." Arthur Colby shrugged. "He would never agree, but you are good for him. You keep him in line. Something, I was regrettably too busy to do when he was a child. Now it is far too late."

"What about his mother?" Fey asked, wondering at why she cared.

"She died in childbirth—part of the reason for Alan's internal angers. He has never forgiven her for abandoning him."

"It doesn't sound as if she had a choice."

Arthur Colby shrugged again. "It is easier to blame someone else for our miseries than to accept and change our own shortcomings. Alan has suffered other letdowns. The women in his life have been far from consistent."

"Meaning?"

"After his mother died, his maternal grandmother blamed Alan for her death. She blamed me for impregnating her, and Alan for being born. She never relented in her verbal attacks even though she insisted on seeing Alan. She went to court and obtained visitation rights. This went on for several years until her mental abuse of Alan became physical and I was able to break the court order."

Fey knew about abuse. "What about his other grandmother?"

"My mother, Lila, was a good woman. My father died several years before Alan was born. When Anna, my wife, died, Lila moved in here. She cared for Alan as her own, and he loved her dearly. However, when the battles with my mother-in-law were at their worst, Lila was killed by a hit-and-run driver. Alan was six. Lila's death devastated him. Every woman ended up terrorizing or abandoning him."

"Growing up is tough," Fey said. The words came out sounding more flippant than intended. Growing up was hard. She'd experience it firsthand.

"Do you know about Alan's wife?" Arthur asked, choosing to ignore Fey's tone.

Fey looked startled. "I didn't know he was married."

"Widowed," Arthur Colby clarified. "She committed suicide a year after their marriage when she discovered she couldn't conceive."

Fey felt shell-shocked. "Another form of perceived abandonment," she said.

Arthur Colby nodded. "Alan was able to blame yet another woman for the disappointments in his life."

Fey wasn't sure she wanted this inside scoop on Colby's background. She might begin feeling sorry for him.

There was a short silence as Fey assimilated the information. Colby needed some couch sessions with a competent shrink. Fey believed blaming others for your own misfortunes was an easy cop-out.

Her brother, Tommy, had taught her a lot about the terrors of misplaced blame. Even if blame was appropriate, it never did any good. She could blame her father for the rotten things in her life, but she could only blame herself if she couldn't get beyond them. Laying blame served no purpose except to provoke the inner devils of anger and hate.

Arthur Colby moved closer to Fey. "Alan tells me you are bound and determined to catch the person who murdered the Goodwinter woman." The change of subject was abrupt.

Fey was surprised. "I'll catch him."

"One way or the other?" Arthur Colby reached out casually and touched the square-headed carousel horses on the shelf, making them turn again.

"One way or the other," Fey agreed. "I can't afford to lose this one."

"You sound determined."

Fey sensed something in Arthur Colby's voice. "Do you mean I sound determined for a girl?" she asked.

Arthur Colby's eyes widened. "No. I mean you sound determined for a detective. I am my son's father, not his keeper."

"The apple doesn't usually fall far from the tree."

"Even the seed from a sweet tree can bear bitter fruit."

A voice suddenly intruded from the workshop entry. "Isn't this cozy?"

Fey and Arthur turned to see Alan Colby leaning against the doorframe with a sardonic grin slapped across his face.

CHAPTER THIRTY-ONE

When Jake Travers entered the Santa Monica district attorney's offices in the morning, he also sensed something was wrong.

"Good morning, Mr. Travers," the receptionist said. "Mr. Vanderwald is waiting in your office. He wanted to see you immediately."

The last thing Jake needed was a formal confrontation with his boss. The two men had never been politically aligned, but their relationship had become more strained since Jake became a threat to replace Vanderwald in the next election. It was rare for Vanderwald to appear at the outlying Santa Monica prosecutor's office. If the two men needed contact, it was accomplished through terse phone conversations, or by Jake traveling to Vanderwald's downtown power base.

"Thanks, Doris," Jake told the receptionist. He reversed his field and moved back toward the entrance. "I'll be right there." He needed a few moments to figure out what Vanderwald's presence foreboded.

"But, Mr. Travers." Doris tried to stop him from leaving. "Mr. Vanderwald said he wants to see you immediately."

"Then let's make out I haven't walked in yet."

"Let's not," said a deep male voice from the hallway leading to Jake's office. Simon Vanderwald stepped into sight, a black frown thundering across his forehead. His unsmiling face was round-cheeked from too much rich food and too many lunchtime martinis. Below his face the stocky body had once earned him honors as a Notre Dame lineman. Now, it was pear-shaped and soft. He was dressed in a dark gray suit, a starched white shirt, red power tie, and highly polished slip-ons with tassels. "What time is this to be getting into the office?" he demanded.

Jake glanced at his watch. It was five minutes before his usual eight o'clock start time, but he realized there was no acceptable answer to give to the aggressive question. It didn't matter Jake rarely left the office before six or seven at night. Vanderwald was never in his downtown office before ten, took a two hour lunch, often went home early, and played golf every Friday. But nothing was going to satisfy Vanderwald in his current mood.

"Get in here," Vanderwald said, turning on his heel and disappearing down the hallway again.

Jake looked over at the receptionist. She was discreetly shuffling papers. Steeling himself for the ordeal ahead, Jake followed in the direction of Vanderwald's echoing footsteps.

As he entered his office, Jake saw Vanderwald had taken center stage by sitting in the black leather chair behind Jake's large rosewood desk. Knowing Vanderwald, Jake had anticipated this move and was determined not to be put off by its pettiness. It was the person sitting in one of the two comfortable visitors' chairs who threw Jake off his stride. Janice Ryder was the last person he had expected to see this morning.

Jake set his briefcase in the middle of his desktop then walked behind where Vanderwald was sitting. He turned and rested his butt on a low bookshelf below the window, which dominated the main wall of the office. The move was calculated to not only usurp Vanderwald, but also to force him to swivel around to face Jake. It also served to gain extra distance from Janice Ryder—whom Jake considered the biggest threat in the room.

"What's this about?" he asked aggressively, dispensing with any pleasantries. There were no points to be won through politeness.

"I'll cut to the point," Vanderwald said, swiveling in the high-backed leather chair to face his subordinate. He was playing with a letter opener he had picked up from the top of the desk. He smirked when he saw the way Jake had positioned himself with the light behind him.

"Good of you, Simon," Jake said. Two could play at the condescending first-name-usage game.

Vanderwald gave him a dirty look. "Ms. Ryder contacted me on behalf of her client Isaac Cordell."

Jake looked at Janice. "Is he ready to turn himself in?"

"And take a chance on a justice system which has already wrongfully deprived him of ten years of his life, Mr. Travers?" Janice raised a perfectly plucked eyebrow. "I don't think so." She wore a sleeveless, umber-colored blouse, which set off the creamy texture of her skin. Below the blouse was a subdued yellow suede skirt short enough to make the best of her trim legs, and yellow high heels. Pearls at neck, wrist, and ears were the only accents to her outfit.

A viper in disguise, Jake thought. He knew an ax was about to fall.

"This meeting isn't directly related to Mr. Cordell's

status as a fugitive," Vanderwald stated flatly, trying to regain the upper hand in the situation. "This is about unethical behavior on the part of this office—more specifically on your part—possibly leading to the dismissal of this case and opening this office to civil prosecution."

"Explain," Jake said, rising to the bait and partially losing his temper.

"Ms. Ryder has presented me with a writ from a San Francisco judge—with jurisdiction over the original false conviction of Mr. Cordell—clearing his parole status."

"Wait..." Jake said.

"We're done waiting, Mr. Travers," Janice Ryder interrupted. She stood up and walked to the front of the rosewood desk. She spread her hands along the front edge and leaned forward. Out of the corner of his eye, Jake saw Vanderwald lean forward unobtrusively to look down the front scoop of the umber blouse.

"My client is obviously not guilty of the initial charge of murder from ten years ago. He should never have been sent to prison. Whether you agree or not, he should never have been on parole in the first place. Therefore, the parole search was invalid. The weapon seized during the illegal search is inadmissible in court."

"The judge will make a ruling at the prelim."

"No, he won't," said Vanderwald, cutting in sharply. "The question should have been evaluated by this office before charges were formally filed."

Jake jumped to defend his position. "We have an eyewitness who places Cordell at the scene, and we've got more than enough motive."

Fey had broken the bad news about Kathleen Bridges' identification, but he was looking for any port in a storm. It turned out to be a hazardous harbor.

"You are aware, counselor, your eyewitness isn't worth pig swill," Janice Ryder said. "If you put a feeble old lady on the stand, I'll rip her to pieces. Motive by itself counts for less than nothing."

Jake shifted his gaze from Janice to Vanderwald. If he hoped to find backing, he was disappointed.

Vanderwald gave him an ice-cold stare. "This is poor showing, Jake. If you hope to win the next election, you'll need to exercise better case judgment."

There it was, Jake thought sadly. Out in the open. Jake hadn't even declared as a candidate yet, but Vanderwald was already moving to shut him down. It was clear how Vanderwald survived in office term after term. This scenario had nothing to do with the case against Cordell being good or bad. It was about declaring political war.

Vanderwald didn't care about Cordell's guilt or innocence. With its constitutional arguments concerning double jeopardy, the case was far from an out-and-out winner. It was a bad risk. The press would have a feeding frenzy, making Jake's position like sitting on a straight razor—either way he slid, he'd bleed.

The case wasn't worth diddly to Vanderwald except for use as political ammunition—giving Jake, as the deputy DA who filed the case, a big fat black eye.

To milk the political advantage, Vanderwald could hold a press conference to stroke every liberal bleeding heart in the city. At the same time making Jake look unprofessional and vindictive.

Jake felt the weight of the process on his shoulders. Welcome to the grand old American game of political infighting and mudslinging. He'd played his share of office politics to gain his appointment as the head filing DA under Vanderwald, but the experience was nothing compared to what was to come.

"Are you telling me you're going to overturn my filing on this case?" Jake asked Vanderwald.

Vanderwald threw out an arm expansively. "There is

no case. Come up with admissible evidence against Cordell and you can file any charges you want. Until then, this office must remain impartial. You can't allow yourself to become personally involved. Your whole career at the bar could be in jeopardy."

"How am I going to be disbarred over filing a border-line case?"

Vanderwald looked smug. "The filing alone won't get you disbarred."

"What then?" Jake glanced at Janice Ryder. In a flash of insight, he saw what was coming before the words fell from Vanderwald's mouth.

"If it became public knowledge you were screwing the investigating officer in this case—showing your interest in filing and prosecuting Cordell is a personal vendetta—you would find yourself dismissed from this office, and perhaps even disbarred if someone pushed the point."

"Personal vendetta," Jake exploded. "You're talking a bunch of unmitigated crap."

"I know it and you know it," Vanderwald agreed. "But the press would love it, and they would tear you apart."

Jake pushed himself up from the bookcase and looked angrily across the desk at Janice Ryder. "Was it you who made up this stuff about me sleeping with the investigating detective?"

"Don't waste breath denying the allegation. I have in my possession a list of police officers, detectives, and DAs who are apparently aware of your relationship with Detective Croaker. I hope you won't make it necessary for me to take depositions from all of them."

Jake felt the bile in his stomach churn. "All right," he said. "I'll play along for a minute. But tell me why Fey and I would involve ourselves in a conspiracy to frame Isaac Cordell?"

"Because he's convenient."

"What?" Jake shook his head in bafflement.

"There are other dynamics occurring you are unaware of, counselor," Janice told him.

"Enlighten me."

Janice paused a beat before speaking. "Your lover may be directly involved in this case."

"Of course, she is," Jake said, not bothering any longer to deny his relationship with Fey. "She's the investigating officer."

"I'm not talking about her involvement as a detective. I'm talking about her involvement as a suspect."

Jake felt as if his legs were going to go out from under him. He leaned back against the bookcase again.

Janice Ryder placed a photo facedown next to Jake's briefcase. It was a copy of the one in the envelope delivered to her earlier in the morning. She continued to stare at Jake, but she spoke to Vanderwald. "Can I assume the warrant for my client's arrest will be withdrawn?"

"Immediately," Vanderwald replied with a smooth smile.

Jake reached forward and picked up the photograph. "What about the escape charges and the assault against Fey?" he asked before turning the photo over.

"Look at the photograph. I think you'll agree those charges are moot," Vanderwald told him.

Jake turned the photo over. He had trouble focusing, but the images were clear.

Janice Ryder picked up her briefcase and turned to leave the office. "Thank you for your cooperation, Mr. Vanderwald. I hope you will keep me abreast of developments."

"Certainly."

"Good-bye, counselor. I'm sorry I had to be the bearer of bad news."

Jake didn't reply. Janice opened the door to the office and exited gracefully, a soft scent remaining in her wake.

Vanderwald stood up and placed the letter opener on the desk. Jake hadn't moved. He was still staring at the photo.

"I'd dump the bimbo quick if I were you," Vanderwald said. "I don't understand what you see in her anyway. I know some men prefer women who are built for comfort instead of speed, but a couple more years and her body will be beyond even the comfort zone."

Jake clenched his jaws, useless anger threatening to explode from his interior.

Vanderwald walked to the open door and turned back to face Jake. "By the way, there's a five-hundred-dollar-a-plate dinner coming up next week to benefit my campaign fund. I'll expect to see you there."

He closed the door gently as he left.

CHAPTER THIRTY-TWO

The morning had been busy for Fey. The overnight reports were unusually heavy, and there were two bodies in custody. Hatch was up for handling the arrestees and took off for the city attorney's office to get quick filings. When Colby arrived at his desk, he found three ADW reports and an attempted kidnapping case waiting. Fey had been dragged into a dispute involving rival Gypsy palm readers trying to kill each other because—according to unwritten Gypsy law—their businesses had been set up too close together.

Over the years, Fey had become the unofficial Gypsy detective in West L.A. It wasn't a role she cherished, but since she knew more about the strange characters—who run their lives by a set of rules far outside those of normal society—than anyone else in the division, it was a role with which she was increasingly tasked.

Handling Gypsy disputes successfully was a matter of respect. Fey knew if she tried to impose traditional law enforcement remedies on the situation, things would only get worse. However, she made a couple of discreet phone calls to private numbers, and within an hour she was meeting with the rival palm-reading families and the matriarch of the local Gypsy clan.

After explaining the situation to the matriarch, Fey left the Gypsies alone behind the closed door of Mike Cahill's office with the blinds drawn. Cahill couldn't stand Gypsies and would have gone crazy had he known Fey was leaving a half dozen of them alone in his office. But as Cahill was out of the station at a department bureau meeting, Fey figured what he didn't know wouldn't hurt him.

Fifteen minutes later, the Gypsy matriarch quietly led everyone out of the office. With much smiling and gesturing, all charges and countercharges were dropped, and everyone went happily about their business. Everyone except for Mike Cahill, who, returning to his office later in the morning, couldn't figure out what happened to the antique letter opener he kept on his desk.

Fey knew the situation had only been resolved as far as the police were concerned. The actual dispute would be settled later under Gypsy law in more private surroundings. Fey's hope was if it ended in a blood feud, the carnage would be kept off her patch.

Before lunch, Monk Lawson bounded into the office and approached Fey. She had let him escape the dint of daily reports because she wanted him to chase down any information he could find on Janice Ryder. Over coffee, they sat down together to go over what he'd gathered.

"There wasn't a whole lot I could come up with in a hurry," Monk told her. "But I was able to come up with some basics."

"Always a good place to start," said Fey. "If anything clicks, we can follow up further."

Monk produced a stack of index cards filled with neat, precise handwriting.

"Since Ryder is a lawyer, I started looking for information via the law library. I checked in *Martindale Hubble*—"

"Martindale who?"

Monk looked up from his notes, distracted for a second.

"It's the law profession's version of Who's Who."

"Okay," Fey said, satisfied.

Monk looked back at his notes. "Ryder's listing showed she entered law school through Berkeley's Boal Hall in nineteen-eighty-two."

"Ended up at the top of her class, I expect," Fey put in semi sarcastically.

"How did you guess?" Monk asked in the same tone. "She was editor of the law review from eighty-three to eighty-four and graduated with the Order of the COIF in late eighty-four."

"COIF is a fancy way of saying summa cum laude?"

"Yeah. She was real smart. Took the bar in eighty-five and passed the first time."

"What year was Cordell originally convicted for murdering his wife?" Fey asked.

Monk shuffled through the papers on his desk before pulling one out and consulting it. "The latter part of nine-teen-eighty-two."

"When little Miss Brains started law school."

"You think there's a connection?"

Fey shrugged. "It's hard to tell. What else do you have?"

Monk went back to his notes. "Taking on Cordell's case and getting him paroled was a big deal. There had to be coverage."

"And?"

"And after exhaustive research—"

"I get the point," Fey said. "My heart bleeds. What

did you do? Have the law library librarian find the stuff? Quit messing around and spell it out."

Monk only looked slightly chastened. "A month ago, there was an in-depth profile of Ryder in *The Recorder*—the daily legal newspaper for the Bay area."

"Compiled as a result of her winning parole for Cordell?"

"Yeah. MacGregor, the cop you talked to in San Francisco, was right. Cordell's case was high profile in Bay area society ten years ago, but interest dwindled until Ryder began fighting to get him paroled. Cordell had been a model citizen up until he supposedly murdered his wife, but he had not done his prison time quietly. He'd twice been turned down for parole due to the violent nature of his behavior inside. He was suspected in two prison stabbings and a long list of minor offenses. When Ryder finally convinced the parole board to spring Cordell, the prison hierarchy must have breathed a sigh of relief."

"Did the article cover the motives behind Ryder taking on Cordell as a cause?"

"Not much. She'd done a lot of *pro bono* work in private practice, and a reputation as a liberal cause carrier."

"I can't think of anything the world needs more."

"She did pay her dues on the way up. After she passed the bar, she spent two years with the public defender's office then jumped over to the DA's office for another two years."

"What do you think made her change colors?"

"I'd say a bad marriage."

"What? Miss Brains isn't completely perfect?"

Monk chuckled. "Make you feel better?"

Fey shrugged. "Who'd she marry?"

Monk went back to his notes. "A hotshot private lawyer named Howard Ryder. Corporate type. Entertainment law, contracts, civil stuff. They were married shortly after she joined the PD's office. They lasted a year together. His profile indicates he had big bucks but didn't want to spend them on his wife's liberal causes."

"I bet she took him for a bundle when they split."

"Are you talking from experience?"

Fey's face clouded. "Don't start. I get enough crap from Colby. I don't need you chipping in."

"Sorry. Didn't know it was a hot button."

"Now you do. Who was this bimbo before she married a bank?"

"You mean her maiden name?"

"Yeah. Where did she come from?"

Monk flipped through his notes. "It's mostly sob-story stuff. Her mother abandoned her when she was eight. Left her in Daddy's care and ran off with the mailman or someone similar."

"Rough."

"Then things got worse."

"Make me cry," Fey said.

"When Janice was eleven, Daddy married again. This time to a woman named Madeline Walsh."

Fey felt the hairs on the back of her neck prickle.

"Two years later," Monk continued, oblivious to the change in Fey's attention focus, "daddy died in a car crash, and wicked step-mommy split with the insurance money, leaving Janice to be brought up by her grandparents—"

Fey leapt to her feet. She grabbed Monk's notes and started scanning them. "Where do you have her maiden name written?"

Monk reached for the cards. Fey thrust them back at him.

"Come on. Come on."

Monk was getting flustered. "Er...Here it is. Fletcher. Her maiden name is Fletcher."

"You're making my head hurt," Fey said, flopping back in her chair. She stared into space, her mind whirling.

"What? I don't get the connection."

Fey was still looking thoughtful. "The conniving spawn sprung Cordell from jail and pointed him like a gun at our victim."

"What are you talking about?"

Fey focused her eyes on Monk. "Yesterday at the bank, Colby and I talked to an IRS agent named Craven. He's been tracking our victim for years. According to Craven, she was a black widow killer who drained her mates financially before bumping them off for the insurance money."

"Okay. So?"

"One of the identities Craven uncovered for our victim was Madeline Fletcher—a woman who took off with an insurance policy after her husband died in a car crash. Craven told us she left a penniless thirteen-year-old stepdaughter behind to be raised by grandparents."

"And you think—"

Fey leaned forward. "I don't know how she managed to track her stepmother through all her various identities, but I have no doubt she either sprung Cordell and pointed him right at the woman, or she killed the victim herself and set Cordell up for the rap again."

Monk nodded. "After she set him up, she planned to use this double jeopardy hocus-pocus and get him off."

"It needs hammering out, but the scenario fits," Fey said. Her heart was racing at the same pace as her brain.

She needed time to bring the situation into perspective, but she wasn't going to get it. The lightning storm started at Jake Travers's office was about to splatter all over her.

Earlier, Fey had noticed two suit-and-tie types go into a closed-door session with Mike Cahill. She'd recognized one of the visitors as an Internal Affairs investigator, but she'd been too busy to think much about it. Even when Cahill interrupted her thought process and motioned for her to join him, Fey's first thoughts were directed toward which of the other detectives on the homicide unit might be the focus of IA's attentions.

The instant she entered Cahill's office however, she felt the atmosphere close around her like an ice-cold fog. When Cahill closed the miniblinds covering the windows into the squad bay, she knew there was big trouble brewing.

One of the IA investigators stood up. "Detective Croaker, I'm Lieutenant Baxter, and this is Sergeant Hilton." He indicated the younger man next to him, who hadn't bothered to stand. "We're with Internal Affairs." His last pronouncement had been merely routine. IA cops wore an air of paranoia as a protective cloak. If possible, they dressed even more conservatively than cops who carried rank. No striped or colored shirts. No wildly patterned ties. No pointed shoes or boots. No sport jackets. Only dark blue, single-breasted suits with white shirts, dark ties, and polished wing tips.

"We've met before," Fey said to Baxter. When he didn't acknowledge her, she switched her gaze to Cahill. He was fiddling with something on his desk and refused to meet her eyes.

Oh, no, she thought. *We've got big trouble right here in River City.* She couldn't understand why one of Colby's favorite sayings popped into her mind, but she couldn't help thinking it was appropriate.

"What can I do for you?" she asked. Her voice was strong, belying the tremors in her knees.

"Have a seat." This came from Hilton, the younger IA officer. He had short-cropped dark hair, bushy eyebrows growing together across the bridge of his crooked nose, and an unsmiling mouth with thin lips. Heavy eyelids gave him a hooded look, as if he were a vulture waiting for something to die.

Fey sat, but kept her mouth shut. She realized she was taking the first steps into an uncharted minefield. This was IA's show. She would gain nothing by charging ahead.

"Are you currently in charge of investigating the murder of Miranda Goodwinter?"

Fey looked at the two oversized black briefcases on the conference table in front of the IA investigators.

"Is this interview being taped?" she asked.

Hilton scowled and started to say something, but Baxter beat him to the punch. "Yes," he said calmly. Baxter's sun-seamed face held the weary wisdom of knowing too many dirty cops. Fey knew his reputation. Most cops bucking for promotion put in an eighteen-month tour with Internal Affairs and then get out. Investigating dirty cops is not a job for a weak stomach or a thin skin. Baxter had been with IA for fifteen years. He was a crusader. He was also fair—a tough reputation to earn in IA.

The *them against us* syndrome cops developed was magnified a thousand times when you worked IA. Nobody trusts an IA investigator. Even clean cops can't walk through the sewer of a big city and not have crap rub off.

If IA targets you, it doesn't matter how good a cop you are, they'll find something. If a cop couldn't be had for something, then he or she wasn't doing the job properly.

Citizens' complaints, *beefs* as they were called, were part of a cop's everyday life. Even if a cop did everything properly, there were people who made complaints—suspects with a grudge; victims who did not get everything they wanted; citizens who felt they were unfairly ticketed because *nobody ever stops for that stop sign*; witnesses to an arrest who had no idea what they were seeing but felt a cop had been far too harsh on the nice man who had tried to kill the cop's partner. All of them made life rough for cops through the offices of Internal Affairs.

There were legitimate complaints. Cops on the take; illegal use of force; cops taking or selling drugs; cops involved with gambling and prostitution; and many other variations. The real heavy-duty stuff came in the form of cops who became assassins for hire; organized cop burglary rings taking down thousands of dollars a week; political corruption; protection rackets; and a myriad of other stomach-turning activities besmirching the badge, making Internal Affairs a necessary evil.

Fey had been under the microscope several times, but all charges had been cleared as *unfounded*. It had been a number of years since her last beef, however, and Fey did not feel like going through the routine again without a fight.

Most good cops had a tendency to go overboard when trying to clear themselves with Internal Affairs, allowing their rights as a citizen and a police officer to be trampled. Fey had been around too long to not protect herself. She wanted to know what was going on, and she wanted to know now.

"What are the charges against me?"

"Nobody has said anything about charges, Fey," Mike Cahill spoke up.

Fey immediately shot him down in flames. "These guys aren't here to interview me for officer of the month." She looked back at Baxter. "Well?"

Baxter tried a smile, but it didn't seem to fit on his face. "There are no formal charges. We are simply investigating a conflict-of-interest allegation in your investigation of the Miranda Goodwinter case."

"There is no such thing as an informal Internal Affairs investigation," Fey said. "I have no idea what you're talking about, but I'm not saying anything until you advise me of my rights, and I get defense rep."

"Detective Croaker, there's no need for this," Baxter told her.

"The hell there isn't," Fey replied evenly. "Don't give me this father figure, good guy crap. Either you let me get a defense rep and then read me my rights, or I'm walking."

"Listen, lady." Hilton half rose out of his chair, but Baxter put a restraining hand on him.

"Can it, sonny," Fey told him. "Mind your elders or we'll send you out onto the freeway to play with the traffic."

Hilton's face turned bright red, but he sat down.

"Get yourself a rep," Baxter said.

Fey stood up and opened the door to the office. She scanned the squad bay until she spotted Nate Collins. Like Fey, he was a detective supervisor, but he was also a lawyer. "Nate," Fey called out. "I need you."

Every cop was entitled to have a defense representative present when being interviewed by Internal Affairs. A defense rep was a fellow officer, usually with advanced legal skills, who would sit in on the interview to advise the cop who was being questioned.

Collins looked questioningly from where he was sitting at his desk. When he saw the expression on Fey's face, he instantly knew what was going on. He'd been a defense rep enough times to recognize a cop in trouble.

"What's up?" he asked when he reached Fey.

"I don't know yet, but there's a couple of IA butt hairs who are going to railroad me given a chance. I need you to sit in as my defense rep."

"You got it," Collins said. He followed Fey back into the office.

When everyone was settled, Fey asked the recorder briefcases be opened so she could be sure they were working. Baxter sighed heavily but complied.

"Satisfied?" he asked.

"Hardly," Fey said. "As I told you, I have no idea what you want to talk to me about, but I know not to give Internal Affairs an even break. It's nothing personal, understand."

This time Baxter simply grunted.

"If there's any chance criminal charges may result from this interview, you need to read Detective Croaker her Miranda admonition," Collins spoke up for the first time.

Baxter looked Collins over calmly. "Hilton," he said to his partner, while still maintaining eye contact with Collins.

The younger IA investigator pulled a small officer's notebook from his pocket and read verbatim from the Miranda admonition printed on the cover. He knew the admonition by heart, but should he ever be required to testify, there could be no technicality problem if he could say he read the rights directly from the card.

"You have the right to remain silent," his voice droned. "If you give up the right to remain silent, anything you say can and will be used against you in a court of law. You have the right to an attorney. If you so desire and cannot afford one, an attorney will be appointed for you without charge." He paused for a second and looked up from the card. Everyone in the room remained silent.

"Do you understand these rights?" he asked.

Fey's reply was a simple, "Yes."

"Do you wish to give up your right to remain silent?"

"No."

"Do you wish to give up your right to have an attorney present during questioning?"

"No."

Hilton sat back as if he were a well-trained puppy, and Baxter took over the interview again.

"As you have refused to waive your constitutional rights—" Baxter was as formal in his speech as Hilton had been in reading the rights "—I must advise you to answer our questions for administrative purposes only."

"Are you ordering me to answer your questions?" Fey asked, playing her part in the game of well-rehearsed Q and A.

"Yes."

"By whose authority are you ordering me?"

"By the authority of the Chief of Police of the Los Angeles Police Department. I must also advise you any refusal on your part to answer our questions may result in departmental charges being brought against you for insubordination."

"I will answer your questions as ordered," Fey said. "But only for the purposes of this departmental investigation. In no way should my answering of these questions be construed as a voluntary waiving of my Miranda rights." She leaned forward to check the briefcase recorders were still working. She then turned toward

Collins, who was sitting next to her. "Okay?" she asked him.

"Letter-perfect," he replied, indicating Fey had protected herself correctly.

Fey sat back and tried to relax the stiffness in her neck. "The ball's in your court," she said to Baxter.

"What was your relationship with Miranda Goodwinter?"

Fey opened her mouth to speak, but Nate Collins put his hand on her arm to stop her. "Hold on," he said. "Bad question. It's like asking, *have you stopped beating your wife?* You're making the assumption Detective Croaker had a relationship with this Miranda Goodwinter."

Baxter's expression soured. "Let me rephrase. Detective Croaker, have you at any time had a relationship with Miranda Goodwinter?"

Fey shook her head. "You've sent your dog up a bad trail. Beyond investigating her murder, I have never had any sort of relationship with Miranda Goodwinter."

Baxter took Fey's declaration in stride. "You never had contact with Miranda Goodwinter prior to the beginning of this investigation?"

Fey nodded. "The first time I saw the woman, her blood was leaking all over the floor."

"Real sensitive," Hilton chipped in.

"Comes with the territory. You'll catch on after a while."

"Fey." Nate put a restraining hand back on her arm.

"This is crap, Nate," Fey said to him. She turned back to Baxter. "Make your point."

With a deliberate movement, Baxter removed a photograph from his jacket. It was a duplicate of the photo Janice Ryder produced in Vanderwald's office earlier.

Baxter held the photo toward Fey, but Nate reached out and took it.

"If what you are telling us is true, Detective Croaker, how do you explain this photo?"

Nate took a quick glance at the print and handed it to Fey.

Fey's hands were trembling slightly as she took it. Her eyes glanced down. It was a photo of two women with their arms around each other in a nightclub setting. They were both smiling.

One of the women was Miranda Goodwinter.

The other was Fey.

CHAPTER THIRTY-THREE

Fey placed the bottle of vodka on the bar as soon as she'd arrived home. She'd been sitting and staring at it for the past hour without cracking the seal. Her mind was running on overload—spinning and spinning, but unable to process. Anger and despair buzzed through her in alternating fits and starts. Absently she stroked Brentwood's coat as the cat nestled in her lap.

Finally, rousing herself from the depths of the recliner, she placed the complaining cat on the floor and walked to the bar. She threw ice in a glass, opened the vodka, and poured a healthy measure over the cubes.

She brought the glass to her lips and gulped. The alcohol tasted foul but succeeded in washing away the traces of bile regurgitating from her stomach. The back of her throat felt raw when the alcohol hit, making her wince. After the one swallow, she banged the glass down so hard two ice cubes bounced out and slithered away.

"Arrrrrrg," she screamed inarticulately, knocking the glass flying with a sweep of her hand. Brentwood screeched and flew out of the room almost without touching the ground. Still standing, Fey folded her arms on the bar, dropped her head, and began to sob.

Twenty-two years on this thankless job, she thought, *and it goes to hell in one afternoon.* She knew she was being maudlin, but she believed she'd earned the right.

The rest of the interview with Internal Affairs had been a nightmare. Once the photograph was revealed, the kid gloves came off and the bloodbath started.

"How long did you know Miranda Goodwinter before she was murdered?"

"I didn't know her. I never met the woman when she was alive."

"What was your relationship with Goodwinter?" Hilton barked. "Were you lovers?"

"No!"

"Are you a lesbian, Detective Croaker?"

"Not pertinent." Fey felt fire burning in her cheeks.

"Then you admit you are a lesbian?"

"I'm admitting nothing."

Hilton kept up his barrage. "If you and Miranda Goodwinter weren't lovers, what were you? Good friends?"

"We weren't anything," Fey said wearily. "I've told you repeatedly, I didn't know the woman existed until I was assigned to investigate her murder."

"A murder you committed because she left you for another woman."

"Unbelievable," Fey retorted angrily.

"Okay," Hilton said congenially. "She left you for a man instead. Someone who had the equipment to take care of her needs."

Fey shook her head. "You're insane. What about all the history on Goodwinter dug up by the IRS?"

"What about it?" Hilton asked. "Maybe you're in on the scheme as well. There's still the matter of two million dollars in bearer bonds taking a walk. There's a good motive. Perhaps we'll find them when the search of your house is completed."

"My house—" Fey felt the shock reach to her core.

"As we speak, a search warrant is being served on your residence. Don't worry, it's all nice and legal. A copy of the warrant will be left for you."

Fey closed her eyes and sighed.

"When did you first meet the victim?" Baxter asked quietly as he took over the questioning.

Fey's voice was tired and defeated. "I never had contact with Miranda Goodwinter while she was alive."

Baxter slapped the photograph down on the desk in front of her. "Wrong answer! Here's the proof. Photographs don't lie."

"This one does."

"Is there a jury anywhere who are going to believe you?"

"The photograph is a fake! And why should a jury care? Are you seriously suggesting I murdered Miranda Goodwinter knowing I would be the detective assigned to investigate the case?"

"Fits facts."

"Ridiculous!"

"Is it? This photograph proves you knew the victim while she was alive."

"Your photograph proves diddly. It's a fake."

"SID has examined the photo and pronounced it an original with no signs of tampering."

"Half the time our vaunted Scientific Investigation Division can't find its ass with both hands, a flashlight, and a map. It's why we send our hot cases to the Sheriff's Department's lab. Our people have dropped too many clangers."

On and on the questioning went in the same circle. Hilton and Baxter continued to badger and accuse. Fey continued to deny.

Finally, Nate Collins called a halt. "Gentlemen, this has gone on long enough."

"Butt out of this, Collins," Hilton told him.

Collins stood up. "Don't try to intimidate me. This interview is over. If you're going to charge Detective Croaker with something, then let's get to it. If not, back off."

Baxter put a restraining hand on Hilton, and everyone sat back in their chairs.

Baxter picked a pencil up from the table and began to fiddle with it. "All right," he said. "This interview is terminated, but the investigation is far from over." He put the pencil down and looked directly at Fey. "Detective Croaker, you are relieved of your investigative duties and assigned to your residence until further notice. You will be on full pay, but you will remain at home during your work hours unless directed otherwise."

"Mike—" Fey appealed to her immediate supervisor.

Cahill shrugged. "I'm sorry, Fey. I have no control over this situation."

"Right," said Fey. "I suppose Colby is going to be put in charge of the Goodwinter murder inquiry?"

"He's been on it since the start," Cahill tried to justify.

"The hell with you, Mike." Fey stood up. "If you need me, I'll be at home, like a good little detective." She reached to turn off both tape recorders. "Come on, Nate," she said to Collins. "I can't stand the stench of hypocrisy in this office any longer."

"There's more." This came from Mike Cahill.

"More," Fey said. "How can there be more?"

"It's about Cordell."

Fey felt her stomach flip-flop as she fought for control of her emotions. "What about him?"

"The District Attorney's Office have pulled the arrest warrant and dropped all charges."

Fey was speechless.

"I'm sorry," Cahill said. He sounded and looked sincere. "This is coming directly from upstairs."

Nate put a firm hand on Fey's shoulder and eased her out of the room. There didn't seem to be anything left to say.

Now, standing amongst the shards of glass from the broken tumbler, Fey still didn't know what to say or how to proceed. Her house had not been overly disturbed by the searchers from Internal Affairs, but it was clear everything had been moved. Fey felt violated. Her inner sanctum had been invaded—her privacy ripped from her and spread out for strangers to see—it was a form of rape.

She tried telling herself everything would work out, but she didn't believe it. The photograph showing her with her arm around Miranda Goodwinter was something out of the *Twilight Zone*. It was enough to make her doubt her sanity. Had she'd been leading a double life she didn't know about.

Fey had an advantage over Internal Affairs. She knew she wasn't lying about the photograph. She had never come into contact with Miranda Goodwinter before the murder investigation. She had never gone out with her to a nightclub. No matter what SID said, the photo had to be a fake. She also only had Internal Affairs' word the photo had been cleared by SID. She knew neither Baxter nor Hilton were above lying.

Lying was a favorite investigative technique. Tell a suspect his partners were putting all the blame on him, and separately tell each one of his partners the same thing. Tell a suspect his fingerprints had been found on the murder weapon even though you hadn't even found the murder weapon. Promising a suspect you'd file a lesser charge or get his sentence reduced were the only lies you couldn't tell—anything else was fair game.

The photo bothered Fey for other reasons as well. There was a sense of déjà vu about her own image. She had seen it before, but she couldn't remember when or where. As for the part of the photo showing Miranda Goodwinter—where had it come from? There had been no pictures of any sort at the murder scene.

She had to get her own copy of the photo. Internal Affairs would be forced to give her a copy if charges were filed, but they would delay as long as possible. There had to be some other way.

Getting a grip, Fey began to clean up the mess she had made with the vodka. She felt better realizing she was thinking about fighting back. She was angry charges against Cordell had been dropped.

Twice since she'd been home the phone rang, but she'd let the machine pick up. On both occasions, she'd vaguely heard Jake's voice imploring her to call him. She knew she should, but right now she didn't need explanations, sympathy, or a man who wanted to cry on her shoulders. What she needed was time and space to think things through—to find an objective viewpoint and make clearheaded decisions.

Charges against Cordell being dropped didn't change anything as far as Fey was concerned. He was out there, and Fey knew he was demented enough to follow through on his threats. He might not even realize charges had been withdrawn.

After throwing the glass shards away, Fey walked

through the house checking weapons were easily accessible in every room. She was vulnerable, but she wasn't going down without a fight.

She picked up a shotgun, checked the load, and walked into her backyard. The horse sheds needed to be cleaned. It was the automatic, menial work needed to free her subconscious to work on more academic problems.

The dusk of evening had given way to the deeper darkness of early night. Fey switched on the corral pole lights and found her neighbor, Peter Dent, had already placed the horses in their boxes for the night. She tried to remember if she had seen or heard him at work, but realized she'd been too deep in her own troubles to notice.

She checked her horses and found them comfortable. The straw in their boxes was fairly fresh, appearing to have been there since early afternoon. Wanting physical activity, Fey decided to muck them out again. She could have let the horses into the corral as she worked, but there was something reassuring about their closeness.

Keeping the bottom half of the Dutch doors on Constable's box closed, Fey leaned the shotgun against the back wall and patted the horse on his rump. She picked up a pitchfork and began to muck the straw as Constable nudged her playfully with his nuzzle. "Stop it, silly beast," she said softly, the unconditional affection from her horse easing her frame of mind.

When she finished, she spread fresh straw, filled food tubs, put in fresh water, and retrieved her shotgun. She patted Constable affectionately before moving on to Thieftaker's stall.

In the second horse's stall, Fey began the same routine —closing the bottom half of the Dutch doors and leaning her shotgun against the stall wall. She turned to look at the horse but was amazed to see a flaming bottle flying through the air to smash at her feet. Thieftaker reared back as gasoline exploded, flames flaring to roaring life.

Fey ducked away from the horses' flashing hooves, lunging toward the stall entrance. She almost reached it when the top half of the Dutch doors slammed closed with a decisive thud.

CHAPTER THIRTY-FOUR

Fey threw herself at the door, her body jarring hard when it refused to budge. Behind her, Thieftaker's eyes rolled wildly as he thrashed around in fear. A thin line of gasoline had flown across the horse's back. Fey watched in horror as flames erupted along its length.

Moving with the speed of desperation, Fey grabbed Thieftaker's blanket from a peg, throwing it across the terrified horse's back to smother the flames. The horse twisted and kicked out, catching Fey a glancing blow on her left arm. She grunted and spun away into a wall.

Regaining her balance, she tore off her blouse and, dodging another wild kick, dunked it in the horse's water bucket. Trying in vain to calm the horse, Fey danced around in the confined space and threw the soaking wet blouse over the horse's head to cover its eyes and muzzle.

The flames in the tiny stall were gaining the upper hand. Fey had to do something fast or she and her horses would perish. Blinded by smoke, reacting strictly on instinct, she grabbed Thieftaker's mane and swung herself with reckless abandon onto the horse's back. She knew it would hurt the horse across the burned area, but better hurt than dead.

Retaining her seat by squeezing her legs tightly into Thieftaker's sides, she drove her heels into the horse's flanks. With the damp blouse still covering his head, Thieftaker bucked wildly, but Fey clung on with fierce determination. Yelling encouragement, she settled the horse slightly and urged him forward.

The big animal reacted to Fey's commands, but there was precious little space available before he smashed blindly into one of the stall walls. As the horse backed away in shock, Fey hung on then spurred Thieftaker forward again.

Fey had helped build the horse boxes. She knew they were not sturdy enough to withstand the pounding of a ton of terrified horseflesh.

Three times Thieftaker smashed into the burning wooden walls, shaking the structure, but seeming to make no headway. The horse was maddened with fear as it rammed its powerful chest into the wall for the fourth time. There was a loud cracking sound as boards separated from posts and the night air rushed in to feed the flames.

Seeing her last chance, Fey dug her heels into Thieftaker's side. The horse twirled, out of control, then ran forward to hit the same wall for a fifth time. There was more splitting of boards and horse and rider sprang into the open.

Thieftaker, sensing freedom, bolted forward until he ran into the iron railing enclosing the corral. Fey was thrown off by the impact, hitting the dirt hard. Instinctively, she rolled away from the pounding hooves above her, scrambling to her knees and then her feet.

With no time to hesitate, she part ran part stumbled her way toward the burning horse boxes. There, she unbolted the bottom Dutch door keeping Constable confined. The second horse box was filled with smoke but had not yet been invaded by flames. Constable blasted out into the corral to join Thieftaker.

Another part of the structure collapsed, flames and sparks leaping into the night sky. Fey staggered into the corral. She stumbled to her knees twice before reaching the railing. The horses were running wildly around but were mostly out of danger.

Gasping for breath, Fey pulled herself through the gaps in the railing and ran for the house. She only noticed there were sirens blaring when five firemen charged through her back gate dragging a hose. Peter Dent was with them. He ran to Fey, catching her as she almost sagged to the ground in relief.

"You hurt?" Peter asked urgently.

"I don't know."

Peter eased her to a sitting position. "I saw the flames from my back window," he said. "I didn't even know you were home yet—"

"Ever have one of those days, Pete?" Fey said calmly, causing Peter to look at her strangely. She caught his glance and gave a soot-blackened grin. "I'm fine," she reassured him, before breaking into a fit of coughing. She flapped her hands. "Make sure the horses are okay, please."

Peter looked unsure, but Fey pushed him away. Two paramedics moved in to take his place.

Fey coughed again. Her head felt like a spike had been driven through it. All the various aches and pains shed recently accumulated had intensified tenfold. She turned her head to the side and vomited.

From the farthest corner of Fey's property, hidden by the night and the depths of an overgrown bougainvillea, Isaac Cordell watched the activity with interest.

He smiled.

Things had not gone as expected, but he'd gathered information for another time.

Croaker was proving to be extremely resilient. It was remarkable she was still alive. Beaten and battered, but still alive.

Cordell pulled a blanket tightly around his shoulders, burrowed down into the root of the huge bougainvillea, and closed his eyes. He was happy for now with the way things were.

There would always be another time.

———

The house was quiet in the early hours of the morning. Alone and exhausted, Fey sat again in her favorite armchair. Peter Dent had moved Thieftaker and Constable to his own corral for safekeeping. The firemen had rolled up their hoses and disappeared back into the night.

Having showered and slipped into her white terrycloth robe, Fey had wrapped her wet hair in a towel. Physically, she felt scrubbed and clean. Emotionally, she felt a hundred years old.

She reviewed her situation for the millionth time. Someone was trying to kill her. Her job was at risk. Internal Affairs involvement put even her freedom at risk. Her case against Isaac Cordell was in shambles. Her love life had jeopardized a man she cared for deeply. And she was sure Colby would find a way to blame everything on her because she was a woman.

On another level, she had a brother who hated her; a dead father whose abuses haunted her personal reality; and a self-esteem as fragile as fine crystal threatened by a diva's high notes.

Anything, even death, was preferable to how she felt in the moment. She briefly considered the service revolver in her purse. It wouldn't make as much mess as the shotgun on the floor by her feet. She thought of other cops who had sucked bullets—the irrational guilt felt when learning of their suicides.

Suck starting your gun was a pathetic, self-absorbed, useless gesture. A waste of ammunition. It said the bad guys had won. It said there was no justice—no God.

Fey refused to believe it.

She mocked herself with a wry smile. She'd never commit suicide. She wouldn't give the bastards the pleasure. She was at the bottom of her personal barrel where life's detritus languished—the slimy, unattractive things nobody wants in the light. It was not a pleasant place, but it forced you to consider options.

Fey was surprised to find something there. A dirty, slimy, unattractive idea. One nobody would want in the light. It needed work. It needed shaping and research. It needed luck. However, if she hadn't been at the bottom of the barrel, she never would have found it, let alone considered it.

To see if her dirty, slimy, little idea would work, she needed to drag it kicking and screaming with her as she swam back to the top.

A line from the Bible flitted through Fey's mind... *Vengeance is mine, sayeth the Lord.*

No problem.

Fey would give it back to him when she was finished with it.

CHAPTER THIRTY-FIVE

"Eddie? It's Fey Croaker."

"Fey! What's going on?"

"What have you heard?"

"Somebody is messing you around with a photo given to Internal Affairs." Eddie Mack, the department's top crime scene photographer was starting his day at work when Fey called. She'd been lucky to catch him as he already had a full card of photo assignments for the day.

"Did you see the photo?"

There was silence.

"Eddie?"

"I saw it."

"It's a fake."

"If you say it's fake, I believe you."

Fey felt gratified. "Internal Affairs said your people at SID verified the photo hadn't been tampered with."

"Not true," Eddie said. "We said it didn't appear to have been be tampered with. There's no way to be sure."

"Why not?"

There was more silence, but Fey realized Eddie Mack

had covered the receiver in order to talk to somebody. After a few seconds, his voice came back on the line in a low whisper. "I can't talk right now."

"You have unfriendly ears around?"

"Yes."

"Then listen. I need a copy of the photograph."

"Come on!" Eddie's voice went first high and then low again. "It's more than my job is worth. IA would be all over me if they found out."

Unfriendly ears around or not, Eddie was engaged.

"Who's going to tell them? I have a right to examine the evidence."

"Then ask them for a copy."

"And wait until they decide to give it to me."

"I can't, Fey. You're one of the most professional homicide dicks I know, but Internal Affairs has clamped down hard on the photo. They took all our copies."

"I know you, Eddie. You keep copies of all your work, because you know stuff gets lost. It's a habit. It saved several detectives over the years."

"Fey..."

"You're my only chance, Eddie. They're talking about prosecuting me. I'm a suspect in this case because of the photograph. I've got to clear it up before it goes further."

"But..."

"No *buts*! You said you believed me. Help me get the bastard who's trying to shaft me."

Silence.

"Eddie. I need you."

Silence.

Then finally, "I'm sorry."

"Eddie!"

The line went dead.

Fey sat next to the phone with her head in her hands. She had already called Mike Cahill and reported her *on duty at home* status. Cahill had been formal and cool over the phone. Fey dreaded what kind of scuttlebutt was being issued by the squad room's rumor control.

Cahill asked her briefly about the events of the night before but was not forthcoming when Fey explained about the attempt on her life. The photograph of her with Miranda Goodwinter had turned her into a leper. Mike Cahill was proving to be a fair-weather friend.

Fey was bound and determined she wasn't going to sit back and wait for the department to proceed with their case against her, or their investigation into the attempt on her life. With Cahill covering the department's collective political butt, waiting for Internal Affairs to conclude their investigation would be anticipating the guillotine blade to drop.

Steely resolve was fine, but Fey needed a starting point. She had hoped for more from Eddie Mack. The dirty idea she'd formulated was slightly less reasonable in the morning, but she had no choice except to crack things open and see what fell out.

The logical starting point was the photograph. It was the one piece of the case Fey knew to be true. It didn't matter what anyone else believed. She knew she had never had contact with Goodwinter while the woman was alive. Therefore, the photo was a loose thread. If she pulled on it hard enough, it might unravel the whole case.

The phone rang.

Fey picked it up. "Hello."

A whisper came down the line. "Ajax Photo Supply. Eleven o'clock. See a guy named Rhino."

The phone line went dead, but not before she was able to recognize Eddie Mack's voice.

Fey listened to the hum of the dead wire. She hung up and smiled. It was like coming out of darkness into the brightness of a gorgeous summer day. Her brain was clicking over at a thousand miles per hour. She didn't know what she was going to find at Ajax Photo Supply, but it could be the starting point.

Meanwhile, there was Isaac Cordell. He was part of the main problem of solving Miranda Goodwinter's murder, but he was the largest part. He was the wild card.

Fey's gut told her even if Cordell knew the charges against him were dropped, he was still going to come after her. She had heard his voice on her answering machine. She'd seen what he'd done to her brother. She knew he wasn't going to back down.

Whatever Cordell had been before he went to prison had no bearing on the animal he was now. Ten years in a hellhole doesn't turn anyone into a model citizen. Incarceration was only procrastinating dealing with a problem until the problem was again unleashed on society.

Rehabilitation was simply a word used to fill dictionaries. A word used by liberal prison reformers to spark the emotions of other bleeding-heart knee-jerks who didn't understand a thing about the rights of a victim.

Prison never cured any serious criminal. Nothing short of God could—and the only way to get them an interview with God was to fry them.

Fey had seen Cordell's eyes when he had turned to attack her. What she saw there was a soul devoid of mercy or fear.

The threat of Cordell had to be faced and defused. Carrying around shotguns was not a solution, especially since it had proved of little use the night before.

The department was not going to back her where Cordell was concerned. She believed Monk and Hatch would be there for her, even if it would put them squarely on the hot seat if things turned sour. But it was a moot point. Fey had another solution.

She picked up the phone and dialed.

Ajax Photo Supply was tucked away in a relatively new industrial complex behind Union Station in downtown Los Angeles. Fey walked through the door at eleven o'clock and found herself surrounded by three walls of photographic blowups. Scenes of graphic tragedies everywhere: car crashes, famine, the aftermath of plane crashes, photos of abused children, familiar shots from Vietnam, Afghanistan, WWII concentration camps. Blood, gore, pain, and anguish assaulted the eye from every direction. The effect was overwhelming.

The wall behind a lower counter was filled with smaller snapshots of smiling children, family outings, office parties, and other festive gatherings stuck every which way with drawing pins.

The most startling thing about the setup, however, was the total absence of photo supplies.

Behind the low counter, on a high stool, sat an elfin-like girl dressed in black. Her miniskirt rode high on her crossed thighs, revealing long legs encased in sheer black stockings capped by black chunky pumps. A black Lana Turner sweater hugged pointed breasts, between which ran a cheap string of black beads. On her thin face the girl wore bottle-cap sunglasses superficially poised to offset her trendy, spike-cut black hair. The elf was even smoking a black cigarette.

"Yes?" she said with an air of artful detachment as Fey approached.

Fey took another look at the photos on the walls before asking, "Is Rhino here?"

"In back," said the elf. She extracted the cigarette from her mouth with the uniquely European underhanded gesture, pointing it in the direction of a door at one end of the wall behind the counter.

Fey lifted up the counter gate top and let herself through. She walked to the doorway. Like the rest of the back wall, it was covered with pinned-on snapshots of happy scenes, a stark contrast to the blowups on the other three walls.

Not knowing what to expect, Fey took a breath and forged ahead. She had a lot riding on this excursion. According to the rules of being *on duty at home*, Fey was supposed to remain at her residence unless she was contacted by her supervisor to do otherwise. At the risk of inciting further departmental wrath, she had driven from her house to West L.A. station, where she made an unannounced appearance.

She had gone directly to Mike Cahill's office and had closeted herself in there with Cahill for the fifteen minutes it took him to ream her out for disobeying the stay-at-home order.

Fey insisted her only motive in coming to the station was to make a direct plea to Cahill to reinstate her. Cahill told her, in no uncertain terms, the decision to reinstate her did not rest with him. It was a decision to be made by Internal Affairs.

Fey knew Cahill wouldn't and couldn't do anything for her. But she suffered the humiliation for two reasons. First, she needed an excuse for being away from her residence in case Internal Affairs tried to contact her while she was gone; second, she needed some things from the wall of the station's coffee room.

As she entered the back room of Ajax Photo Supply, those precious items were burning with hope in the pocket of the windcheater wrapped around her shoulders.

The room was dim, filled with a permanent haze of

cigarette smoke. It was twice the size of the lobby, and the walls were lined with VCR machines stacked floor to ceiling. All had red-glowing recording lights. What space wasn't filled by VCRs held bins of videotapes and printed tape boxes. Fey saw the photos and titles on several empty tape boxes—lots of flesh tones. It was a porno reproduction plant. By all appearances, probably a pirate operation.

Under the lone overhead lamp, a hunchbacked man with long, greasy hair sat at a battered table. He was using a mouse attached to an expensive computer setup. A small stub of a cigarette threatened to burn his lip while shrouding his head in smoke.

"Rhino?" Fey asked.

"Yeah. Shut the door behind you," he said, in a British accent. "And if you want my help, you'll keep a set of blinders on."

Fey's reply was immediate. "I see *nuthink*," she said, in a mock German accent.

"Thank you, Sergeant Shultz," Rhino said. "Come sit down." He cleared a stack of magazines off a hard-back chair.

Fey did as she was told. The cigarette smoke was getting to her, the craving deep from within her chest waking up.

At close range, Rhino was no better a prospect than he was from behind. His haggard face was grimy with neglected patches of beard, and there was a blob of dried egg at one corner of his small mouth. Thick glasses, each lens having an additional watchmaker's magnifying glass on a wire to be dropped into position, rested on a long nose with a full crop of hair sprouting from wide nostrils. He smiled at Fey, revealing a dazzling array of large, sparkling white teeth.

When Fey looked slightly startled. Rhino simply

shrugged and stated, "I believe in good oral hygiene." He must have experienced similar reactions to his teeth before. He continued to fiddle with the computer in front of him. From her position, Fey couldn't see the screen.

"How do you know Eddie Mack?" Fey asked, when she tired of listening to the hum of the VCRs recording.

"We has a shared business interest, don't we?" Rhino tossed his head in a gesture encompassing the whole room. "He must really trust you to let you in on his little secret."

Fey looked around at the stacks of busy VCRs. Through the gloom, she could make out another room farther back filled with camera equipment. She was surprised. Eddie Mack didn't seem to be the type to be a pirate video king, but she wasn't going to complain. Especially if Rhino was going to help her.

"Did Eddie tell you what this is about?"

"He said you was havin' a spot of bother with a photo snap of you with your arm around another bimbo. You say it ain't a possible scenario since you didn't know the other tit."

"Not until she was dead and cold anyway."

Rhino wrinkled his nose. "Not my style. I don't know 'ow you do *it*."

While he talked, Rhino never took his eyes off the computer screen or stopped twiddling with the mouse.

Fey held her breath while asking her next question. "Did Eddie give you a copy of the photo?"

Rhino kept pushing the mouse around. Eventually, he looked up at Fey. He gave her another quick look at his teeth and said, "Yeah. He says you owe him big time."

Fey shrugged. "Before this is over, I'm going to be in debt over my head."

Rhino rolled and tapped the mouse again.

Restlessly Fey asked, "Were you able to do anything with the photo?"

Rhino tapped the mouse a final time and turned the computer screen toward Fey. Fey took one look and burst out laughing. The screen was a very high-resolution monitor. The picture displayed was crisp and clear. In the dim light of the back room, Fey was looking at the same photo of Miranda Goodwinter in the nightclub setting—only this time Fey wasn't in the picture. This time there was a man with his arm around Miranda Goodwinter. A well-known man—Richard Nixon.

"Whoa," said Fey.

"I thought you'd like it," Rhino said, and flashed his teeth.

"*I am not a crook*," said Fey.

"Your impersonation is lousy. Stick to Sergeant Schultz."

Fey looked at the screen again. "Okay, I'm impressed, but how do you get it off the screen and into the form of a photo print?"

Rhino rolled the mouse and tapped it. A machine at the other end of the table began to whirl and click. The machine was about a foot wide by three feet long by one foot high. A sheet of Kodak print paper rolled out. Rhino picked it up, took it over to a cutting board, trimmed the sides, and gave the finished product to Fey. It was as perfect to look at as the original photo with Fey next to Miranda Goodwinter.

Rhino tapped the print with a chewed fingernail. "You want prints, slides, or negatives? I can give 'em all to you. Nobody will ever be able to tell for sure they're not originals."

"Amazing," Fey said. "Do you know what this means where photo evidence is concerned?"

Rhino snorted. "Pretty soon there won't be any such

thing. This technology has made it outmoded. Should provide blackmailers with a load of business, though, before it becomes common knowledge."

"The criminal mind," Fey said. "Always a step ahead." She took a harder look at the new photograph. Richard Nixon still had his arm around Miranda Goodwinter. "How does the system work?"

Rhino sat back down again. "Simple really. It's called digital imaging. You take a photo, use a top-quality scanner to put it into a computer with the appropriate software, delete or add whatever you want, start up a high end printer," he pointed to the machine which had produced the print, "and presto, a new negative with no signs of tampering. But photography is child's play compared to doing a whole video."

"You can do this on video?"

"Sure. The technology is the same, but it takes a real artist to do it right. Give me enough time and I could produce a video of JFK assassinating himself. You have to be real careful about shadows and mirrors and stuff. Here, I'll show you." He pushed his chair across the room and flipped on a television screen Fey hadn't seen nestled among the VCRs. He took a tape off a low shelf and plugged it into an empty VCR. Within seconds, an erotic coupling of Britain's ex-Prime Minister Maggie Thatcher and Ronald Reagan appeared on the television screen.

"Wow," Fey said. She was as amazed by the film's quality as the identities of the faked images it portrayed. "And at their age."

"I wanted to send a copy to Nancy, but I remembered to *just say no*," Rhino said. He shut the VCR and the television off before wheeling himself back to the table.

"How common is this technology?" Fey asked.

Rhino shrugged. "Common enough. The equipment and software are expensive, but this stuff is being done all the time in the movies today. *Terminator 2* is an example. The silver guy who keeps forming and reforming was all done through digital imaging."

"How about small jobs, like putting my image into the photo?"

Rhino belched and rubbed his tummy. "There are a few photo freak guys like me around. We're not hard to find if you know where to look. Then there are larger image developing businesses who could do the job."

"How many freaks or legitimate businesses would you say are in the L.A. area?"

Rhino thought for a moment before shrugging. "Two dozen freaks. Maybe twenty businesses."

"You think you could track down the guy who put me into this photo?"

"Maybe. What's it worth?"

"My job."

"Don't mean nothin' to me."

"How about your freedom to exploit the free enterprise system?" Fey waved her hand at the illicit videotapes being recorded around her.

Rhino shook his head. "I told Eddie letting you come here was a bad idea. But I don't think you'd screw Eddie over."

"Probably not," Fey said.

Rhino let loose with his orthodontia. "Didn't think so. I'll do what I can."

"Thanks."

Fey looked back at the computer screen again. "If a person is deleted from a photograph, can you reverse the process?"

"You mean from the new negative?"

"Yes."

Rhino picked his nose and flicked away the prize.

"No way. The original image never appears on the new negative, so there's no way to recover it."

Too bad, Fey thought. It would have been nice to confirm who was sitting next to Miranda Goodwinter in the original photo, but she already had a good idea.

"However," Fey began, "you could put any of these people into the photo next to the woman?" She pulled out the promotion party photos she had taken off the wall of the station's coffee room.

The only photo she hadn't been able to find on the wall was the one of her with the two other female officers —the one labeled *The Crack Squad*. But she knew what had happened to the photo...and how her image had appeared next to Miranda Goodwinter's. She'd always had a vague feeling she'd seen the image of herself in the photo before.

Rhino looked at the photos in Fey's hand. "Yeah, I can put those folks in the picture. Simple as wanking in bed."

"Wanking?"

Rhino flashed his teeth. "You're not old enough for me to explain the term."

"I'll take that as a compliment."

"Take it how you like." Rhino took the photos. "You want glossy or a matte?"

CHAPTER THIRTY-SIX

Fey could feel the momentum of the investigation building. It was as if she had been on a steam train groaning its way up the side of a mountain and was now gathering speed as it crested the top for the run down the other side. From experience Fey knew—like *The Little Train That Could*—the investigation would soon be moving at speeds threatening to turn it into a runaway.

At the conclusion of most successful investigations, a detective should be able to look back and see where the trainload of clues, hunches, and information crested the mountain and began the steep descent toward the final destination of arrest and conviction.

On the downward slope, however, the final destination was not guaranteed. A detective had to hang on, doing everything possible not to let the whole thing derail in a spectacular crash leaving dismembered alibis, broken laws, and bloodied witnesses strewn along the tracks for defense lawyers to pick through like so many scavengers.

As she left Rhino's with a stack of interesting prints in her pocket, Fey knew she should go directly back to the station and confront Mike Cahill. It would be the right thing to do—she could have immediately cleared up the doubts about her contact with Miranda Goodwinter and been officially put back in charge of the murder investigation—but it wasn't what Fey was going to do.

She was tired of playing by the book, tired of relying on other people who had her back only when it was convenient, politically correct, or in their best interest. There was a good chance, even after clearing herself of having had previous contact with the victim, Mike Cahill, or someone above him, would feel putting her back on the case would still be a conflict of interest.

Internal Affairs could also raise objections, dragging their feet before eventually clearing her of any wrongdoing. IA hated to be wrong. They would mess about, picking at nits, leaving a cloud over Fey's head, while the case got cold and finally found its way to the unsolved-inactive file—for which Fey would be blamed because she was officially the supervisor of the unit.

The possibility the case may be solved by another detective was something Fey never considered. The ugly little idea becoming stronger and stronger in her mind left her no doubt she was the only cop who had a chance of bringing the guilty to justice. It wasn't a matter of conceit, but rather a matter of being the only detective in a position to see the trees instead of the forest.

Because of her suspension, Fey was forced to reevaluate everything she'd seen and heard since the beginning of the investigation. This second look had been taken with the desperation of personal perspective. It had cleared away the clouds of subterfuge, allowing the truth to surface.

The method of the attempt on her life, coupled with other small clues, solidified the vague rumblings Fey was originally reluctant to consider. Her problem now wasn't *whodunit*, but how to prove it. When she did, it would be a thunder and a satisfaction she wasn't going to allow anyone to steal.

She drove the dozen blocks from Rhino's back room to the central branch of the Los Angeles Public Library with no conscious memory of how she arrived there. Her mind was busy ticking off the numerous threads she needed to gather. She didn't care if IA found out she wasn't at home as ordered. She'd deal with it later. Right now, her train was running down the track at speed, and nothing was going to stop it.

Finding an empty spot at the curb, Fey parked, fed the meter, and made her way into the library building. Within fifteen minutes, she'd secured a private booth and access to a Lexus-Nexus machine. Lexus-Nexus was a computer system giving instant access to the files of over five hundred newspapers and one thousand magazines nationwide.

The department had access to two Lexus-Nexus terminals situated in Parker Center, one under lock and key in the Antiterrorist Division, and the other slightly more accessible through the Organized Crime and Intelligence Division. Neither were open to Fey, so she was shelling out her own cash to access the library's terminal.

After thirty minutes, she came up with good value for her money.

The IRS agent Kyle Craven had given Fey the first pieces of the puzzle. Monk Lawson had filled in background with the information he provided on Janice Ryder.

Fey had fit some of those pieces together revealing Janice Ryder's father—Peter Fletcher—was one of Miranda Goodwinter's first victims. It gave Ryder a great motive for murder. It also gave her a strong reason for unleashing Isaac Cordell to either do her dirty work for her or take the blame for her own murderous actions. It looked good, but Fey still wanted more information before she went anywhere with it.

The Lexus-Nexus machine gave it to her.

Although the computer system gave access to the files of many newspapers, the system's files on the *Los Angeles Times* were more extensive than most of the others, going back thirty-years. Fey's first Lexus-Nexus inquiry produced the obituary for Peter Fletcher. Most of the information was a rehash of what Kyle Craven already shared. The obit did, however, pinpoint the location of the drunk-driving accident in which Fletcher had been killed—a particularly nasty section of Mulholland Drive.

After uncovering this nugget of information, Fey spun her wheels trying to track down further information on Miranda Goodwinter's other identities. She came across a few possible tidbits, but nothing to make her blood rush.

She was running out of ideas when she thought about the scam Miranda Goodwinter ran on Isaac Cordell. It was the one time in her murderous career Miranda Goodwinter varied her usual method of operation. It was also the first time she had involved somebody else in her scheme—Adam Roark, Cordell's business partner.

Fey keyed Roark's name into the Lexus-Nexus machine, focusing the search date to a two-year period after Cordell was sent to jail. Kyle Craven had followed up on Roark, but only to confirm Roark hadn't filed any further tax returns after taking off with the proceeds from the insurance policy, which had sealed Cordell's fate.

After thirty seconds, the Lexus-Nexus terminal indicated fifty possible articles related to Adam Roark. Fey scanned the entries, finding most dealt with a popular architect also named Adam Roark. However, Fey came across several mentions in about the right Adam Roark.

There was a particular article in *The Los Angeles Times*,

which made her whole effort worthwhile. It was a short piece—filler on a slow news day—a few lines of type detailing another drunken-driving death. The name of the deceased was Adam Roark, late of San Francisco. His car skidded over the edge on Mulholland Drive. Fey had no doubt it was the same nasty section of Mulholland Drive where Peter Fletcher died.

In the criminal mind, what works once should work again. *Lady M* couldn't keep coming up with new and innovative ways to kill lovers and husbands. Somewhere along the line, she would have to go back to tried-and-true methods, which had worked before. Sticking a drunk body in a car, pointing the car wheels toward the edge of a cliff, and jamming the accelerator down was simple, but effective.

It was a lot of years since Peter Fletcher went over the edge on Mulholland Drive. Since then, there had been numerous other legitimate accidental deaths on the treacherous road, which ran through the Santa Monica Mountains to the beach.

Who was going to notice one more?

Fey had noticed—and she believed Janice Ryder had as well.

Ryder had done an inspired job tracking down the stepmother who murdered her father and abandoned Ryder. She had done a better job than even Kyle Craven. But then Craven had lots of other distractions, while Janice Ryder had a single-minded vendetta to pursue. Cordell's case must have appeared made-to-order, and she pursued her plan with a hatred fueled by the pure white heat of vengeance.

Fey had another of the keys to break the case wide open—but there was still a hidden killer to catch. Her train was on track, but there were a lot of twists and curves to come.

Isaac Cordell came out of hiding early enough in the morning to watch Fey leave her house. He gave her a few minutes to make sure she wasn't coming back before jimmying the lock on her back door.

Half-starved, he ravenously ate a sandwich with items from Fey's fridge. He even made several cups of instant coffee, being careful to clear up and leave no sign of his presence.

Ever since Fey took him down in the back alley, he had burned with an obsession to strike back at her. Destroying her would strike back at everything and everyone who had ever turned against him. In a dark, still partially civilized recess of his mind, he knew prison turned him into an animal.

In order to survive, he'd been forced to unleash the primitive savage at the very base of every human's nature. It had been explained to him by the prison psychiatrist, and he accepted the information on face value. But it did nothing to change or control the monster he had become.

The chain of psychiatrists, psychologists, and priests who had taken up his cause all told him he could change. But they failed to realize he did not want to change. He was delighted with what he had become. For the first time in his life, he was in charge of his actions. The cause behind the pains in his head freed him to embrace his angers. No more did he have to bow down to the whims of an overbearing mother or a manipulative wife. Others bowed down to him now. If they didn't, he broke them into tiny pieces. He had the power and he had to use it while he could.

The only way to keep the power was to crush

everyone who challenged you, tried to take the power away from you.

Fey Croaker had challenged his power. She had not bowed down before him. She had to be crushed. Isaac would enjoy the crushing.

His hunger satiated Isaac set about the work he had come to perform. Finding Fey's toolbox in her garage, he removed a hammer and chisel then returned to the house. Without much problem, he found the shotgun Fey had been carrying with her the night before. With a slight struggle due to unfamiliarity, the shotgun was eventually stripped down. Isaac took the chisel to the firing pin. When he was satisfied the gun would never fire, he reassembled the parts and put it back where he found it.

He put the hammer and chisel back in the garage and returned to the kitchen. Hungry again, he removed several cans of fruit and a box of stale crackers from Fey's pantry. The items would be enough to hold him until it was time for the next move in the game.

CHAPTER THIRTY-SEVEN

Brentwood startled Fey when he leaped at her from behind the living room couch. Fey had come home early in the afternoon, her head full of the information she had gleaned from the library and other sources. Dumping her huge purse containing her gun on the couch cushion, she was totally unprepared for the screeching cat who flung himself at her and attacked her shoes.

Fey's heart rate took off for the stratosphere in the split second it took her to recognize the cat. Surprised and off balance, she almost fell over as the cat completed his hit-and-run attack. Twisting, Fey managed to flop onto the couch, pluck one of the decorative pillows from the end, and throw it in the direction of Brentwood's departing backside. The cat sauntered away unconcerned.

"You, too," Fey yelled at the animal. "You disappear whenever you feel like it, scare the hell out of me, and then expect dinner."

Brentwood twitched his tail at her in response.

Fey flopped back on the couch, her heart still pounding. "I swear cats are worse than men!"

A stray thought entered Fey's head as she stared at the ceiling. Talking aloud to Brentwood, she realized her animals were like her children. The thought set her wondering about Miranda Goodwinter's relationship with her cat. Fey believed the woman would feel the same way about her animal as most pet owners did.

Fey wondered how long and through how many identities Miranda Goodwinter had kept her cat with her. Had she discarded an animal or pet with every identity change, or had Brentwood been a long-term companion? Thinking about the question, the more Fey favored the latter response. It could explain a nagging point in her whodunit theory.

Earlier in the afternoon, Fey abandoned her library research in favor of a pay phone and a pile of quarters in the corner of a downtown greasy spoon where she knew the owner, Max Monroe, and his wife. Their specialty of the house was a Polish sausage and egg sandwich coupled with gallons of hot coffee. While Fey's order sizzled on the grill, she took her first cup of the strong, black coffee and muscled the local bookie away from the phone.

Her first call pulled coroner Harry Carter away from a late autopsy.

"This better be important," Harry said in greeting. "I'm already late for a lunch date, and I'm only half done with a stinker from last night."

"It is important, Harry. The stinker will still be there after lunch. I know you have a cast-iron stomach."

Harry blew a raspberry down the line.

"I love you, too," Fey said. "But I don't have time for phone sex at the moment."

"What's on your mind, if it isn't my libido?"

"Do you remember telling me your original assessment of the murder weapon in the Goodwinter case might be wrong—rather than a screwdriver, it might be some other type of tool with a thin, flat edge?"

"I remember," Harry said. "I also remember you said you had the murder weapon in custody, and it was a screwdriver."

"I've had second thoughts."

"Sounds as if you've had third and fourth thoughts."

"Yeah, them, too."

"What are you thinking?"

Fey put her thoughts into words for Carter to consider.

"Sounds reasonable," Harry said when she finished. "You come up with one, and I'll do my best to match it to the wound."

"Do me a favor, Harry, and keep quiet until I get back to you."

"You think I got nothing better to do than run around blabbing to folks about your off-the-wall theories? I got more stiffs hanging out down here than a whorehouse during a Brotherhood of the Weasel convention." Harry broke the connection.

Max Monroe pulled a table close to Fey and placed her sandwich on the corner nearest to her. Fey smiled at him as she used a second quarter and dialed a number from memory. She set her half-empty mug next to the sandwich plate.

"Eat it while it's hot," Max said, gesturing with a pair of bouncing eyebrows.

"Okay, Mom," Fey said, taking a quick bite and then having to swallow it almost whole as somebody answered the phone.

"Is Annie Thaw there?" she asked, choking down sizzling hot sausage and bread-crumbs.

"I'll put you through," said the Scientific Investigation Division receptionist.

Fey waited, sipping coffee to clear her throat and burning the roof of her mouth in the process.

Almost two minutes passed before Fey's fingerprint expert friend came on the line. "This is Annie."

"Hi, Annie. It's Fey."

"What's cooking, sister?"

Fey noticed she'd dribbled egg on her blouse. "My lips and the roof of my mouth at the moment," she said in distraction, rubbing the stain.

"What?"

"Forget it," Fey said, focusing her attention. "Those unidentified prints from the Goodwinter crime scene..."

"The one on the door handle and the one in the blood smear?"

"Yeah. I have some comparisons I want you to make."

"You got suspects? Let me grab a pencil...okay, shoot."

Fey told Annie the names of the people she wanted checked.

"Anything on file locally for comparison?"

"Two of them may have something," Fey said, "but you'll probably have to get on to DC for a service record for the last one."

"It'll take time."

"I don't have time. Get DC to fax you a set."

"You'll be pushing your luck for a positive ID. Prints aren't always real clear on a fax."

"Give it a shot, Annie. I trust you. Do the fax comparison and give me your best bet. We'll worry about proof positive for court later."

"I thought you were out of the loop on this thing. Someone said you were in the ringer big time."

"Since when did you worry about protocol? This is important, Annie. You wouldn't let a sister down, would you?" Fey cringed at her own cheap shot.

"Jeez, Fey. A low blow, even for you."

"You'll do it?"

"Of course. What do you want me to do when I get a result?"

"Call my beeper. I'll get back to you," Fey said. She gave Annie the number.

"Hang tough, babe," Annie said to her friend.

"I am woman, hear me snore," Fey said, and hung up.

Having set wheels in motion, Fey finished her sandwich and headed for home. She was unsure what direction to take next in the case. She wasn't ready to confront Mike Cahill or Internal Affairs with the information she had gathered. The time would come when she had everything tied up tight, so they couldn't deny the scenario.

She gave brief thought to Isaac Cordell, but his situation was partially beyond her control. Her phone calls early in the morning before leaving the house had brought positive responses, but the whole issue was a waiting game at best. Cordell would take a run at her, Fey had no doubt. But he had the advantage of choosing the time and place. All Fey could do was wait patiently and be prepared.

Back at home, however, her thoughts about Miranda Cordell's relationship with her cat opened a course of action. Fey rooted through her purse for her notebook containing the entries she made while talking to Kyle Craven and the bank manager.

The account Miranda Cordell established at the bank was in the name of Monica Blake. Fey had copied down Monica Blake's details, including the address she listed as her residence in Beverly Hills.

Gathering up her purse, Fey hit the road again. Within an hour, her efforts returned a jackpot of information.

Monica Blake, aka: Miranda Goodwinter, had lived in

the penthouse of an upscale apartment complex with a doorman, car jockeys, maintenance staff, managers, assistant managers, flunkies, and assistant flunkies. Fey knew the price range for typical penthouses in the area was between four and five grand a month. Killing spouses and collecting insurance policies was a lucrative profession.

Fey tracked down the complex manager, Hector Ibarra. He was a small man with a sense of self-importance and a scraggly gunfighter's mustache nowhere near as impressive as he thought it was.

"Ms. Blake had been with us for six months before she suddenly left us," Ibarra told Fey, after she identified herself.

"Did she have a lease?"

"A year's lease, but she didn't try to break it. She simply paid it off and didn't come back. It was all very sudden and strange."

"Why strange?"

Ibarra gave a shrug. "She was a strange woman. All of the furniture in the apartment was rented so, of course, she left it behind. But she also left behind all her clothing and personal items. She told me to donate it to Goodwill."

A strange woman indeed, Fey thought. What woman could bear to leave behind the favorite sweater that brings out the color of her eyes, or the comfortable pair of shoes you never want to give up? No treasured books or high school love notes. No memories, no keepsakes, no connections to the past. Only an order to bundle up what was there and give it away. The human equivalent of a snake shedding its skin.

She could understand why the woman paid off the lease. When you were trying to disappear, there was no sense bringing extra heat on yourself. If you tie up all your loose ends, nobody gets upset and nobody makes the effort to look for you.

Fey surprised herself by finding she felt sorry for Miranda Goodwinter, or more specifically the child who had become Miranda Goodwinter...The child who had grown into a savage, calculating serial murderer with no conscience and no goal beyond adding dollars to a bank account.

Fey's thoughts flashed to the hell of her own upbringing and the effects it had wrought upon every relationship, every decision, every day of her life since. She could only venture the vaguest guess about the depths of depravity it took to cause a child to grow into a Miranda Goodwinter.

"What do you think caused Ms. Blake to move out? Did she give any explanation?"

"No. One day everything was fine, the next she said she was moving out."

"Did she have any regular visitors?"

Ibarra shrugged again but picked up the phone and asked the head doorman to come into his office.

"This is Diego Mazina," Ibarra said, by way of introduction. "He would know about Ms. Blake's visitors."

Diego nodded at Fey, giving her a wide smile displaying a gold incisor. He wore the same style company blazer as Ibarra, but without the fancy trim.

Fey identified herself and asked him about Monica Blake's visitors.

"Not many," said Diego. "There was one man who came to take her out regularly."

"When did he first show up?"

Diego looked thoughtful. "About a month after she move in." His Latin accent was more noticeable than Ibarra's. Fey knew he would have to sanitize his speech a lot more if he hoped to move into management. Bland was what the world was coming to expect. Being a foreigner, or a minority, was becoming more accepted, but you better not appear ethnic.

"Did she ever have any women visitors?"

"Not on my shifts," Diego said. "And I am here most of the time."

Probably working as much as he could, Fey thought, to send money back to his family in Central or South America.

Fey articulated several descriptions of males to Diego.

"The first one sounds like the man who came to take her out."

"Did he ever stay overnight?"

Diego shook his head. "Sometimes, he would go up to the penthouse with Ms. Blake. But he would always leave later in the evening."

Monica Blake, the black widow spinning her web around a new victim before devouring him.

"The man was very upset when Ms. Blake moved," Diego offered of his own accord.

"Really?"

"*Si*. Very angry."

"He also became very upset when I told him Ms. Blake had not left a forwarding address," Ibarra chimed in. "He didn't believe me. I was forced to call the police, but the man left before they arrived."

"Since you seem to recognize my description," Fey said, "I'm sure you would recognize this man if I was to bring back a photograph."

Both Ibarra and Diego nodded in the affirmative.

"What about the second man I described?"

"It could be he was here also," Diego said. "It was the day before Ms. Blake moved out."

The second description Fey had given had been as close as she could get to describing Isaac Cordell.

"Did anything unusual happen?"

Diego gave the same ethnic shrug displayed earlier by Ibarra. "After the man's visit, Ms. Blake came down the elevator in a big hurry. She seemed upset. She was very nervous while she was waiting for her car to be brought around."

"Nothing else?"

"No. Nothing."

"Did Monica Blake have any pets?" Fey asked Ibarra, refocusing on the interview.

Ibarra grunted. "We don't allow pets in the building."

It surprised Fey, but she thanked the two men. Diego accompanied her out of the office and walked with her to her car.

"Why did you ask if Ms. Blake had a pet?" Diego asked as Fey was about to get in her vehicle. She halted her process and stood up again, leaning one arm across the top of the open car door.

"Is there something you want to tell me, Diego?"

Diego looked back over his shoulder, as if regretting he had spoken.

"It's okay," Fey told him. "Whatever you say stays between us."

Diego licked his lips. "Senor Ibarra does not know, but Ms. Blake had a cat."

"A cat?"

"*Si.* She pay me to feed it if she was going to be out or away." Diego said in a hushed voice.

"What kind of cat?"

Diego shrugged. "*Blanco*...A white one."

Bingo. Fey felt her pulse increase. Brentwood.

"What happened to this cat?"

Diego looked around again, nervous he would be seen talking too long to Fey. "The lady, Ms. Blake, she call me. Ask me to get the cat and his things and save them for her." The more nervous he became the more broken Diego's English became.

"Did she come back for the cat?"

"*Si.* It was the night after she left. The same night the first man you described became so upset when he found out the lady had moved."

"What happened?"

"Nothing, except she came to the maintenance room and got her cat."

"Monica Blake came back here and picked up her cat?"

"*Si.* She pay me a hundred dollars."

"Was she driving her regular car?"

"No, she had another. I don't know what kind."

"She came and picked up the cat, nothing else?"

Diego looked, if anything, even more uncomfortable.

"Come on, Diego, give."

"It was the man..."

"Which one?"

"The first one you described. The one who was so upset because she was gone."

"What about him?"

"He was still here when the lady come for her cat."

"Here? In the building?"

"No, in his car. Parked at the curb across the street. He was sitting there when the lady came back to get her cat."

"He saw her? Even though her car was different?"

Diego nodded. "I think so."

"You didn't tell Ms. Blake."

Diego didn't reply. Fey realized he hadn't wanted to lose his hundred bucks if Monica Blake had taken off without her cat. "It's okay, Diego. What happened next?"

"When the lady left, the man...he follow her."

"He followed her car when she drove away? Did she see him?"

Diego cast his eyes down and shrugged.

Fey slid back into the driver's seat of her car. "Thank you, Diego. *Muchas,* very much, *gracias.*" She dug a twenty-dollar bill out of her purse and handed it over. "Send something home for your kids."

Diego's face lit up with pleasure.

CHAPTER THIRTY-EIGHT

Fey had most of the pieces she needed, except for the biggest one—Isaac Cordell.

Putting a case together was like working a jigsaw puzzle. First you turned all the pieces face up. Next you tried to fit together all the straight-edged pieces to form the outline of your picture. This gave you a framework on which to hang the pieces of the big picture—the solution.

Unlike a jigsaw puzzle, when you were investigating a case you didn't have the picture on the front of the box to work from. All you had were experience and intuition—the tools a detective needed to put together the leads, clues, and evidence making up the substance of an investigation. However, if Fey could capture Cordell, crack him open like a walnut in a vise, she would have the key to unlock the entire scenario without relying on assumptions and long shots.

She didn't need what she wanted from Cordell in order to present the case for filing. However, pinning him down would end any argument regarding her slant on the case.

She also knew Cordell wasn't going to go away. He would continue to fester until he burst all over her. Fey wasn't willing to live with the anxiety of anticipation.

True bottom line was she wanted Cordell. Wanted him bad.

She wanted him for the case.

She wanted him because she wanted to silence the naysayers.

She wanted him most, however, for what he tried to do to her; for what he did to her brother; for the fear he stirred in her.

She hated the fear most of all. It made her want to destroy Cordell, blow him away the second he made his move.

You can't always have what you want.

She wanted Cordell dead, but she needed him alive.

She also needed him broken and to find her own strength in the breaking.

Picking up the shotgun from against the wall in her living room, she hefted it under her arm and walked out the back door. With a casual pace belying the tightness in her stomach, she sauntered to the gate in the slump-stone wall giving access to Peter Dent's backyard corrals.

She had not thought about the cleanup needed to her own corral. The charred mounds of her horse boxes were a sodden, blackened mess, filling the evening air with the odor of smoke. Taking care of those repairs was for another day.

Peter Dent had more acreage and used inherited money to build larger stables. They were beautiful, but labor intensive. Fey was grateful for Peter's help but didn't envy him the extra work.

Thieftaker nickered when he saw Fey. The horse trotted over to the steep-poled corral fence to meet her with Constable following. Fey fondled her horses' muzzles, whispering in a soothing voice. Taking the shotgun, she climbed between the corral's railings, Fey checked the alfalfa, hay, and water supplies. As usual, Peter had everything in order.

As darkness fell, Fey spent a few more moments with her horses before returning toward her own residence. With the shotgun held loosely in her left hand, she considered taking Thieftaker on a night ride through the surrounding foothills.

As she passed through the gate between the properties, a muscular arm whipsawed around her neck. A knee dug into the small of her back, and she was pulled back into an off-balance arch. She gasped for breath.

"Hello, bay-bee," Cordell grunted in her ear. "I've been waiting for you. I'm going to make you real happy to see me."

Three days of hiding in bushes and sleeping rough had added to Cordell's unpleasant disposition. The smell of him overwhelmed Fey as she fought for breath. Her throat felt it was being crushed. She tried striking backward with the butt of the shotgun. Cordell sensed the movement, bending Fey farther backward to avoid it.

"Naughty, naughty," he said. He pushed forward, forcing Fey to move with him. Her head pounded from lack of oxygen. Blackness blurred the edges of her vision. Desperately, she threw her legs straight up and out, crashing down to the ground. The movement tore her head free of Cordell's grasp. She had landed hard but rolled onto one knee with the shotgun at the ready.

Cordell laughed.

Fey wasn't taking chances. She had a round in the shotgun's chamber. She thumbed the safety off and pulled the trigger. She had the barrel pointing at the ground in front of Cordell, intending the blast to be a warning shot. She still wanted Cordell alive if possible.

She heard the shotgun's hammer fall, but there was no explosion of shot. Fey was confused, but when Cordell laughed, she realized the weapon had misfired.

She expected Cordell to jump at her, but he stood looking at her, his hands on hips, and displaying a wicked smile. She wasn't going to ask why. Pumping another round into the chamber, Fey pulled the trigger a second time. Again, there was no response from the weapon.

She looked at Cordell. He was watching her, waiting. When he saw her comprehend what had happen, he lunged at her.

Fey swung the shotgun hard. Cordell stepped inside the roundhouse swing, parried the blow, and drove a hard left jab into Fey's forehead.

Bells clanged and whistles exploded in Fey's brain as she fell backward with the force of the hit. Staying with her momentum, she retained the presence of mind to roll with the blow—summersaulting completely over—to put space between her and her attacker.

She came up on hands and knees, eyes straight ahead, trying to anticipate Cordell's next move.

"I'm going to kill you," Cordell said from where he was casually standing. He picked up the shotgun Fey had dropped.

"Apparently, not with my shotgun," Fey said. Her voice was a croak. *I am a frog lady*, she thought ridiculously when she heard herself.

Cordell looked, hefted the shotgun. "It's still a good club." He hoisted it like a baseball bat. "Bottom of the ninth. Bases loaded. Cordell at the plate looking for a grand slam." He swung the shotgun hard, letting it go spinning away at the apex of the movement. Fey watched as it flew through the air, hit the ground, and skitter into the burnt debris of Fey's horse boxes.

"I ain't using no gun to kill you," Cordell said. His demeanor was casual. "What I'm gonna do is a lot more fun."

"Why?" Fey asked, stalling, trying to get her breath back.

"What do you mean, *why*?"

"Why are you doing this? You didn't kill your wife ten years ago. I know you didn't kill her this time. You can walk away from this."

"I don't have anywhere to walk. People like you took everything away from me. How are you going to make up for ten years of my life?"

"Nobody can. But what about the next ten years?"

"There won't be a next ten years."

"Why not?"

"Because of what nobody else, but the prison doctor knows."

"What?"

"The hellhole you call a prison gave me a disease."

Fey thought fast. "AIDS? You got AIDS in prison?"

"Not AIDS. I punked a lot of boy-girls behind those bars—something to pass the time—but I never got no AIDS."

"Then what?" Fey didn't care as long as she could keep him talking. Her vision was clearing and her breath coming back. Cordell thought he had all the time in the world to play with her. Hoping not to set off a reaction, Fey stood up.

"When you go to prison, there are two choices," Cordell told her, his voice still surprisingly in control. "You're either a punk or the punkee. The way not to become a punkee is to get big. Big and strong. I was big to begin with, but I had to become bigger."

"Steroids," Fey said, leaping ahead to what she knew was coming.

Cordell nodded. "You ain't stupid."

"How did you get steroids in prison?"

"I take back what I said about you being stupid. You can get anything in prison. Steroids are no problem."

Fey knew the question was stupid, but she was still stalling.

"What do steroids have to do with anything?" she asked. "Give yourself up. Help me crack this case wide open and walk away a free man."

Cordell moved his hugely muscular body a step closer to Fey. She did not give ground. Even in the darkness, she could see Cordell's face was a cloud of anger. *Here we go* she thought.

Cordell screamed, "Because the steroids gave me brain cancer. I'm going to die!" He grabbed his head with both hands as if he wanted to shake out the disease.

Fey took her chance.

Shuffling a step forward, she lashed out and drove the toe of her foot toward Cordell's groin. The big man reacted instantly, but still grunted with pain as he took the brunt of the blow on his thigh.

Fey broke contact and ran. She stumbled as she headed for her backdoor, caught her balance and sprinted.

Cordell was right behind her. He grabbed a hank of her flying hair, pulling it out by the roots. Fey yelled in pain but refused to slow.

The back door was unlatched and slightly ajar. Fey slammed through it, stumbling again and sliding across the linoleum of the kitchen floor.

Cordell burst through the door, intent on catching Fey, and was blindsided by Kyle Craven who seemed to come out of nowhere. Cordell crashed into the kitchen refrigerator. As he rebounded, Card MacGregor appeared and drove a baton into Cordell's solar plexus.

Air whooshed out of Cordell's lungs and he dropped to the floor in a fetal position.

Kyle Craven bent down to help Fey to her feet. She put a hand to her head where Cordell had pulled out the fistful of hair. It came away bloody.

"Thanks," she said.

"Are you all right?" Craven asked.

"Yeah. But you guys took long enough to swing into action."

Craven and MacGregor had agreed to help when Fey had called them earlier in the morning. Craven had been maintaining a loose tail on Fey since she left to go to Ajax Photo Supply. MacGregor, who had grabbed the first plane from San Francisco, joined Craven when Fey headed for Beverly Hills.

Both men wanted to be in at the finish of a case with major meaning for them. Fey had known Cordell would come for her. Without police department resources to back her up, she was forced to come up with alternate manpower. Craven and MacGregor were the obvious choices—They had a stake in the case, and neither was happy with loose ends. Like most law enforcement types, they were anal-retentive enough to want to be in on the kill and put a final finish to the case.

"Cuff him," Fey said to MacGregor, who took a pair of Smith & Wesson stainless steel ratchets out of the back pocket of his jeans.

MacGregor was bending over Cordell, ready to slap a cuff over a wrist, when the big man exploded. Nobody was prepared. Everyone had let down, thinking the situation was defused.

Everyone except for Cordell.

Before anyone realized what was happening, Cordell

slammed Card MacGregor backward into Kyle Craven. The short and burly retired detective hit the tall, rapier-thin IRS agent like a bowling ball taking out a single spare. Both men ended up on the floor in a heap of confused arms and legs.

Fey cried out, seeing Cordell scrambling for the open back door. She reached to grab him, but Craven and MacGregor were in her way. By the time she maneuvered around them, Cordell was out the door and moving.

How he'd found his breath so quickly after MacGregor hit him with the baton, Fey didn't know. But the jaws of Fey's trap had snapped open as quickly as they had snapped shut.

Fey pursued Cordell. Seeing him running for the open gate into Peter Dent's yard.

"Cordell!" Fey screamed. "I'm coming for you!"

Adrenaline coursed through every capillary in her body. Her blood was up, and she felt hot and loose. For the first time in years she felt invincible, capable of anything. She felt as she had as a young officer with five or six years on the job, when nothing could hurt you—there was no ass you couldn't kick. On the job it was known as the Wyatt Earp syndrome.

Minutes before, Fey had been running from Cordell. But she hadn't been fleeing. She'd been the bait to lure him to his capture. Now, so close to having it all, she wasn't going to let him get away.

In Peter Dent's yard, Fey saw Cordell duck between the rails of the corral, making a beeline across the yard to escape up the side of Peter's house.

A hundred yards behind, Fey ducked through the rails herself, calling out to her horses. Constable galloped straight past her, spooked by Cordell's passing, but Thief-taker trotted straight to Fey. She grabbed his long mane. In a smooth movement, she swung onto his back.

Clamping her thighs to Thieftaker's sides, she kicked her heels into his flanks, urging him forward. For the second time in as many days, the big horse fed on the urgency in his master's demeanor and moved with a surge of power.

Cordell was already through the other side of the corral, but Thieftaker easily cleared the top railing at Fey's direction and galloped toward the fleeing man.

In desperation Cordell fled up the side of Peter's house, knocking garbage cans over in his wake. Running full tilt at a flimsy side gate, he crashed into it, blasting it off its hinges as if he were a middle linebacker blitzing a third-string quarterback.

Out on the street, he turned toward Fey's residence, but saw Craven and MacGregor running out the front door. He changed directions instantly.

MacGregor had his gun out and leveled in a regulation two-handed stance.

"Don't! He's mine!" Fey yelled as she clung to Thieftaker's back in pursuit.

Several cars screeched to odd angle stops as Cordell ran between them. Fey followed without hesitation—in her element on the back of a horse.

Cordell had nowhere to go. Fey ran him down like a cheetah after a lame gazelle. Thieftaker's broad chest, moving at four times the speed of Cordell, slammed into the big man and sent him sailing into the air. Cordell crash-landed face-first, sliding along the pavement as Thieftaker trampled over him.

Pulling hard on the horse's mane, Fey slid off his back. As she gained her feet, she ran to where Cordell lay, but her haste was wasted. Cordell wasn't going anywhere.

Fey looked down at her quarry, her chest heaving with exertion. Cordell stared back at her, tears welling up in his eyes, his right leg and his left arm at unnatural angles, blood seeping from the road rash down one side of his face.

"You bitch." Cordell's voice was a low rasp. He spat out a tooth as an exclamation point.

"Yeah. I'm a bitch," Fey replied, as MacGregor and Craven ran up beside her. "And proud of it."

CHAPTER THIRTY-NINE

Fey should feel tired, but she'd never felt more alive. The instincts and experience honed to a fine edge by her years as a detective were fizzing with adrenaline.

Fey believed great athletes must feel the same overwhelming euphoria before a championship game. The power coming from within—the positive knowledge you can't be stopped.

Fey was entering the interrogation room—final play of the game; ten seconds left on the clock; fourth down and forever. Fey was going throwing the investigative equivalent of a *Hail Mary*.

Since Cordell's capture, she'd been busy. Two uniform officers had taken Cordell for medical treatment. Craven and MacGregor went along to ensure Cordell didn't escape. The men were unquestionably on Fey's side—protecting her from all interference.

Fey used her contacts with the ER staff to expedite Cordell's treatment. His left arm was broken in his fall and needed setting in plaster. His right knee required a Velcro walking cast to stabilize the damage.

Cordell was then transported to West Los Angeles

Area station and booked into the jail. Because of his injuries, he would eventually be transferred to the jail ward at County Hospital, but right now Fey wanted easy access. She had other plans for him.

At the hospital, Cordell had screamed for his lawyer and demanded his phone call. When MacGregor complied, appearing to dial the number Cordell requested. In actuality, he dialed Fey's second home phone, which simply rang and rang.

"No answer," MacGregor told Cordell, holding the phone so Cordell could hear the endless ringing.

When Fey gave MacGregor the all clear, he would dial the right number and Janice Ryder would be added to the mix of converging suspects.

While Cordell was being processed, Fey contacted Mike Cahill at home, telling—not asking—him to meet her at the station at six a.m. She also told him to get Baxter and Hilton there.

"What's this about, Fey?" Cahill asked.

"Just do it, Mike." Fey didn't tell him about Cordell's arrest or other evidence she had uncovered. "You had faith in me once. Have a little more. I won't let you down. Not like you did me."

"Unfair."

"Life's unfair, Mike."

Cahill could have been a world-class sailor, always prepared to blow with the wind. "I'll be there," he said after a pause. "I can't guarantee Baxter and Hilton."

Fey sent a derisive laugh down the line. "Maybe you can't, but I can. Tell them I'm ready to confess."

Next, Fey called Vance Hatcher and Monk Lawson using the conference call feature of her telephone.

"Feel like some unpaid, unauthorized overtime?" she asked them.

"What do you need?" Monk asked.

"I need search warrants and arrest warrants written and served," Fey said. "We're going to find a murder weapon and put a suspect on ice for the murder of Miranda Goodwinter, aka Monica Blake, aka Miriam Cordell, aka ad infinitum."

"We're in," Hatch said.

"Meet me at the station in an hour," Fey told them.

"Is Colby part of this?" Monk asked.

"Soon," Fey said.

The next call was tough, but Jake Travers's feelings for Fey ran deep. Having time to get over the shock of Simon Vanderwald's accusations, Jake decided he was standing against Vanderwald over Cordell's prosecution.

When Fey called and explained circumstances, Jake was immediately on board. Fey's plan would allow Jake to strike his political opponent, but Fey knew Jake would have helped anyway.

At the station, Monk and Hatch pushed the paperwork hard. They were skeptical at first, but when Fey explained, there was no argument.

Jake roused a judge from a warm bed to sign the warrants with a minimum of scrutiny. The documents were solid, but there wasn't time to go into every small detail some judges demanded—especially cranky judges awakened after midnight.

"Find the weapon—get the confession," Fey told Hatch and Monk, relying on the two detectives to serve the warrants while she took on Cordell.

"We've got this," Hatch said. "Don't worry."

Fey mentally released everything except her focus on the next step. Cordell was downstairs in the jail. In a back cell. All by himself.

Fey went to see him.

Alone.

———

Baxter and Hilton had sleep in their eyes when they rolled into WLA station at six o'clock. They were surprised to find Fey waiting for them with coffee and doughnuts. Mike Cahill had arrived a minute earlier. He knew Fey better than the IA investigators did. He knew the coffee and doughnuts were not a bribe. They were a setup.

"Good morning, gentlemen," Fey said. "Nice to see you again."

Hilton grunted in his obnoxious fashion. "You ready to give yourself up?"

"Have a doughnut," Fey said, shoving the box across the conference table in Cahill's office. "Maybe your personality problem is a permanent sugar low."

Baxter was quicker to sense the atmosphere change. He could tell something was going on. He reached over Hilton, took a doughnut, and then poured himself a cup of coffee from the pot in the middle of the table.

"Thanks," he said to Fey. "It's not often someone offers us breakfast."

"Not unless they're trying to kiss up," Hilton said.

"Shut up," Baxter said to his partner. "You're out of your league, kid."

"What?" Hilton looked like an injured puppy.

"Eat your doughnut and drink your coffee, Sergeant," Baxter said, subtly pulling rank on his partner. "Use your mouth for something other than a place to put your foot."

Hilton looked mortified. Fey turned away to keep from laughing.

"Is there a point to this meeting?" Baxter asked, after an appreciative sip from his cup. His inquiry was polite, not aggressive. He was almost as good a sailor as Mike

Cahill. He could tell Fey was experiencing favorable winds.

Fey explained the events surrounding Cordell's arrest. She kept strictly to what happened the night before at her residence. She didn't mention the frantic activity since.

When she was done, Baxter knew there was more, so he prodded gently. "I don't see how this changes the situation regarding your relationship with Miranda Goodwinter."

"Yeah," Hilton said. "Your lieutenant said something about you wanting to confess this morning, so why don't we get to it." He began to open his briefcase-recorder.

Baxter slapped his palm down on the top of the briefcase, slamming it closed. He didn't look at Hilton. "I'm not going to tell you again, Sergeant. Sit down and shut up or go play with yourself in the bathroom."

Fey smiled at Baxter. She was enjoying Hilton's discomfort, but realized she wasn't going to get the same kind of rise out of Baxter.

Mike Cahill was doing what he did best—keeping quiet until he saw which way was going to be safe to jump.

Fey spoke directly to Baxter. "The situation regarding my suspension came about because of this picture." She tossed the photo, showing her with her arm around Miranda Goodwinter, on the table.

Baxter glanced at it. He didn't bother asking how she got a copy. "It was the main issue," he said.

"You told me SID said it hadn't been altered."

"Well..." Baxter started to hedge.

"Exactly," Fey said.

Baxter was backpedaling. He knew Fey was aware SID said they couldn't guarantee the photo hadn't been altered.

"You wanted to get me to crack, so you bolstered your

story," Fey said. "Every good detective does it. You tell your suspect he's been made on prints, when you haven't even dusted for them. You tell one suspect his partner has squealed on him, when you haven't even interviewed the second suspect yet."

Baxter shrugged. "You never made those kinds of moves?"

"I'm telling you it was a low thing to try on a cop with a good record."

Baxter looked Fey in the eyes. "It's my job," he said.

"Your job is like your partner's rectum. It stinks."

"Make your point."

"Why didn't you investigate this photo before you pulled me off the case?" Fey tossed one of the photos Rhino had created on the table.

Baxter picked it up, looked at it with a frown, and handed it to Mike Cahill.

Cahill glanced at the photograph casually then with sudden interest. "Wait a minute," he said.

The new photo showed Cahill in the same position Fey had been, with his arm around Miranda Goodwinter.

"Or how about this one?" Fey threw another photo on the desk. "Or this one?"

The two new photos showed Monk and Hatch with their arms around Miranda Goodwinter.

"Tell us about it," Baxter said, indicating he was willing to listen.

Fey talked long and hard. She explained the developing process and everything else she learned from Rhino. She explained how she obtained the photo images of the other detectives from the promotion party snaps pinned on the walls of the coffee room. She told Baxter and the others about the photo of herself with two other female detectives originally among the collection in the coffee room.

"Why set you up this way?" Baxter asked.

Fey rapidly explained. Mike Cahill looked shell-shocked when she finished, but Baxter looked thoughtful as he digested the facts.

Hilton simply looked lost. He opened his mouth to speak, but Baxter cut him off with a softly spoken, "shut up," before Hilton got any words out.

"What is your plan going forward?" Baxter asked, bringing his attention back to Fey.

"You saying I'm back on the case? You're satisfied with my explanation of the photo?"

"The allegations in the IA investigation will be unfounded. Lieutenant Cahill will decide if you're back on the Goodwinter case."

"Mike?"

Cahill was perturbed by the photo in his hand. "Can you nail your suspect?" he asked.

"Right to the wall," Fey said.

"Then go for it."

CHAPTER FORTY

Coby felt sick when he saw Fey sitting in her usual position at the head desk of the homicide unit. It was eight o'clock.

Fey motioned him over. "I'm glad you're here," she said. "I want you to sit in on an interrogation with me." She rapidly explained about the arrest of Cordell.

"I thought I was in charge of the Goodwinter case now. Aren't you supposed to be assigned on duty at home?" Colby said.

"Not anymore," Fey said. "Internal Affairs' evidence imploded. Allegations have been unfounded. I'm back to full duty." She smiled, and squeezed Colby's arm. "Isn't it great?" She fought not to cringe.

"Yeah. Uh. Great," Colby managed. He was off balance, didn't know what questions to ask or which way to turn.

"Come on," Fey said, not giving Colby a chance to think. "Cordell and his lawyer are in the interrogation room." Fey stood up. Without looking to see if Colby was following, she headed for the interrogation room.

The room she entered was the larger of the squad's

two interrogation rooms. There were four chairs in the room, two on either side of a battered metal table. In the two chairs farthest from the door, Isaac Cordell and Janice Ryder waited. On the wall behind them was a window with an old-fashioned Venetian blind in the closed position.

Jake Travers was also in the room, sitting in a chair on the door side of the table. The atmosphere buzzed with tension. Fey slid into the only open chair, leaving Colby to lounge against the wall behind her. She opened a notebook and perused its contents, gathering her thoughts.

She knew the hidden interrogation room microphones were *hot*. Mike Cahill would be in the tape room listening and recording the session. She also knew Hatch and Monk would be busy carrying out their part of her plan. A lot depended on their success, and she silently wished them luck.

Fey played her opening move. A pawn. Nothing fancy or flashy, a simple opening gambit designed to get the game under way. "I understand your client wants to make a statement?"

Janice Ryder nodded her head. "Yes. However, he is speaking against advice of counsel."

"Noted," Fey said. "Be aware, the conversation in this room is being taped."

Janice Ryder looked uncomfortable. Her hair and clothing were immaculate, but Fey noticed Ryder's right index fingernail was chewed to the nub. She also saw the lawyer was sitting with her legs and arms crossed—the definitive body language of apprehension.

"Before I listen to Mr. Cordell," Fey said, "I would like to ask you a few questions, Ms. Ryder."

"Me?"

"Yes."

"Are you going to read me my rights first?"

"If you think it's necessary. Are you guilty of something?"

"Of course not." Janice Ryder's face flushed. She refused to make eye contact with either Fey or Jake Travers.

Despite this, she tried out an offensive move. "I want to lodge an objection to the presence of Mr. Travers. His association with the investigating detective in this case is prejudicial to my client."

"Save your objections for court, Counselor," Jake told her. "By then, you may have more to worry about than unsubstantiated rumors." Jake gave Ryder his patented deadpan face with blazing eyes, which never failed to get a point across to a jury.

"What are you implying?" Janice asked.

"I'm implying…" Jake leaned forward with his elbows on the metal table. Fey's hand on his sleeve stopped him from saying more.

"This is my race," Fey said gently.

Fey looked at the notebook she had placed on the desk. "Your father was Peter Fletcher," she said to Janice. "Correct?"

A black look clouded Janice Ryder's face. "What's the pertinence?"

Isaac Cordell was sitting, quietly watching Fey. His plastered arm rested across his chest his injured leg thrust out in an immobilizing cast.

"Don't play stupid," he said to his lawyer. "They know about the tricks you've been pulling with your fancy law degree."

Fey had spent an hour alone with Cordell in a small jail cell before dawn. They had been two deadly adversaries forced—within the cramped and private confines of the cell—to confront not only each other, but also themselves.

The confrontation began in anger with ranting and raving on both sides. Forgiveness and understanding were concepts neither was willing to extend.

Fey's anger at Cordell for his physical attacks paled by comparison to her anger over the memories his treatment had refreshed of her father's abuses.

Cordell's desperation over the tumor within his head was as fierce and frustrating as ever. His warped senses perceived Fey as the tumor's living manifestation.

Each saw the other as the perpetrator of abuse.

But each had something the other needed and wanted more than revenge. Joining forces to fight a common enemy, they struck a bargain binding them in common hatred.

Cordell knew he was going to die quickly from the malignant walnut in his brain. His bargain with Fey kept him in the game a little longer, providing him with the irony and demented pleasure of taking someone down with him.

Fey would handle her disgust over bargaining with Cordell after her other agenda was achieved. Only then would she know if the price she was paying with her soul would be worth the cost.

In the interrogation room, surrounded by the other players in the farce, the two co-conspirators were fulfilling the agreed obligations of their devil's pact.

Janice Ryder turned her head toward Cordell, surprised at his outburst.

Cordell smiled mockingly. "Don't look shocked," he told her. "I should have known you wouldn't help me without an ulterior motive."

Janice turned back to Fey. "I'm not here to answer questions. I suggest we focus on my client."

"Let's stay with your involvement," Cordell said. His voice was husky.

Fey wondered if he was going to explode. She was unsure of how far to let him run, but he would be difficult to stop.

"Tell me you didn't set me up after you sprung me from the joint," Cordell continued. "Look me in the eyes and tell me. I'll believe you. I'll believe anything a woman tells me."

Ryder snapped at him. "I suppose you believe whatever yarn this woman detective has spun?"

"Why not?" Cordell asked. "She ain't helping me from the goodness of her heart. Ten years in prison teaches you the only way to get respect is by kicking ass. She's kicked mine—twice!"

Fey decided to take back control. "When you were paroled in San Francisco, Cordell, whose idea was it for you to move to Los Angeles?"

"Hers," Cordell said, jerking a thump toward Janice Ryder.

"I don't have to sit here for this," Janice Ryder said. She stood up and grabbed her purse from the table. "I've done all I can, Mr. Cordell. You're on your own."

"Sit down!" Fey said, her tone brooking no argument.

"Am I under arrest?" Ryder asked.

"Not at this moment," Fey said.

"Then I'm leaving."

"No, you're not," Fey told her. "You are not under arrest, but you are legally detained pending further immediate and ongoing investigation." Fey glanced at Jake, who nodded his concurrence.

Janice Ryder sat.

The interrogation room was beginning to heat up with the presence of too many bodies and rising emotions.

"Ms. Ryder was responsible for your relocating in Los Angeles?" Fey rephrased her question to Cordell.

"Yeah. She cleared it with the parole board."

"Were you aware she had located your wife—the woman you were supposed to have murdered?"

"No. I figured she was still alive, but I didn't know where."

"Did Ms. Ryder tell you the woman who got you sent to prison was the same woman who murdered her father?"

"No."

Janice Ryder made to jump start, but Fey froze her with a glance.

"Did you tell Ms. Ryder you wanted to find your wife?" Fey asked Cordell.

"Yeah. I told her when she first came to see me in prison."

"What happened when you got to L.A.?"

Cordell scratched his casted arm. "She told me she'd tracked down a woman who might be my wife."

"Did you ask her how?"

"I didn't care."

"Then what happened?"

"She took me to an apartment building in Beverly Hills. We parked on the street until a woman came and got into a car."

"Was that woman your wife?"

"She'd changed some in ten years, but I still recognized Miriam. Ryder told me Miriam was now calling herself Monica Blake—but she was the same old Miriam."

"What did you do?"

"What did I do? I wanted to kill her. This time for real."

"Did you?"

"No way."

"Why not?"

"Because I wanted money first. Miriam and Roark

ripped off a million bucks in insurance when I got sent down. I wanted my share."

"What did you do?"

"I went to her fancy apartment and confronted Miriam. It was worth ten years in jail when I saw the look on her face. Scared her out of her skin."

"Then?" Fey encouraged. She was surprised Cordell was being this open, but he had nothing to lose.

"She was my wife. It had been ten long years. I screwed her."

Fey felt her stomach roll thinking about what Miranda Goodwinter had faced. But the dead were dead. It only mattered now in the context of dubious justice.

Cordell continued his story. "When we were done, I told her I wanted what I was due. She and Roark got a million bucks while I was sitting in jail. I wanted the million. If she didn't have it, I was going to kill her right then."

"What did she say?"

"She said she'd give me two million if I let her live. Who was I to argue? I was going to take the money and kill her anyway. I'd learned about bearer bonds in jail. I told her it was how I wanted the money. I followed her to the bank the next morning, watched her go in. When she came out, she had a receipt showing she ordered the bonds. I followed again in the afternoon to get the bonds. This time, she didn't come out. I thought I had the exits covered, but she slipped by me and I never saw her again."

"What did you do?"

"I went back to the halfway house. A couple of weeks went by. Then you were banging on my door and chasing me out windows."

There was an extended silence in the room.

"Are you trying to prove I had Mr. Cordell murder

Miranda Goodwinter?" Janice Ryder asked with contempt.

"I believe it's what you originally had in mind," Fey said. "But I don't believe it's the way it happened. When Monica Blake slipped out of the bank and became Miranda Goodwinter, not only did Cordell lose track of her, but so did you. It took a lot of years, but somehow, you managed to track down the woman—your stepmother—who you believed murdered your father. When you identified her as Miriam Cordell, you also discovered Isaac Cordell was in jail for her murder. You had found the perfect weapon. Your plan fell apart when Cordell let Monica Blake get away. You were stumped, but when we arrested Cordell, you came to his defense thinking he had somehow tracked his wife down again and killed her again."

"You can't prove anything."

Fey laughed. "I don't need to prove anything. I can produce a paper trail showing Miranda Goodwinter was a black widow killer of long standing. I could probably prove she was your stepmother. Cordell's business partner dying in a car crash—in the same way and same place your father died—prove all of Miranda Goodwinter's identities were connected.

"By circumstantial evidence I can also show your intentions regarding your client, which will be enough to prove them to the Bar Association and get your law license yanked. However, I do not need to prove anything in court because neither you nor Cordell murdered the woman."

There was silence again.

Janice Ryder spoke. "Then what are we all doing here?"

Fey stood up, hoping her timing was right. She

walked behind Cordell and Ryder to open the blind on the window, revealing the squad bay.

She glanced out.

Sitting at Fey's desk, bracketed by Hatch and Monk, was Colby's father.

Hatch saw Fey looking and gave her a thumbs-up. He lifted a clear evidence bag off the desk. Fey could see it contained a wood chisel. She turned back to the interior of the interrogation room and stared directly into the eyes of her partner leaning against the back wall.

"You want to tell us about it, Colby? Or do we need to give your daddy the third degree?"

CHAPTER FORTY-ONE

Colby's face was chalk white. For a moment, Fey thought he was going to faint.

"How did you know?" he asked simply, his voice a disembodied echo.

"A fingerprint left in the blood and a pathologist who wasn't afraid to change his original assessment of the murder weapon. But those things would never have been caught if you hadn't stupidly overplayed your hand."

Fey knew she had one chance to turn Colby. If she let him off the ropes for a second, he'd gather his wits and clam up. She had to push hard and fast. "You tried to cover yourself too many ways. You were shoving on me right from the start of the investigation. I originally put your actions down to a personality conflict, but you were pushing too many buttons. I finally began to wonder why."

"How much do you know?" Colby was beginning to shake.

"Most of it," Fey said. "Between what I can prove, what I know, and what I can guess, I'd say your dad was scheduled to be Miranda Goodwinter's next victim—until

Isaac Cordell reappeared on the scene, causing her to dump everything and run."

Colby slid his back slowly down the wall until his buttocks touched the floor, his knees rising in front of him as if they could protect him from the onslaught of the truth.

"Dad had dated occasionally since my mother died. He even had a few steady girlfriends. But he was obsessed with Miranda Goodwinter. She cast a spell over him he couldn't shake." Colby's voice came forth in muffled tones. His head was down. Fey thought he might be crying.

"Where did your father meet Goodwinter?" Fey asked.

She had to play this right. A veteran of hundreds of interrogations, she knew Colby would only give her as much as he thought was safe or what she already knew. She hoped it would be enough.

Cops rarely made good crooks. It didn't mean there weren't crooked cops. It did mean, however, the handful of bent coppers—those who made every other cop look bad—rarely had the true lack of conscience to be effective liars.

"He met her at an antique toy show. Dad was there with a display of his original toy designs. There were a lot of well-heeled collectors, and Dad's stuff was in demand. She thought if all these rich guys were throwing money at Dad, he must be richer than any of them."

"But he wasn't?"

Colby shook his head. "Not anymore. He has enough to get by, but the big money was gone years ago. I don't think she realized all Dad was doing at the show was selling off a few originals to make ends meet. There was no demand for any of his new stuff."

"He started seeing Miranda Goodwinter on a regular basis?"

"Yeah, but he knew her as Monica Blake. It was cool at first. Dad was acting as if he were a teenager..." he trailed off.

"But something soured you on the deal?" Fey encouraged.

"I ran a check on Monica Blake. You know how it is?" Colby said, looking up for the first time. "As a cop, you check out your new neighbors, or the kid who's dating your daughter. You don't take chances."

"Monica Blake didn't check out?"

"Only so far. She didn't have any kind of history I could trace."

"Did you tell your father?"

"Yeah. He got pissed off. Told me he was old enough to know what he was doing. It caused a big rift between us."

"Did you try checking further?"

"Not until Dad told me she'd disappeared on him."

"It must have been when she was confronted by Cordell and decided to run," Fey said.

Colby nodded his head. "I knew nothing about Cordell, but. Dad was acting strange. He was out all night and would not tell me where he'd been."

"Let me guess," Fey said. "You followed him one night?"

Colby nodded. "The night he killed her. He told me later he'd gone to the apartment where she used to live, trying to find out what happened to her. She came back to the complex while he was still there, parked on the street. She didn't see him, but he saw her. He followed her to the new town home she leased as Miranda Goodwinter.

"For a couple of weeks, Dad drove to the new town

home and watched her place. He got to know the guards
—told them he was thinking of buying a place inside.
They let him go in and out thinking he was a harmless
old man."

Colby snuffled and wiped his nose on his sleeve.
Nobody in the room said anything. Everyone was
waiting for more. Eventually, it came.

"The first night I followed him, I parked outside the
complex and climbed over an exterior wall. I found his
car, but it was too late. Dad had finally worked up the
nerve to confront the woman he knew as Monica Blake. I
waited by his car because I didn't know which town
home he was in. When he finally came out, he had blood
on him, and I knew the worst had happened."

"He had the murder weapon with him?"

"Yeah."

"A wood chisel?"

"One of his original set. He refused to let me get rid of
it. Said he'd turn himself in and confess if I did."

"Did he want to turn himself in and confess?"

"He was a foolish old man. I couldn't let him. He is
my father." Colby hung his head again.

"Instead, you got yourself assigned to the murder
investigation to run a cover-up," Fey said.

Colby didn't reply.

"Touching," said Fey, then lost her temper. Jumping
around the table, she bent down, grabbed Colby by his
collar, and dragged him upright. It was unclear who was
more surprised, the other observers in the room or Colby.
"You smug, self-serving bastard," Fey screamed into
Colby's face. "You want us to believe you did this to save
your poor father. There is a lot more to this than a cover-
up. I was getting too close, wasn't I? Not to your father,
but to you. So, you tried to kill me!"

"Take it easy, Fey," Jake said. He reached out to restrain her.

"Keep your hands off me," Fey yelled at him.

Even though Colby was supporting his own weight, Fey was still holding him by the front of his shirt, pressing him against the wall.

"When we found out about Monica Blake's financial affairs, we found two million dollars in bearer bonds had taken a walk." Fey nodded her head in Cordell's direction. "Cordell didn't get the bonds, even though he made her get them out of the bank. They had to be somewhere else."

She banged Colby against the wall. "I'm betting you found them in the town home, while cleaning up after your father, and decided to keep them for yourself." Fey slammed Colby back into the wall again. "You must have missed the stash in the dryer, or it also would have been gone."

"Fey!" Jake yelled, but he didn't move toward her.

"You slimy piece of gutter wash," Fey said to Colby, her face right up next to his. "You knew I was going to keep hammering away until I found those bonds, didn't you? It's the first rule of investigation, *money, money, who's got the money?* You follow the trail of the money and it will lead you to your suspect." Spittle was forming in the comers of Fey's mouth.

"You used your trick photography to get me thrown off the case," she continued. "But you still weren't happy. You knew sooner or later I'd get back, so you decided to kill me off. I knew it wasn't Cordell who threw the gasoline bomb into the horse box. He wanted a piece of me up close and personal. He wasn't about to miss out on doing away with me face-to-face. I thought about it for the rest of the night, and I began to think about you."

"You'll never prove it!" Colby said. The look on his face changed.

Fey dropped her hands from Colby's shirt and backed away smiling. "At least you've stopped being the put-upon son defending his poor old dad." Her own voice was calm. "It didn't suit you."

"Nobody will believe you," Colby told her.

"Yes, they will," she said. "I have an eyewitness."

Colby's eyes darted around the room. Cordell was grinning from ear to ear.

"Funny, ain't it?" Cordell said. "Me, the prime witness for the prosecution." He let loose a huge laugh. "I was hiding in the bougainvillea at the back of Croaker's property waiting for my chance to get her. I saw the whole thing. I was pissed 'cause I thought you'd ruined my fun." Cordell laughed again. "I'm going to plead guilty to attacking Croaker, so I can be inside waiting for you. We're going to have good times."

Fey opened the door to the interrogation room. She called for Hatch and Monk. "Get Colby's sorry ass out of here and book him," she said when they approached.

CHAPTER FORTY-TWO

The Gunnery was a small, quiet bar a dozen blocks from West Los Angeles station. In a large double booth in the rear of the establishment, Fey was holding forth while Hatch, Monk, Jake, Mike Cahill, Card MacGregor, and Kyle Craven sat in leather seats and coaxed her through the fine points of the case again.

"There were a lot of little things," Fey said. "I didn't start to put them together until Colby tried to burn me out in the horse box."

"How could you be sure it wasn't Cordell who threw the gasoline bomb?" Mike asked.

Fey shook her head. "I never even considered it. You weren't there in the alley when Cordell was trying to beat the crap out of me. I saw the madness in him. I knew if he got another chance at me, he wouldn't do it from a distance. Cordell wanted to strike out at the system. I represented the system to him, so he wanted to personally destroy me. When I talked to him in the cells, it was easy to turn his anger toward Colby, to get him to tell me about seeing Colby throw the gasoline bomb. Cordell didn't care who he took down as long as he could have a personal role in doing it."

"You automatically eliminated Cordell as a suspect in the firebombing," Hatch said.

"Yes," Fey agreed. "I spent the rest of the night thinking about methods and motives. I considered Janice Ryder, but her position was secure. She may have set Cordell up to take out Miranda Goodwinter, to get revenge for the death of her father. She maybe even believed Cordell had murdered the woman, but she already had a constitutional argument with her double jeopardy defense. Vanderwald was also in her corner. He dropped the charges against Cordell for political reasons, so her conscience was clear."

Fey continued, "She may have set Cordell up, but she also was close to getting him off clean. The only fly in her ointment was Cordell wasn't going along with the game plan. She didn't know about Cordell's anger or his brain cancer. She simply thought he'd gone against his best interests by escaping from custody. She still felt if she could bring him into line again, they'd be home free." Fey stopped and took a sip from her drink.

"Those moves are going to cost her," Jake said.

"Disbarment?" Fey asked.

"If we push it. I think we can show conspiracy to commit murder on her part," Jake said. "It wouldn't hold up in criminal court, but it will be enough to shaft her in a state bar court."

"Hang on," Monk Lawson said. "Let's get back to how you came up with Colby and his father as suspects. I know I'm low man on the totem when it comes to murder squad experience, but I still don't get it."

Fey smiled at him. "What is it Sherlock Holmes used to say? Something about when you have eliminated the possible, whatever remains, no matter how impossible, has to be the answer? Once I'd eliminated Cordell and Ryder, Colby was the only other person floating around who could have been responsible for the sequence of events. It was easy for me to accept Colby was behind the photos and the other information given to Janice Ryder. Cordell didn't have access to the information, and Ryder didn't generate it herself. Only an insider would know about my relationship with Jake. When I remembered where I'd seen the picture of myself that appeared next to Miranda Goodwinter, Colby was the most likely suspect."

"Didn't you think he did it to get back at you for Two-Step's?" Monk asked.

Fey laughed at the memory. "At first but setting up the photo would have taken longer than the time frame between the incident at Two-Step's and the information coming to light. He was pushing too hard to get me off the investigation." Fey paused as a waitress brought another round of drinks. "I couldn't imagine what type of relationship Colby could have with Miranda Goodwinter. But a relationship must have existed for him to have a photo of her. There weren't any photos at the crime scene, so he must have found one elsewhere."

"How did his father become a suspect?" This from Cahill.

Fey shrugged. "He was the right age. From Colby's lifestyle, I made the same mistake Miranda Goodwinter did. I assumed there was family money. Annie Thaw told me about the fingerprint found in the blood at the crime scene. Colby must have wiped most of the surfaces his father could have touched, but he missed one print. Thinking about Colby's father, I remembered two things. First, Annie Thaw told me the fingerprint in the blood showed signs of scarring."

"And the second thing?" Monk asked.

"I remembered shaking hands with Colby's dad when I went to talk to Colby. His hand was rough. The fingertips were in bad shape from all the woodwork. The woodworking led me back to Harry Carter's theory the murder weapon wasn't a screwdriver. In my mind, I could see the rows of wood chisels on the tables and walls of Colby's father's workshop, and the pieces began fitting together."

"Such as Colby discovering the murder weapon in Cordell's pad," Vance Hatcher said. He was hooked into Fey's wavelength.

"Along with the missing bearer bonds. Cordell and Ryder didn't have them. Then my trip to Colby's residence spelled out financial troubles. You guys did great with the search, finding everything we needed."

"Colby didn't think things out," Monk said. "He was winging it—scrambling to stay ahead of the investigation. He didn't have time to dispose of the evidence or cash the bonds."

Monk agreed. "The tower he was building would have crashed down sooner or later. His father was the weak link. The minute we turned up on the doorstep, he started to spill the story. He may have murdered in a fit of passion, but he's not a criminal. His conscience was eating him up. He'd never have survived a tough interrogation."

"We had the goods anyway," Fey said. "Annie Thaw ran the print from the bloodstain against Colby, Cordell, and Ryder to be sure, but I knew she'd get a match from Colby's father's service records. However, when you guys came up with the murder weapon, the original nightclub photo—Colby's father with his arm around Miranda Goodwinter—the bonds, and a confession, it sealed it. I'm grateful and proud."

"I never imagined this outcome when I investigated

this case ten years ago," Card MacGregor said. "I'm thankful to be in for the kill."

"It ties up a lot of my loose ends," Kyle Craven said. "I would have hated for this one to get away."

"Face it, Craven," Fey said, "You hate for any of them to get away. Do me a favor and stay out of my tax returns."

"You should be able to write off your equestrian expenses this year," Craven said. "I witnessed you use your horse to catch a felon."

Fey laughed. "I'll get you to fill out my *ten-forty*."

Hatch had been toying with his glass. "We got the case clearance," he said. "But the price was high."

Fey gave him a penetrating glance. "If you mean because we had to take down one of our own—you're wrong," she said. "Colby was not one of us. By trying to murder me, he crossed to the other side. How high would the price be if we hadn't caught him. We do our job because we believe in being good cops. If you stop believing, the depths become murky and deep."

"Hear, hear," said Mike Cahill. He raised his glass in a toast.

Everyone followed in kind.

There was a beeping noise, and Mike Cahill reached for the pager on his belt. Before he could turn it off, the pager in Fey's purse sounded. They both checked the readouts.

Cahill looked at Fey.

"It's another cold one," she said without hesitation.

"I've learned not to argue with your intuition," Cahill said.

Monk and Hatch stood up. "Here we go again," they said in sync.

"No rest for the wicked," Fey said, finishing her drink in a gulp. "Only for the dead."

A LOOK AT CROAKER: GRAVE SINS

Her personal life is in shambles, but no cop does it better than Fey Croaker – as she fights for respect in the L.A.P.D. . . . and for justice in a city on the edge.

All of Los Angeles is thrust into chaos when a popular NBA athlete is charged with a series of gruesome murders. The evidence against the defendant appears overwhelming, but old evils die hard. For L.A.P.D. homicide detective Fey Croaker and her appealing crew, the race for the truth will tax each of them to the limit.

Under the scorching light of media attention, Fey's own demons are brought into sharp focus with the life of her wayward brother literally hanging in the balance. It's a race to get to the truths hidden beneath layers of lies, secrets, and deadly perversions – and Fey must win while there is still an L.A. left to protect and serve.

AVAILABLE DECEMBER 2025

ABOUT THE AUTHOR

Paul Bishop is the author of fifteen novels and has written numerous scripts for episodic television and feature films. A novelist, screenwriter, and television personality, Paul is a nationally recognized behaviorist and deception detection expert.

A 35 year veteran of the LAPD, his high profile Special Assault Units produced the top crime clearance rates in the city. Twice honored as LAPD's *Detective of the Year*, he currently conducts law enforcement training seminars across the country, is an adjunct professor at the University of California Channel Islands, while also focusing on numerous writing projects.

Find Paul online:
www.paulbishopbooks.com

www.ingramcontent.com/pod-product-compliance
Lightning Source LLC
Chambersburg PA
CBHW010823250626
47169CB00010B/2935